DESTINY

DESTINY

OR, THE

ATTRACTION

OF

AFFINITIES

John David Morley

LITTLE, BROWN AND COMPANY

A *Little, Brown* Book

First published in Great Britain in 1996 by Little, Brown and Company

Copyright © 1996 by John David Morley

The moral right of the author has been asserted.

*All characters in this publication are fictitious and any resemblance to real persons,
living or dead, is purely coincidental.*

A CIP catalogue record for this book is available from the British Library.

ISBN 0 316 87807 3

Typeset in Garamond by M Rules
Printed and bound in Great Britain by
Hartnolls Limited, Bodmin, Cornwall

UK companies, institutions and other organisations wishing to make bulk
purchases of this or any other book published by Little, Brown should contact
their local bookshop or the special sales department at the address below.
Tel. 0171 911 8000. Fax. 0171 911 8100.

Little, Brown and Company (UK)
Brettenham House
Lancaster Place
London WC2E 7EN

1934

1

They spoke to him in Swedish and were surprised when he didn't understand. Everyone took him for a Scandinavian. He got off the post packet from Oslo to Malmö and walked into the office of the shipping line on a summer evening, a tall blond, young man with hardly any luggage, nothing that would detain him, to inquire about passage to Copenhagen, and from there on to England. There was a boat leaving for Copenhagen the next morning, they said, and directed him along the wharf to a lodging-house where he could spend the night. But he chose not to stay at the lodging-house. He was getting short of money. He could save by sleeping out. He might also have been vaguely aware of the lodging-house as an enclosure he was reluctant to exchange for the space and light of the northern sky; a reluctance that ran deep, not only because he was an outdoor sort of person, but because at this moment in his life being closed in meant a restriction of the freedom that was his only for as long as he had not made up his mind. Sitting in a sleeping-bag on the wharf, he could watch the harbour traffic and the gulls wheeling above in the dusk all the summer night long, the constant comings and goings of a port in which he could share and to which he was not committed. He was free. He sat in his sleeping-bag, hugging his knees and exulting in his freedom, as he looked out over the harbour. Here was the turntable swinging each vessel round in the direction it had been assigned, the dial pointing to the place that would become its destination. From here the ships ran out across the sea. In a grove on the far side of the sea hung a golden fleece. He had taken his finals at Cambridge that summer; his head was full of Latin and Greek poetry, history and mythology, and what he imagined as he sat watching the harbour in the gravelly light were the seafarers of antiquity, Odysseus, Jason and the Argonauts, adventurers setting sail on a dusky sea. Rejecting the lodging-house in favour of the open sky, he was instinctively resisting the confinement of his future life, which would begin when tomorrow his vacation was brought to an end as he boarded the boat to return to search for a job in England. He spread a map out on the ground and idly followed a dotted line marking the ferry route that led straight across the Baltic from Malmö to Stettin. Suddenly, almost with a shock, Sophie von Kutzow came into his mind. The Kutzows had an estate somewhere in Brandenburg or Pomerania, but he had forgotten the name. He remembered the sense of strangeness coupled with the excitement he felt when he first saw her in his parents' house. Sophie was a distant relative of his mother's who had come to stay with the family almost ten years ago. As he drifted off to sleep, he thought of Sophie's curious habit of shaking hands when she came down to breakfast in the morning, and how they had teased her about it, and he remembered her laughing as she stood at the garden gate, saying she would shake his hand just one last time. In the morning, recalling the name of the Kutzows' estate, he decided on impulse to visit his German relatives, and boarded the next ferry bound for Stettin.

Holm lay a hundred and twenty miles inland and he walked there in three days. He was a great walker. In the summer of 1933 he had walked through the Lake District into Scotland, making detours to scale extra peaks on his way, and the following year he crossed Norway on foot, from Trondheim to Oslo, in a matter of weeks. His parents had brought him up to be self-sufficient, to be frugal, to be honest and to pay his way. He respected his father, his mother he adored, but displays of affection within the family were not allowed to be more than dutiful. Restrained emotions crept out, like weeds, and found expression at best as sentimentality. Somewhere inside his mother's north German reserve were feelings associated with what she called *Fernweh*. He used to think of it as homesickness for where she came from across the sea. It was a longing for somewhere or something that would always remain in the distance, perhaps for distance itself, but he had not known that until he sat watching the boats in Malmö harbour. He looked at the map and saw straight lines, and walked them, translating enormous distances into his legs without questioning that he would arrive at the place for which he had set out. But now something unexpected had happened. He was arriving somewhere other than the place for which he had set out, and the longing for distance seemed to grow in proportion as the distance was closed, the unaccountable yearning he felt even as he reached Holm on the evening of the third day and walked down the linden avenue towards the house.

2

Wherever their English guest had been, it seemed he had walked there. The initial incredulity of the Kutzows that so young a man could already have so much mileage in him gave way to an ironic amusement, and by degrees to a familiar teasing.

Etta, the ancient aunt who ruled the roost at Holm, put her head on one side, mustered him, and pronounced her verdict: *Nun, lieber Magnus, unser Nachbar Herr von Strehlitz ist Flieger und Sie sind eben unser Wanderer.* From then on he was known in family parlance as the Wanderer. The Wanderer, who had never had a nickname in his life and was rather pleased to have been given one at last, correctly interpreted this as a sign that he had met with approval at Holm. They liked his open face, the manliness of his bearing, the modesty of his manners and his tastes; and he was their relative, however distant a one. Magnus Gould became part of the family at once.

'Where's our Wanderer?' Etta, who liked having the young man around, soon began to ask. When told that he was out somewhere she smiled and added softly to herself, 'Wandering, of course.'

Holm had collected Aunt Etta, in the way that estates seemed to do, when she was a young woman, and never let her go of her, not for marriage, not for anything. She had lived half her life in the nineteenth century, fifty years of it at Holm, and most of those years with her cousin Maria, who nominally inherited the estate when her husband died in the 1920s. Although still in her early fifties, Maria seemed a much older woman – perhaps because she had prematurely taken on the manner of the much older woman who had been her closest companion for so many years. Neither had seen very much of the outside world. Etta had the childlike qualities of a nun, preserved and protected in isolation. Life at Holm continued at the same level and unchanging pace as the estate itself had for generations, lying in a fertile plain with nothing to interrupt the view from the upstairs windows to the horizon, almost as far (or so visitors were told) as the Baltic coast.

Maria's daughter came back to Holm with her two children when her marriage failed and she could not continue living in Berlin. Sophie was much smaller than Magnus remembered; at their last meeting he had been ten and Sophie twenty-two, and he had had to look up at her when they shook hands. Otherwise she did not seem to have altered. Only her name had changed – she was called Sophie Romberg now. Magnus looked at her and saw a divorced woman of whom his parents might not entirely have approved. Spirited, even sparkling, like the fresh colours in her face, with a warm skin, a warm complexion, she was petite rather than small, perfectly proportioned within the scope she had been given. Despite the brightness of her appearance, Sophie seldom laughed.

Her brother Dietrich was different; large and sprawling, always in a good humour, usually audibly so, for the benefit of the rest of the house. He worked in Berlin and spent his vacations at Holm. In his mid-thirties, still a bachelor, Dietrich was the favourite of the maid and the cook who had been on the estate since he was a boy. There was a gardener who also did jobs about the house and lived in the village. Since the death of Maria's husband, when the owners of a neighbouring estate rented and began farming the Kutzow land, these had been the only staff at Holm. Life on the estate was simple; the Kutzows were not demanding, nor could they afford to be.

Their tenants had installed an estate manager in the second, identical house on the other side of the park. The manager and his wife, a childless couple by the name of Kurtz, lived alone in the enormous house with a parrot and six dogs. Most of the house had been shut down. From time to time a young man came from Berlin to stay in a wing sub-let by the tenants. He had a passion for flying and housed his aircraft in a barn on the edge of the field adjoining the park. This was the airman to whom Aunt Etta had been referring when she dubbed Magnus 'our Wanderer', contrasting him ironically with their neighbour, Botho von Strehlitz.

In fact, the Wanderer was not as pedestrian in comparison with the Airman as he allowed himself to be made out to be. The barn where the young baron kept his aircraft was locked, but on taking a peek through the chinks in the boards Magnus was able to identify, among other machines he had never seen before, a stick-and-wire braced biplane very similar to the De Havilland he had learned to fly during his time with the Cambridge Flying Corps. Magnus could feel his scalp tingle when he saw the aeroplanes locked away in the gloom of the barn. He couldn't wait for their owner to arrive from Berlin.

In the meantime, the Wanderer kept it to himself that he could not only wander but also fly. He made inquiries about the Kutzows' neighbour and learned that he was a few years older than himself, had studied at the University of Jena and had already taken his doctorate at an advanced college of engineering in Berlin. Aunt Etta said he came from a wealthy background, and she sounded approving. Dietrich's views about Strehlitz as a person, however, were non-committal.

Magnus was happy at Holm. He could imagine no better way of spending his life than as the administrator of a country estate. He at once became friends with Kurtz, a professional manager who was paid a salary to do his job, and as he accompanied the *Verwalter* on his rounds he found himself wondering whether there were similar positions in England. His family were middle-class people who lived in a small provincial town and owned no land. Magnus knew nothing about landowners or estates: they belonged to the grand world. The situation seemed to be different on the Continent. On his long walk down from the coast he had passed dozens of similar estates, and from what he saw of life at Holm, the landowning class was not special or grand, as had seemed to him to be the case in England. But Magnus didn't really know. He had never mixed with that kind of people.

Aunt Etta and Maria, at any rate, were quite different from what he imagined 'that kind of people' to be like. Every evening, the two

ladies sat in Etta's salon playing patience. The ritual was always the
same. The ladies went up after dinner, sat down at the baize-covered
table and took the cards out of the box. The maid brought tea, reappeared at nine o'clock to take out the pins from Miss Etta's coiffure
and comb her hair. Her hair was so long that she had to sit on an
elevated chair to facilitate this procedure while she continued to
play patience and chat with whatever company cared to join the
ladies in her room. The Wanderer's attendance for an hour every
evening was obligatory, to improve his language, Etta said. Magnus
either read to the ladies, and they corrected his pronunciation, or he
made conversation, and they corrected his grammar. Etta, sitting
hunched in a high chair, a wizard of apparent agelessness, her face
smooth-skinned and scarcely lined, with her quaint, sometimes arch
manners, her hair falling in a cascade almost to the ground, seemed
to Magnus to be less an old woman than a marvellous child.

Sophie had already seen so much more of life than the two older
ladies. Sometimes she got impatient with them; unfairly, it seemed
to Magnus. He could not see that Sophie's irritation was not really
with Etta and Maria but with herself, forced as she was to mark time
on the estate for the best years of her life. He could not discern that
the restlessness driving her on to constant activity was not so much
motion towards something as away from it. She lived in flight from
inaction that would remind her oppressively of herself.

Every morning at half-past five, she cycled off to swim in the lake
a couple of miles from the house. Her children spent all their time at
the lake. Sophie went down there at midday to take them their lunch,
and in warm weather she often swam in the evening as well. As
Magnus was in the habit of joining the estate manager for breakfast
before setting out with him on his rounds, he accompanied Sophie on
her early-morning swim on the way there. He loved the ride to the
lake along roads lined with poplars, the mist rising off the fields as
another beautiful summer day began to spread across the sky. All day,
with Kurtz, he saw only the land under his feet, but when he cycled
with Sophie in a rush of wind the horizon tilted away at the end of
the poplar avenue and showed them nothing but the sky.

'There's no one here, I always go in as I am,' she said the first time they went swimming together, turning away and quickly undressing a few yards along the shore. They stood a little apart, getting undressed with their backs to each other, and plunged straight in. Each of them swam on their own for a while, but somewhere out in the lake their paths usually converged. Treading water, they chatted in the middle of the lake, and Magnus experienced a feeling of joy as they swam back side by side.

Sophie's children had complete freedom at Holm. She expected them to look after themselves during the day while she was busy in the house. She was brisk with them and took their obedience for granted, never hesitating for a moment to let them know when they did something that displeased her. She gave them a clear measure, as dependable in the definition of the limits they were not to cross as it was in the extent of the freedom they were allowed. But within those clear boundaries the children knew they were surrounded by their mother's love and care. She was predictable, like everything at Holm, and the children's life was carefree for that reason.

Elena and Bernhard slept in a room at the far end of the house, away from the grown-ups, because that was more exciting, but Sophie left the lights on in the corridor so that it wasn't *too* exciting and the children would not be afraid if they needed to come to her at night. It was such a long way from their room at the end of the corridor that Sophie let them travel to and fro on their bicycles. The corridor was lined with linen chests, dowries brought into the family by generations of brides who had come to Holm, and to a child they must have loomed frighteningly in the dark.

Elena, who was five, liked the grown-ups to come and sit on the chests, as her Uncle Dietrich did whenever he was home, and tell her stories about spooky things that might be inside the chests but would be unable to get out as long as there was a grown-up sitting on top of them. Sometimes, to make Elena happy, her mother called everyone to come and sit on a chest and talk for a while in the corridor. She understood that, because it helped to ward off ghosts, it was a comfort to the child. The girl was like her mother. She had the same brightness and lightness of manner overlaying the same seriousness in her nature.

What was Sophie's burden, the weight she already shared with her daughter when Elena was still a child?

Her burden was having to come back to Holm and carry the estate and the family, as her sense of duty required, almost entirely on her own shoulders; a degenerate family line which, after generations of inbreeding, produced men like her brother Dietrich, who were sweet but unstable and weak, or women like Aunt Etta, whose wombs were so far atrophied that they were unable to bear children. That was one reason why Sophie had preferred to marry outside the landowning aristocracy. She had escaped Holm and gone to Berlin, but when the marriage had not worked there had been no alternative for her but to come back with her two children. Sophie felt physically trapped by Holm as mentally she did by her disposition, by the *Schwermut* she had inherited, a heaviness of heart that dragged down the lightness in her nature that could so easily have floated her up into the sky.

How refreshing it was when something out of the ordinary happened on the estate, how happy she was to greet a new face! Magnus's arrival seemed to be the event Sophie had been waiting for ever since she had returned to Holm.

Magnus was someone different and he had the feel of somewhere else. His speech, his walk, his sense of humour – in almost everything his manner was a little out of line. His shirts, the smell of the soap he used, even his boots seemed different. He kept her on the edge of surprise, alert, as Sophie wanted herself to feel. She frequently glanced at him, as if by watching him she could acquire his secret and possess that difference which was the spring of life. She felt quickened by it. The apparent strangeness of Magnus in these surroundings served to sharpen Sophie's own sense of estrangement, but the restlessness which had been taking her away from herself was now bringing her back, towards an appreciation of the fixed things in a life so lacking in perspective it had become unendurable to her.

Since the arrival of Magnus, a long spell of *Schwermut* had magically dispersed. Sophie felt cloudless.

She stood on the shore of the lake with her back to him when she got undressed. Plunging into the lake, she felt it rise to catch her and zip up her body in a sheet of cold water. Their wakes converged somewhere out in the lake. She trod water as they talked, cloudless, she thought, *weightless*, and swam back with strong, easy strokes. She felt drops of water running down her back as she rubbed her breasts with a towel. Her eyes traced the wakes she and Magnus had left to the spot where they had trod water together, still sending faint ripples out over the lake.

'Where's our Wanderer?' Aunt Etta must have asked one evening when Magnus failed to appear after dinner, but Sophie, swimming up weightlessly to surface from her daydream as she darned her daughter's frock, heard her ask instead: 'Where's our weightlifter?', and burst out laughing.

'Well, my dear,' said Etta slyly, her hand hovering over the baize table with a card, which she laid down with an audible slap, 'and what are we to make of *that*?'

'He wanted to finish writing a letter. He said he'd join us in ten minutes.'

Sophie snapped the thread with her teeth and asked her mother, who had just come into the room, to turn on the radio so that they could hear the news.

The main item on the evening news was a bulletin on Hindenburg's state of health. The dying president had lingered on for weeks, but now his condition appeared to have taken an irremediable turn for the worse. Herr Hitler would be meeting for consultations with von Blomberg, the minister of defence, and was expected to make a statement shortly.

Hindenburg died the same night, and Hitler, having satisfied the army's demands for measures to diffuse the tense political situation at home, assumed the title of *Führer und Reichskanzler*, in which office he was to be confirmed by plebiscite two weeks later.

3

Magnus was helping to bring the wheat in from the field on the far side of the lake when the Fokker biplane dropped out of the sky. He was standing by the deafening old steam engine Kurtz had adapted to power a conveyor belt for running bales on to a truck, so he had no warning before the aircraft came in low from behind him and roared past, only twenty or thirty feet overhead. Startled out of his skin, he threw himself on the ground. The farm labourers laughed. He watched the plane skim the lake, gain height and bank in a steep curve that ended out of sight on the far side of the village. Magnus was stunned. He had never seen an aircraft flying so fast. The Fokker must have been travelling at well over a hundred miles an hour. The baron was back, said the foreman with a grin, and the men threw their hats in the air and cheered.

Magnus waited until they had finished the field before he made his way to the barn where Strehlitz kept his planes. He found a man of short and powerful build dressed in grimy overalls, bent over a table measuring a dismantled propeller. Taking off the broad straw hat he borrowed from Sophie when he worked in the fields, Magnus came forward and introduced himself. Strehlitz wiped his oily fingers on his overalls and shook his hand. With a gesture in the direction of the straw hat, he smiled and said, 'I believe I already made your acquaintance from the air – rather too precipitately, I'm afraid. I apologise.'

When Magnus smiled the baron laughed, and the livid scars on either cheek moved up under the corners of his eyes.

Strehlitz introduced his planes, and Magnus listened in awe. The Fokker DVII was the best fighter plane to have come out of the war, the German said. One of the first to be fitted with a steel-tube fuselage in place of traditional wood and fabric, it was armed with two machine-guns and powered by a 160-horsepower Mercedes engine capable of 120 miles per hour, compared with the top speed of 80 mph achieved by its predecessor, the E1, which stood alongside it in the barn. Von Strehlitz walked over and patted it as if it were a horse. The monoplane fighter had been fitted with interrupter gear as early as 1915, he explained, enabling bullets to pass undeflected through a revolving propeller blade. For a year it had shot French and British planes out of the sky. Strehlitz had bought both Fokkers cheap from a scrap dealer ten years after the war and restored them himself.

The third plane in his hangar was a Sopwith Camel biplane his mother had bought him when he was twenty-one, in which he had learned to fly. If Magnus had flown a De Havilland Moth he would be able to fly this one as well, Strehlitz said, pleased to meet another flying enthusiast. He invited Magnus to try out the plane the next morning.

'Here are the beginnings of a new Luftwaffe,' he declared proudly as he locked up the barn, 'rising out of the ashes of the war, even though its wings were clipped by that shameful business at Versailles.'

Magnus found it odd to hear the peace treaty referred to as 'that shameful business'. It had never occurred to him that anyone might see it in that light; but then, Magnus's country had been on the winning side.

Botho von Strehlitz was *deutschnational* and an admirer of Germany's new strong man, Hitler. At dinner that evening, flanked by her Airman and her Wanderer, Etta steered the conversation past political subjects until, inevitably, Hindenburg's demise and Hitler's recent acquisition of power came up. Botho sought to justify Hitler's recent actions in the urgency of the national interest; Dietrich denied their legitimacy. Magnus had difficulty following the argument between them, but on the whole he thought he was on Dietrich's side. He was more or less familiar with names like Schleicher and Röhm. He knew they had been liquidated in some sort of *putsch* earlier that summer, but as he had been sitting his exams at the time his knowledge of these events was hazy.

Viewed from England, at least, through the reports he read in *The Times*, the spectacle of rival political gangs carrying out assassinations in the streets and of people being murdered in their beds had not made Hitler's government appear either reliable or desirable. It was definitely not the sort of thing that happened in England. It was unthinkable. As for what happened across the Channel, however, one had become resigned to the idea that for reasons best known to themselves this was how people on the Continent managed their political affairs. Grand isolationists, conscious of their superiority, the English looked with diffidence across the water at this hurly-burly the Germans chose to describe as a political *Kultur*. Magnus, too, had acquired the superior attitude effortlessly.

But the more the Wanderer saw of the Airman, who, above all else, could fly superbly, exciting his admiration and his envy, the more he felt bound to admit that the difference between them was the difference between the amateur and the professional. Flying, like almost everything in his life, was something Magnus had learned by feel. He knew that in response to certain actions an aircraft would behave in certain ways; Botho knew why it did. The things that Magnus more or less grasped, Botho understood profoundly. Compared with Botho, Magnus was a dilettante.

Of course it was true that Magnus was a classical scholar whereas Botho was an engineer, but the difference was not so much one of aptitude as attitude. It had to do with the German's thoroughness, behind which Magnus sensed a reluctance, even a fear, to leave anything to chance. Germans were unwilling to live with a lack of order. In law, philosophy and science, the presiding spirit of the German language was one of taxonomy, of classification. Like a Roman legion, wherever the language went it imposed order, and by inference, when order was seen to be absent, disorder at the same time, just as the principles of taxonomy were rooted in what was essentially their divisive nature. Living inside the language for a sustained period, while it still remained new to him, Magnus stood a little out of line and could glimpse correspondences that seemed to foreshadow important truths. He saw the difference between himself and Botho, the airman–engineer. He acknowledged the German's professionalism, his thoroughness, while at the same time he saw that these qualities were rooted in a desire to have power over things, just as the methodical arrangement, the administration (*Verwaltung*) of them shared the same etymological stem as the violence (*Gewalt*) that was done to them.

Even life at Holm, evenly spaced and reassuring in the recurring sameness of its days, was taut with the expectations it had of itself, the discipline required to conserve it as it was (or to prevent it from becoming something else). It became vulnerable by reason of its order, in which something apparently quite trivial, like a disturbance of the nightly ritual surrounding the combing of Etta's hair, could hold alarming premonitions for everything that surrounded her, and might even jeopardise the order of the estate itself. An event foreshadowed in this way was Etta's own death, a fatality resulting from a triviality, eleven years later in 1945. One repercussion of the Soviet army's occupation of Holm was that the old lady, forced out of her room, had to sleep in a different bed from the one she had been used to for half a century. Falling out of it on the side where she was accustomed to there being a wall, poor Aunt Etta broke her hip, an injury that led to her death.

Botho, for his part, was astonished by the Englishman's ignorance of technical matters, even more by his negligence. He saw it as an expression of the superior English attitude. He had heard that the main reason for the late admission of engineering as a faculty at British universities was that engineering had not been considered a proper subject for a gentleman's attention. He was unable to understand how a self-confessed enthusiast could get into a flying machine without proper study – without at least being curious to know how the machine functioned – and yet happily entrust his life to it. This showed a lack of seriousness. On the other hand, it was just this lack of seriousness that Botho found attractive about Magnus. He couldn't make up his mind whether to despise the Englishman for his foolhardiness or admire him for his panache.

After ten minutes' theoretical introduction to the Sopwith, a machine he had never sat in before, Magnus rolled out of the barn and took off. Botho watched the plane circle the village. The test would be how Magnus brought it down. He overshot on the first approach, and for some reason changed his mind on the second. Perhaps he wanted to get the feel of the machine before bringing it down. The plane roared off in the direction of the lake and disappeared. Ten minutes later, having almost grazed the top of the barn, the Sopwith made a perfect landing. Magnus got out, grinning.

By the end of the day the Englishman had shown the German that he was also capable of handling both of the Fokker fighter planes. It was straight there and back, basic airmanship with no fancy stuff, but Botho was impressed.

'You have a natural talent for flying,' he said generously.

It was Magnus's turn to be impressed when they staged a mock dogfight with the two Fokkers for the benefit of the farmworkers on their way back to Holm that evening from the outlying fields where they had been harvesting. Botho, in the much faster DVII, flew rings round the E1. But even after they swapped planes it was clear that if they had been using live ammunition Botho would probably have shot Magnus down on the first pass. The underdog climbed out of the cockpit, somewhat chastened.

'That would have been the short end of it for you today, Mr Magnus,' the foreman said with satisfaction, and the farm labourers nodded their agreement as they helped to roll the aircraft back into the barn.

The two young men went for a swim in the lake. Magnus had tanned a deep brown after weeks of working outdoors in the hot weather. When he slipped off his shorts and stood naked on the shore in the fading light, the contrasting white taking on an almost luminous quality, Botho was surprised to see how light-skinned he was.

'You're so fair! I can hardly believe you're Jewish.'

'Jewish? Whatever gave you that idea?'

'With a name like Gould you must be.'

'Good Lord, no.'

Magnus laughed and dived into the lake.

When he had swum out a hundred yards from the shore he turned and floated on his back. Botho submerged as he came swimming towards him, surfacing directly underneath Magnus and tipping him over.

Magnus came up spluttering.

'Just you wait . . .'

'Race you back, Magnus.'

Botho was a powerful swimmer but lay too deep in the water, and Magnus, with the better technique, soon outstripped him. They lay panting in the water, resting on a tree trunk by the shore.

'You're stronger than you look,' said Botho, taking Magnus by the arm and squeezing his biceps.

'Better than the other way round.'

He pulled himself out of the water and jumped up and down to get dry.

'Did you really think I was Jewish?'

'Names having to do with gold are nearly always Jewish, you know. And then . . . well, I couldn't help noticing that you've been circumcised.'

'Does being circumcised here mean you're Jewish? At school in England there were tons of people who'd been circumcised and weren't Jewish. In fact it's the first I've heard of any connection. I thought it was just, you know, hygiene and that sort of thing.'

'Here it means you're Jewish.'

'Ah. But, I mean . . . is that some sort of a problem? I was at school with Jews. They're just like everyone else.'

'Jews are not Germans, that is the point. They can't be seen as part of the German nation,' said Botho sharply.

'That wasn't Theodor Mommsen's view.'

'What's Mommsen got to do with it?'

'There seems to have been exactly the same sort of anti-Jewish business fifty years ago, when Bismarck founded the Reich, you know. Mommsen wrote a rather witty pamphlet saying Jews were just as much Germans as anyone else; as the French, for example, who settled in Berlin after they'd been chucked out by Louis the Fourteenth.

He says that if you were to take the *Germania* of Tacitus as your yard-stick, nobody alive today would qualify as a German national. I mean, Mommsen is sort of the German national historian, along with Ranke, isn't he? One would think he must have known a thing or two about his subject.'

Botho looked at him in astonishment.

'You read Mommsen?'

'But of course. You forget that I'm a classicist, and Mommsen's work on ancient Rome is one of the best there is on the subject.'

'What Mommsen says about Jews is nonetheless wrong-headed.'

They got dressed and walked back to the village. For some reason, the otherwise charming Botho had lost his poise when the conversation turned to Jews. Magnus changed the subject.

'It would be marvellous to try the Fokkers out on a longer run.'

'We could fly up to the coast and perhaps across the Baltic to Denmark, or Sweden.'

'That would be grand. Perhaps Sophie would like to come along for the ride.'

'Women don't much like flying, in my experience.'

'Oh, nonsense, Botho. They *love* flying.'

Botho shrugged.

'Well, ask her if you like. You can tell me in the morning. Good night.'

He shook Magnus's hand and turned off down the avenue leading to the house on the other side of the park.

4

The harvest was mostly in by the time the weather broke. It rained for days. Dietrich cut short his holiday and returned to Berlin. Botho also had business there, and he asked Magnus to join him for a few days. Magnus excused himself on the grounds that he wanted to be on hand to help out with the rest of the harvest as soon as the weather allowed. This was true, even if there was nothing to be done for the time being. Kurtz said that once the weather broke in August it usually meant the summer was over. Magnus felt a pang of sadness.

A letter had arrived from his father in England, with talk of civil-service exams and career opportunities not to be missed 'for frivolous reasons', urging him to return. He considered whether he should join Botho in Berlin after all, and continue the journey home from there. Meanwhile it rained on and he waited at Holm, as if the rain was somehow responsible for delaying his departure, for preventing him from taking any kind of action at all. Magnus didn't want to do anything that might upset the balance. He didn't want the summer to be over or his vacation to end, and this had less to do with anything awaiting or not awaiting him in England than with his reluctance to say goodbye to Sophie Romberg.

He didn't know what to make of his feelings for Sophie. She attracted him. Things with Sophie were so much clearer and to the point than with girls his own age. He let himself be guided by what his feelings *ought* to be for a divorced woman who was twelve years older than himself, and as things stood, clearly his feelings wouldn't do. Nothing good could ever come of a relationship with an older woman.

It seemed rash, even presumptuous, to suppose that a mature woman who already knew her way around in the world could take the slightest interest in him. Magnus nonetheless had the temerity to believe that Sophie liked him. Whenever their paths crossed at Holm, she seemed pleased to see him, but beyond this he didn't know. The early-morning swim they shared had somehow made them allies; but in what kind of alliance? Overcoming his constraints, Magnus had gradually allowed himself to look at Sophie's naked body when she undressed at the lake, and the morning's images came back to him as memories at night; images that stirred a sexual desire. But such desire was inadmissible. It seemed to Magnus to be immoral, a betrayal of hospitality, to be a guest at Holm and at the same time to have erotic thoughts of Sophie Romberg's body. He wavered between disappointment and relief when the weather brought their morning swims to an end.

Kurtz was wrong about the weather. When the rain ceased the summer came back, and Magnus again put off answering the letter from England. For a couple of days the swims with Sophie were resumed, until the morning Botho returned in a flurry and the three of them took off a few hours later. Elena and Bernhard climbed through the skylight and stood waving on the roof as the planes passed overhead. It was the last time Magnus saw them, the last he ever saw of Holm, although he didn't know it at the time. On their way back they took a different route, so Magnus was able to go on directly to England without the detour via Holm. He was confident of being able to defer his return visit until later, but for reasons that would have seemed unimaginable at the time there was never a return visit to Holm.

Botho flew solo in the Fokker monoplane, and Magnus piloted the Sopwith with Sophie as his passenger. Exhilarated, they flew north through a pale blue sky, following the course of the Oder River, a ribbon of light standing out in the ground haze, with the sun travelling below them, a dazzling sphere reflected in the surface of the water. The delta was arranged like textile patterns, greens, browns and greys beautifully mottled, deer bounding through the constantly moving sun reflected in the marshland, giving way to small river craft scattered like matchsticks on the broadening river, and then Stettin, the Stettiner Haff, and the deep blue bay on the edge of the Baltic, with visibility all the way to the Swedish coast. They flew north-west in an arc across the bay, touching down on the island of Rügen, bringing the aircraft to a halt on a beach near the grand spa hotel outside Binz. Guests came out on to the terrace of the Kurhaus to watch the flying machines land by the sea, cheering the pilots as they came up the steps into the hotel, still numb with cold, and asked for rooms for the night.

An intriguing, even problematical threesome – from the moment of their arrival the flying woman and her two companions excited speculation among the mostly middle-aged and elderly guests as to which of them was her husband. Inquiries disguised as polite conversation in the Kurhaus lounge, where they appeared, impeccably transformed, for cocktails before dinner, established that neither of them was, and accordingly both must be her lovers.

The two gentlemen availed themselves of the evening dress offered by the hotel management, while the flying lady had evidently brought her own. It was a striking, aristocratic face that emerged from behind the balaclava and goggles, a striking figure she cut in her sleeveless silk gown. The threesome preferred not to merge with the other guests. At dinner they chose to be seated at a separate table. During the dancing afterwards they also kept to themselves, showing no interest in any other partners. Perhaps they noticed the glances of envy, gradually growing into disapproval, but they didn't seem to care. Just this carelessness and self-absorption (as some of the older onlookers reminded themselves) were the privileges of youth, privileges of which youth was by definition unaware.

Magnus was unaware of anything beyond a radiance that had settled around him from the moment he had climbed into the cockpit that morning. He still saw the river below him, a green-bordered ribbon of light in the glittering afternoon, the brightness of the sky around him; still heard the rush of wind and felt it on his cheeks. He saw the colours of wind and sunlight soaked up in Sophie's burning face across the table, her skin standing out darkly against the waves breaking white on the Baltic strand, the whites of her eyes, as they walked along the beach through the blustery night.

Botho was always there, on the far side of Sophie. She was the older woman, she was beautiful, and she was forbidden. Without Botho there too, Sophie remained unimaginable for Magnus. But they could take her between them, linking arms, walking for miles along the white strand. The wind sank, the moon rose over the sea. They reached a village, capsized on a steep hill. They walked up through the silent streets. It was Sassnitz, Botho said; Brahms had written his first symphony here. One could hear it in the sea – listen! Beneath them the Baltic rumbled, a deep murmur spreading in overlays, rippling out of a shell. Botho led the way up a path along the top of the cliff through a wood lit up by a luminous glow. What is it, Magnus asked Sophie, what's that marvellous light? It's the light reflected from the chalk cliffs, she replied. When they reached the clifftop clearing no further description was possible. The three of them stood speechless on the edge, looking down in amazement. Stark and shadowless in the moonlight, the white cliffs dropped away below them for hundreds of feet. Far beneath them glittered the sea, as motionless as in a painting. Magnus would never forget the scene.

Sophie did not shake their hands, as she usually did, when they brought her to her room and said goodnight. She kissed each of them in turn, and when Magnus reached his own room, and Botho brushed his cheek with his lips as they stood for a moment in the dark, there seemed nothing unnatural in this action, nor in the dream of the three of them making love together that Magnus had that night. He was flying away from a provincial middle-class English background, the morality it had taught him, of which he had never been particularly conscious before; but now, looking down on it, so small and far away, he began to feel ashamed and longed to be rid of it.

Compared with Botho's lifestyle, the abstemiousness and frugality held up as ideals at home looked paltry and unimaginative. His parents made so much of principles only because they had no choice. Puritans were people afraid of their desires who made a virtue of their fear. But Magnus longed to be corrupted – if only he dared! Botho seemed so rich to him, not in the sense that he came from a wealthy background, but because he excluded nothing from a fuller appreciation of life. Indiscriminate, perhaps even amorally curious, the breadth and enthusiasm of Botho's tastes and interests were possible only in someone who knew no snobbishness. Magnus found this engaging, and somehow un-English.

Botho came, already dressed, to his room at dawn. He told Magnus the weather forecast was for high winds building up along the coast during the course of the day, so they should leave earlier than planned. Magnus came out on to the balcony, where Botho was smoking, lounging against the railing and looking out to sea. It was windless now, the sea calm, the strand deserted. Botho ruffled his hair affectionately and lit him a cigarette. Magnus had picked up the habit of smoking from Botho, just as he had begun to imitate other mannerisms and attitudes of his. Together they walked along the beach to check the aircraft before taking a swim. They came back for breakfast, and as they were crossing the terrace Magnus asked Botho where they would be flying. I'm keeping that a surprise, said Botho. At that moment someone called, and they looked up. Magnus saw Sophie waving from the balcony of her room, and his heart leaped. When he went to the reception desk after breakfast to pay his bill, Magnus was told that it had already been settled by the baron.

Botho refused to accept any money from him.

'You should always pay your way,' Magnus could hear his father saying, and when he accepted Botho's hospitality it was in the spirit of rebellion. How trivial! Yet he felt a rush of pleasure at his own daring, a release from his parents' small-town morality.

On a south-east course, again following the Oder River, they flew non-stop for several hours until they were forced down by a thunderstorm, landing in a field not far from Prague. They spent the night in a barn and flew on to Bavaria the next day, coming down over a sheet of bright water late in the afternoon. Botho had friends who lived in a castle overlooking Lake Starnberg, where they were invited to stay. In the distance you could see a chain of mountains, the foothills of the Alps. It was the first time Magnus had seen the

Alps. He had never seen anything more glorious. He caught a train to Innsbruck and walked up over the mountains to Oberammergau, where he arranged to meet Sophie and Botho. But Botho was feeling unwell, and to his delight Sophie came alone.

In the summer of that year the village was celebrating the three-hundredth anniversary of the Passion Play. Magnus sat in the audience beside the woman with whom he had fallen in love and recognised the feeling as the kind of *Fernweh* he had first experienced in Malmö harbour, which had drawn him apparently to Holm, actually to Sophie herself. *Fernweh* measured a human distance that seemingly could never be closed. The longing of the soul seemed to burn brightest after it had completed its journey, still yearning to be at the destination when it had already arrived.

Perhaps the fulfilment of Magnus's first love found expression in its incompleteness. *Durch Leiden Freude.* How true! For Magnus had lacked the courage of suffering, stopping short of experience because he was afraid of the risk. He had been too aware, as Sophie perhaps had also been, though for different reasons, of the distance into which they would release one another when they parted afterwards, and in anticipation of which (although passionately embracing on the dark guest-house landing in the swirl of wedding music that sprang up the stairs), each of them had shrunk back at the last moment, said goodnight and gone separately into their empty rooms.

'Goodbye!'

He stood in a stubble field on the edge of the lake and waved when the biplane took off. The Sopwith turned and came directly at him. He ducked involuntarily as it roared overhead, swooping so low over the water that the compressed whorls of air left furrows on the surface. A shadow briefly tracked its flight across the lake, and then both were gone. He walked back to the castle, wishing he could have followed in the other plane that was parked on the back lawn. Botho had generously lent it to his friends. Magnus went inside to fetch his rucksack, noticing the jagged patterns left by the sunlight on the floor, the sharp coolness of the shadows; aware of the residue in the rooms they had left.

A bruise was coming up inside him. The air stood still around the house. The sound made by a man he could see whetting a scythe on the far side of an inlet bounced off the water, coming across to him clearly. He set off for Starnberg station. It was a warm autumn day. Spiky green chestnuts lay strewn along the avenue. A long drawn-out whine rose from the grass verge, mournfully, an autumn dirge, as if the residue was already fading in the rooms they had left. One could see the softness of the air over the lake. When Magnus stopped to look and listen, the breeze that got up as soon as he walked at once died on him again. He felt the inertia, the speechlessness of his surroundings, their utter indifference.

From Munich there was a night train to the coast. He bought his ticket and wandered around the station. Somebody important must have been about to arrive or depart. A carpet ran down a platform, enormous blood-red banners with swastikas emblazoned black on white hung unfurled from the central arch. At the exit, leading out on to a large square, they were driving piles into the ground with a pneumatic hammer, making a deafening noise, which even from the far side of the square he could still hear as a dully metallic gonging. The trams rushed past him, clanging, and a column of men in brown shirts marched across in front of him, blocking his path. The people on their way across the square waited, like Magnus, and then went on about their business, paying them no attention. He strolled on through an archway down a crowded street and went into a hall with sawdust on the floor, where he drank a beer, before returning to the station to catch his train. The pneumatic hammer was still driving piles into the ground, beating a slow, steady rhythm that got into his head and wouldn't come out, underlying the rattle of wheels on rails, the hiss of steam in the night and the plunging of ships' horns at dawn on the French coast where the sun came up suddenly over a becalmed sea.

5

Sophie's letters to Magnus were at first forwarded from Devon in his mother's careful hand to addresses in Cambridge and then London, and thereafter, in Sophie's own hand, they arrived at the mud-brick town at the mouth of a river that flowed into the Red Sea where Magnus, apprenticed to a colonial trading house in preparation for nothing that would ever be of much use to him, learned to buy and sell spices and skins, carpets and coffee for the first two years of his working life.

He could not say how he had got into the trading house other than that there hadn't seemed to be any way out of it. There had been an offer, and in a hurry he had accepted it. He could not become a farmer on his own land, not even an estate manager, as he had hoped. He lacked the background. But at the end of two years there was the prospect of returning to Europe, perhaps even of spending his first home leave with Sophie in Berlin when the city hosted the Olympic Games in 1936. With joy he thought of her on his way through the air as he dived from a high rock on an offshore island in the Arabian Sea, and in a flash, the instant he sliced the clear green water, he knew that the only reason for him to go to Berlin was to ask Sophie to marry him.

But it was not to be. There was the Abyssinian Crisis. There was one crisis after another, and for some reason the crises of other people took precedence over his own. Overnight, Magnus seemed to become indispensable to the life of a commercial company whose usefulness to his own had never been more than incidental. Informed that his leave was cancelled, and with it the reunion in Berlin when he would propose to Sophie, which had provided the only real focus of his life since the day he had left Holm, Magnus took refuge in his parents' morality, telling himself it was his duty, and obeyed.

The correspondence with Sophie Romberg withered, and after her second marriage died away altogether. But as the years passed, the memory of her did not fade. Curiously, it became ever stronger – the shimmer of gold dust flowing in the river on the far side of the sea where Magnus's other life had been. The war came, and the amateur pilot flew antique planes across Africa, helping to secure the supply lines of the Eighth Army, which was fighting Rommel's troops in the desert. The war ended, and he stayed on as a civil administrator, marrying, raising a family, and reading newspaper accounts of the unspeakable horrors perpetrated in Europe that he could not begin to understand. A curtain came down over Europe and Holm lay on the wrong side, a void in which his letters were swallowed up unanswered. Was Sophie still alive? Somehow Magnus felt a responsibility for the things that had happened, which in time crystallised as a remorse for the things that he had not done, because the course of his life seemed to have lacked a destiny.

The lands he might have farmed had not materialised, nor the estates he might have managed, as Kurtz had done; even Africa crumbled away under the colonial career that had seemed to be shaping there, weaving the pattern that began with his early days as a trader on the Red Sea. The empire disintegrated, and there was no pattern left. One job turned out to be as satisfactory as another, one place as good as the next, but Magnus was capable of disappointment that it had not been otherwise because he had glimpsed the gold dust in the stream, seen it gravitating to a point of convergence that had seemed inescapable. And yet he had let it slip through his fingers. Between Sophie Romberg and himself there had been a common ground, mutual feelings rooting them in place with a sense of belonging that Magnus had recognised as stronger than anything he had experienced in life – unquestionably, then, a destiny, something which had to be; and yet was not. How had it failed to coalesce?

Somehow their bodies had never managed to touch when they swam together in the lake at Holm, and looking back from the shore

in his later life Magnus saw the always separate wakes they had left
behind them. He found it increasingly painful to remember how
casually he had allowed an Italian adventure in Ethiopia to come
between him and the woman he had regarded as his future wife (a
quarter of a century later, he could still clearly hear the music in the
guest-house rooms downstairs when, turning away down the landing
to go without her to his room that night, he had released Sophie forever from his life). With the dread of self-recognition Magnus saw
his flatness where he should have been hollowed out, the tightness
and the brittleness of the vessel into which his destiny had been
poured, a destiny he had been unable to receive. He saw what he
thought of as the deficiencies in his upbringing that were at fault,
and then what had been lacking in his own nature, and he knew it
was his own fault, because in the end Magnus had been afraid to
receive.

Why, then, had Botho von Strehlitz written to him? Why had the
letter come, via half a dozen forwarding stations, fifteen years after
the war, fifteen years after Sophie died in an air-raid on Berlin?
What was the meaning of such a letter when all this had been lost in
any case – everything except a pile of letters and the reproduction of
a painting which Sophie had sent him as a souvenir of their walk
along the Baltic coast that night, Caspar David Friedrich's 'Chalk
Cliffs on Rügen'?

The image of Malmö harbour as seen by Magnus Gould on a
summer evening in 1934 is the image of his life. It is an image of his
own creation. The harbour is the turntable swinging each vessel
round in the direction it has been assigned, the dial pointing to all
the places that will become its destination. From here the ships run
out across the sea. But not for him. Magnus remains in a frieze on
the harbour wall, chin on hand, looking out to sea. He is the man
who has not received a destiny. He does not embark. He leaves that
to his son, whose name he hears them calling faintly across the
water, *Jason, Jason*, as the men pull at the creaking oars and the ship
glides out over the dusky sea.

1961

1

When Jason Gould mythologised his life, he began with the Expulsion from Paradise. He mythologised the scene where he was playing under a table in the house in Africa, and overheard his parents talking about sending him away to school in Europe, as the Expulsion from Paradise. This was the picture that had hung on the wall in the missionary school in Africa. His life there was not in paradise, of course, but his leaving it was nonetheless an expulsion, from the warmth, space and brightness that surrounded him in Africa to the cold narrow enclosures of the boarding schools in England into which he disappeared.

According to the mythology Jason established early in his life, the events that happened to him might be arbitrary but they were still inescapable. Jason's childhood was swallowed up by institutions where arbitrariness was the rule, but from which he could not escape. Memories of the brief spaces between one institution and another were as random as the places they recalled, station platforms, holiday homes, the apartments of people he had never seen before and did not expect ever to see again.

The conversation he overheard between his parents became the caption for the picture on the wall in the missionary school, the picture became the image for the conversation, both; the one gravitated to the other by some mysterious force of attraction, and became a significant mass, for which there was no reason, and from which there was no escape.

In the mythology of Jason's life, the reciprocal attraction of things with qualities in common (the image and the caption drawn irresistibly together) is the process of *Anziehung des Bezüglichen*, or Attraction of Affinities, gravitating to the point of convergence that is his destiny.

2

Jason was walking directly towards the café on the Kurfürstendamm when the elderly gentleman got up and made for the exit. It was one of those pavement cafés consisting entirely of glass, typical of Berlin but still a novelty for Jason, who had arrived in the city only the day before. He noticed the old gentleman inside the café, marching confidently towards him with his walking stick, just seconds before there was a terrific crash.

The old man had walked straight into a sheet of glass. Fortunately the glass was not broken and the old man was unhurt. Jason stopped in his tracks a few yards away and watched the expression on his face. Astonishment was followed by anger. Scowling, the man rapped the glass with his stick, as if it had no business to be there and must get out of the way at once. Jason and someone who was standing nearby burst out laughing at the same moment.

He glanced curiously at his fellow laugher. He was a young man a few years older than himself, perhaps nineteen or twenty, but already with an impressive beard and wearing a sort of flowing cape, both of which Jason could not but envy. Still smiling, the young man turned to Jason, his hand foraging on his chin, plucking at the extraordinary growth there, and said, '*Begegnung mit einer unmöglichen Tatsache. Nicht sein kann, was nicht sein darf!* A perfect demonstration!' in such an ironically amused, intimately confiding tone of voice that Jason at once took a liking to him.

The feeling must have been mutual, for with one accord they stepped into the café (where the old gentleman was still held captive, still protesting angrily at the obstructive sheet of glass), and Holger, waiving introductions, proceeded to expound his view of the case.

3

Holger's first words to Jason refer to the title and the last line of 'Die Unmögliche Tatsache', a poem by the humorist Christian Morgenstern. 'The Impossible Fact' relates how Palmström, a character invented by Morgenstern who figures in many of his poems, is run over by a car at a street corner. A true German, Palmström rises argumentatively from death to discuss the philosophical and legal aspects of having been run over, for surely this accident cannot have been in accordance with the law.

> And thereupon it's crystal clear:
> Cars have no business driving here!
>
> And he comes to the conclusion
> It must all have been an illusion.
> For the good reason (he avowed)
> Things cannot be that are not allowed.

Holger pointed at the elderly gentleman, who was now complaining angrily to the manager. What a ridiculous figure he was making of himself! For he had obviously walked into a sheet of glass, and it was equally obvious that in his pig-headedness he was not going to accept that fact.

'He's declaring the glass out of order. He's denying its right to be there. Soon he'll be denying its right to exist. Did you observe the indignation on his face when his progress through space was forestalled by the intervention of that pane of glass? That is how a German looks who has just had an encounter with an impossible fact. Oh goodness me, no – things cannot be that are not allowed!'

When he learned that Jason was a foreigner, the young law student

eagerly broadened the scope of his diatribe and began to criticise his
fellow Germans, with growing enthusiasm, in much more general
terms, but Jason could not understand everything he said. Holger
talked without stopping for half an hour, until he was almost gleam-
ing with good humour at all the unpleasant things it had occurred to
him to point out about his countrymen. When he got up and
excused himself at last, he inadvertently left Jason to pay the bill, but
also with an invitation to come and visit him. Before leaving, he
wrote out Morgenstern's poem along with his address and telephone
number, and thus it was that 'The Impossible Fact' on the reverse
side of a bill for two cups of coffee and cheese cake became the first
heading in the taxonomy that Jason Gould was drawing up as he
began to make his acquaintance with German life.

The baron who was his father's friend lived in a leafy street with deep
shadows just off the Kurfürstendamm. The baron's major domo and
his mother, a war widow who somewhat resembled the tall narrow
house in which she lived, completed the Strehlitz household. The
atmosphere was ceremonious, a little stiff, like the language, with all
its inflections and conjugations, formal and informal modes of
speech. Jason moved through language and house with the same caution and initial sense of estrangement. Solid nouns stood in their
sentences like fortresses, as impregnable as the oak furniture that
asserted its claims on household space. There was a sense that nothing here would ever be persuaded to budge. There would be no
pirouettes. Nothing would be likely to rise involuntarily on tiptoe
and begin to dance.

Meals were served by Tiedke, the major domo, at a table in an
alcove overlooking the street. Twice a day he stood in the hall and
rang a bell, and to Jason, on his way downstairs, the shadows collecting there seemed momentarily to be dispersed by the brightness
of the sound.

The baron was the youngest of four brothers. The baron's mother
had lost her husband in the First World War, three of her four sons
in the Second. Botho was the sole survivor.

After a week in the death-laden house, with flashes twice a day

when the shadows in the stairwell were fleetingly chased away, Jason's
taxonomy acquired another heading. The German word for gravity
was *Schwerkraft*, the heavy force. A heavy force here was something
that seemed to weigh more than gravity did elsewhere. Levity could
oppose gravity, but not in German. An opposing force of *Leichtkraft*
had never been named. Jason mocked the pedantry and the solem-
nity of the Strehlitz household, but the seriousness at the core of his
high-spirited nature was at the same time attracted by an affinity he
found here. There was no need to disguise himself.

Botho von Strehlitz was not at all like the rest of his household,
however. The baron was convivial, informal, cheerfully obscene. In
the mornings he wandered around the house with a cigarette and a
cup of coffee, his penis hanging over the cord of his pyjama trousers.
He cracked jokes and recited limericks. He offered Jason the informal *Du* from the start, was generous with alcohol and cigarettes
and spoke to him confidentially as if he were his equal, not a sixteen-
year-old boy on his first trip abroad.

There could not have been a greater difference between the
baron and Jason's father, so remote and self-sufficient. Magnus
lived in retirement behind a wall, whereas when Botho was around,
Jason always felt there was a standing invitation in his presence. He
admired his host's silk shirts and old-fashioned smoking-jackets,
his cigarette-holders; he liked the warm dark smells that hung in
his study and the way he interrupted business to come down and
eat peaches in the middle of the afternoon. He rather liked the fact
that this stylish, unconventional man was a baron. Soon he came
completely under his spell.

'Should I call you Botho? It seems such a strange name. It doesn't
seem like a real name.'

'Oh?'

A smile creased the corners of his eyes.

'Then why, for the sake of simplicity, when you join our little
gathering this evening, don't you just call me "Colonel" like the rest
of the boys?'

They both laughed.

For Botho somehow still was the colonel, even though the war had ended. All the young men who came to his seminars every Wednesday evening stood at attention when they entered the house and greeted him with '*Guten Abend*, Herr Oberst!' With all the bowing and clicking of heels that went on in the hall a military chill seized hold of the house, and Jason's heart beat faster when the colonel opened the doors of an enormous, candlelit room which he had never been inside before.

4

Jason had lived as many years as had passed since the end of the Second World War. The war had ended only sixteen years ago – except it hadn't ended, it had just been turned off, in full spate. It dripped on in strip cartoons featuring heroes like Battler Britain, who was always getting the best of stupid German thugs. '*Wham!*' '*Donner and Blitzen, der Engländer!*' 'Take that, Kraut!' Jason knew the war comic books by heart. Battler Britain flew alongside V–2 missiles nearing the cliffs of Dover and flipped them with the wing-tips of his plane, sending them back across the Channel. The protagonists rose from the dead and came back for more, week after week. There were no Jews or concentration camps in these comics. There were teams and team sports. War was fun.

When Jason was eleven an uncle took him out to lunch at a well-known London restaurant. In the course of the meal his uncle raised his hand and crooked his index finger. 'There sits a Jew,' he said.

Jason stared across the room at the table where the Jew was sitting. He looked the man up and down and wondered what was different about him. But as far as he could see, the man looked like everyone else.

Perhaps this was what was sinister about the Jew. He looked just like everyone else, only he wasn't. This was sinister. This was why the uncle crooked his finger.

'There sits a Jew,' says the uncle, crooking his finger, and the Jew first enters Jason's conscious life with something sinister (crooked) about him, because whatever it is, it's invisible, the stigma of the Jew.

*

Once they had been identified, Jews seemed to sprout everywhere. At school they were envied because they needed to shave at an age when most Gentiles didn't have a hair on their chins. They had strange names – Süskind, Berlin, de Hond – which sounded as if they had been made up. They ate kosher bangers that looked like cocktail sausages and had a rubbery flavour. The differences became visible.

There seemed no particular reason why they should have the privilege of special food or of exemption from Saturday-morning class, but those were the rules, part of that order of things which in childhood was still the sole order of things, and which for lack of an alternative was never questioned. It was part of the sole order of things that Jews were different.

The Jews learned German like everyone else who opted for the modern languages course. Süskind always won the German reading prize. He was a Jew, but somehow he was also sort of German, so it wasn't really fair. But when the music master played the first bars of the 'Deutschlandlied' and asked everyone to sing along, the Jews kept their mouths firmly shut. It was a protest, because of what the Germans had done to their fellow Jews in the war.

What had the Germans done?

In the pool of dirty books that were passed from hand to hand and read by flashlight under the bedclothes at night, *Messalina, Whore of Rome*, sex manuals, titles by Harold Robbins, there were also dog-eared accounts of what had gone on in the concentration camps. It was wicked. It was thrilling. You took care not to get caught reading them because they were dirty books.

The dirty books were stowed away in lockers in the house changing-room, where the boys boasted about giving the Yids a bashing as they laced up their rugger boots and went cheerfully out on to English playing fields to engage in team sports.

Battler Britain was on their side. The Germans, and the Jews, were on the other.

5

What is this candlelit room in the house where Oberst a.D. von Strehlitz receives his young acolytes? It is a clearing in the forest, a place for the mystical union of souls. The swastika is forbidden, but two red, white and black flags, banners bearing the naval insignia of the Second Reich and unfurling memories of the Third, stand guard on either side of the fireplace. Below a pair of crossed sabres mounted on the wall above the mantelpiece hangs a picture of a German soldier.

The face that looks out from under the square helmet has high cheekbones; it is a rugged face, the eyes piercing, the jaw thrust firmly forward. The inscription underneath the picture reads: 'The God whose hand let iron grow, he had no love of slaves.' It is a picture out of a comic book that Jason instinctively knows it is forbidden for them to admire. His heart beats faster, sensing in the forest beyond the clearing something that is wicked, and thrilling, and *verboten*. He is thrilled by the shadowy outline lurking in the words *der Gott, der Eisen wachsen liess, er wollte keine Knechte*. It is an incitement to take arms, to free themselves from the yoke – but from what yoke?

Jason strains to understand what the colonel is telling them, about the war of liberation of the German *Volk* under the yoke of Napoleon. He speaks of the courage and the idealism of those student associations which met to proclaim the rights of a sovereign German nation in the fortress where Luther, three hundred years before, had sought refuge from persecution, translated the Bible into high German and laid the foundations for their language; of the subsequent persecution and imprisonment of those early heroes of the German national movement, the enduring glory they have found in the music left to posterity by the greatest composer who ever lived, Ludwig van Beethoven.

At this point the colonel reaches discreetly for the gramophone under the desk and plays them the first movement of the *Eroica Symphony*. They sit in the candlelit room, heads bowed, listening to the glorious music, and their souls are uplifted. They feel noble. They feel ready to undertake acts calling for idealism and courage. There is nothing of which they are afraid in the darkness of the forest. For the moment, however, there is nothing more terrible in the darkness than the barrel of beer that awaits them in the corner. The colonel draws foaming tankards and hands them round, and the young men burst into song. It is the old student song, '*Die Gedanken sind frei*'. Jason doesn't yet know the words, but he drinks the beer and hums along and soon he, too, becomes exuberant. The God whose hand let iron grow, he had no love of slaves! – Tarrah! Thoughts are free! – Throw off the yoke! Moved by these emotions it is his privilege to be allowed to share with the colonel's young friends, Jason has been initiated into the magic circle. He has been seduced, not strictly speaking by Beethoven, or beer, or even a sense of collusion in these dark rituals. By what, then?

A presence has been admitted to the candlelit room. Indistinct, formless, it is a parasite which lives off all of these other feelings, and it is the most persuasive of them all. It comes sidling up to Jason, putting its head in his lap and raising a lump in his throat. He begins to feel sorry for himself. Hold me! Love me! Losing his virginity, Jason succumbs to the insinuations of *kitsch* – most concrete of all German abstract nouns, that user-friendly invention for which there is a universal need – and absolves his first rites of passage on the journey into adult life.

6

Botho was pleased with the new English boy. He was not as physical as his blond, beautiful father had been, but he was more clever. At sixteen he had already finished school, but his parents considered him still too young to go to university. Magnus, in the letter he had written to Botho, alluded to emotional difficulties at home. Emotionally and intellectually, his father thought, Jason was too precocious for his age. He was too excitable. He knew nothing of real life. He should spend the summer abroad, in a different environment, and see something of the world. Botho smiled broadly when he read this letter, savouring the middle-class platitudes Magnus served up, delighted by the irony of Jason's father having chosen him as the boy's keeper.

Magnus could have chosen no one better. Still, at the age of fifty, perfectly at ease with young people, because young people were his preferred companions, by nature sensual, warm and emotionally willing to share himself, Botho represented the opposite of the constrictive English puritanism that ruled in the family from which Jason came. In the Gould family they did not mention sex, not any physical needs, nor intimacies, nor enjoyment of any kind, because things were not done for pleasure. Botho was a discreet homosexual, but not an ashamed one. He had sex, ate, smoke and drank with relish. He talked for the enjoyment of talking. He was a cultivated man, whose ease and pleasure in life flowed from an underlying self-confidence.

Jason, at sixteen, lacked any self-confidence. His self was still forming, his core wrapped in cloud; all that could be seen on the surface was his adolescent enthusiasm. Nothing was more vulnerable than this enthusiasm. Botho's sensitivity to that fact was sharpened by a lustful awareness of what it would be within his power, if he chose, to destroy. Rimbaud and Dylan Thomas accompanied Jason in his suitcase. Botho came to the boy's room the night he arrived, and saw a book open at a poem called 'The force that through the green fuse drives the flower', and soon he noticed Jason taking Trakl and Benn, Hesse and Hölderlin down from his shelves. Having scorched through the pages of poetry, what could such burning-glass enthusiasm reach for without consuming its object as well? For the things that lay beyond experience and could only be known within the cloud of intuition. This was why the enthusiasm, the yearning for things unattainable, was always shadowed by melancholy. Ah! Youth was discovering Mortality. An intuition of the futility of life at its end lay snared within the awareness of its richness at the beginning. The young lyric poet's celebration of the force that through the green fuse drove the flower already anticipated the flower's withering. The life force derived its fervour from the intuition of its death.

The young men invited to the evenings in the colonel's house were sent away each week with a heightened awareness of the thing that mattered most to their mentor, and that was *Deutschtum*, or what it meant to be German. *Deutschtum*, in the diaspora, von Strehlitz said, continued to flourish beyond the merely territorial confines of the German state and the temporal restrictions that had regrettably impinged on it since the end of the war. Knights carried *Deutschtum* north along the Baltic coast a thousand years ago, millions of Germans had gone east into Poland and Hungary, into Russia, bringing culture to an unenlightened people at the request of Catherine the Great, and their descendants still existed as a flourishing culture on the Volga, despite all the Soviet attempts to stamp them out. The superiority of the German contribution to Europe was evident in the frequency with which a nomadic culture had been able to take root in foreign soils and, in time, displace the indigenous one. *Deutschtum* was not bound to a physical entity, as other European cultures were to their native states, in order to survive. It was spirituality, *Geist*. The order and diligence in the national character had been hammered out on the forge of hardship and despair. How could the country have emerged from the devastation of the Thirty Years War, in which half its people had been wiped out, without inner resources of regenerative power, without resilience and a capacity for sheer hard work? Many of the metaphorical rings which Strehlitz drew, encircling *Deutschtum*, also encircled sorrow, ephemerality (*Vergänglichkeit*), darkness, and death. For Jason there was a peculiar fascination in listening to this elegant man (who so evidently enjoyed life), speaking about decay and death with easy eloquence and even a kind of relish. There was easy eloquence and a kind of relish in the word *Vergänglichkeit*, which allowed the bleak perception that all things must decay to merge with a melancholy that was obviously pleasurable. To Jason there seemed to be a kind of masochism in all this.

Week after week the colonel talked confidently about *Deutschtum*, one of the first German apparition nouns with which Jason found himself having to grapple. He talked with a confidence which simply ignored the visitation of *Deutschtum*, this angel of death, on the twentieth century. But if a cult of death belonged to the German identity, as Botho seemed to be implying, did death in Auschwitz, too? Finally Jason asked Botho the unavoidable question.

'What about the five or six million Jews who were murdered in the concentration camps? Are their deaths a part of *Deutschtum?*'

'My dear boy, those figures are entirely exaggerated. We know, from the records, that not more than a few hundred thousand people, at most half a million, were involved in those camps, which of course were rife with all kinds of disease such as typhoid and cholera. So is it any wonder if the death rate was unusually high?'

Confounded (what records?), Jason searched his face and saw Botho looking back at him with a completely steady gaze.

Jason went away in an extremely confused state of mind. Thoughts jumped on him from all directions. He saw the face of the elderly gentleman who had walked into the pane of glass in the café on the Kurfürstendamm, but it wasn't the elderly gentleman. It was Botho, with his nose smudged against the glass and a look of incredulity on his face.

And he comes to the conclusion
It must all have been an illusion.
For the good reason (he avowed)
Things cannot be that are not allowed.

Deutschtum in the twentieth century, fulfilling its destiny as the crowning manifestation of The Impossible Fact: *nicht sein kann, was nicht sein darf.*

Which was where Holger came in.

7

Holger lived in a student commune in Wedding, in the French sector of Berlin, just north of the border with the Soviet sector, which began in Mitte. His room at the top of the dilapidated house in Bernauerstrasse overlooked the broken roofs and desolate streets of East Berlin. During the summer vacation, most of the students travelled abroad or returned to their parents' homes in West Germany. But Holger had broken off relations with his family and stayed in Berlin, in a room where books covered the whole wall except two square yards left for the window. All the books had been stolen, because Holger was a Marxist and he didn't believe in private property.

Whenever Ingrid arrived in Holger's room and noticed a new stolen book on the shelves there would be a row. Ingrid told Holger he was full of shit. If he was a Marxist, why wasn't he living in East Berlin, making his contribution to the workers' and farmers' state? Ingrid lived in East Berlin, although she was not a Marxist. She lived there because there was no help for it. That was where her younger sister lived with her mother, who was a war widow and an invalid, and relied on Ingrid. Ingrid was one of thousands of so-called *Grenzgänger*, border go-betweens who worked in West Berlin and lived in the eastern half of the city.

Early every morning she took the tram from Pankow in the Soviet sector, crossed the border to West Berlin and went to a hotel on the Kurfürstendamm. In the staff pantry she put on a black skirt and white blouse and served breakfast in the dining-room between seven and half-past nine. Then she took off the skirt and blouse and put on her jeans to attend classes at the *Freie Universität*, where she studied medicine. Then she took the tram back to Pankow and did the shopping for her mother. There was less to buy in Pankow, but it was cheaper. Shopping in East Berlin was reserved for people who could prove they were resident. Ingrid's family had always lived there. They were working-class people.

In Holger's eyes, Ingrid lived selflessly. He admired her working-class origins, which made her the real thing. Politically irreproachable, she could even afford to seem uninterested in politics. She had a flawlessly symmetrical face and long blonde hair that hung down to her hips. In Holger's eyes, Ingrid was perfect. It was not so much her beauty that captivated him. He was enthralled by an overwhelming sense of Ingrid's moral superiority. It amazed him that Ingrid was his girlfriend.

'I don't know what you see in me,' he told her, and he meant it. Holger was genuinely modest.

That was what Ingrid saw in him, his modesty and his good nature, both genuine, and she told him so. Holger looked miserable and fiddled with his beard whenever Ingrid mentioned his modesty and good nature. They were such boring virtues, and so bourgeois. Holger came from a very affluent, well-to-do family in Cologne. Ingrid saw that in him, too, but did not speak of it to Holger. Nor did she speak of a feeling of safety in Holger's company which somehow reassured her. At twenty-one, Holger had already managed to acquire the indulgent aura of a pipe-smoking, bearded father figure whom women found attractive for that reason. Ingrid recognised this. In the domain of moral superiority she had another edge over Holger, which was her shrewdness in exploiting that advantage.

In the domain of moral superiority, sixteen years after the war, the cutting edge she had over him was identical to the cutting edge Ingrid's father had had over Holger's father. Ingrid's father was a priest turned communist who had joined the resistance and opposed the Nazis until he was caught and shot by them. Holger's father was a conservative industrialist who had joined the gravy train because it looked good for business and then left it because it looked bad, stepping off before it ground to a halt.

Holger felt ashamed of his father, who had been a Nazi and an opportunist. He would have preferred to have had Ingrid's father. Instead he had Ingrid and was overwhelmed by her moral superiority. Sometimes he felt quite limp beside her blamelessness. When this had a dampening effect on their sexual activities, Holger turned to his imagination for assistance, which it promptly provided in the form of cartoon strips showing Ingrid wearing a black skirt and a white blouse, succumbing to a forceful intruder who raped her in the hotel pantry. Holger did not tell her about these images, because they made him feel ashamed.

Ingrid, whose father had been a victim of the Nazis, and whose mother had been buried for three days under the rubble of a bombed house in Dresden when she was pregnant with Ingrid's sister, seemed to care little about the Nazis and took no particular interest in the war that was past. Holger, whose family had enjoyed substantial benefits during the war as a result of his father's political opportunism, was obsessive about the Nazis and couldn't let go of the past. One wall of the bookshelves that lined his room was devoted exclusively to the Third Reich. Unfortunately, the Nazis refused to be confined to the books on the wall in Holger's room. They stepped out of the books, they came down from the shelves. They hurried down the stairs and out into the streets in an endless column which reached over the horizon. Holger frequently had this nightmare and awoke in terror.

Ingrid didn't know about Holger's nightmare, because at night she wasn't there. She was in East Berlin, in her mother's apartment in Pankow. She came to West Berlin only during the day, when she knew Holger as always cheerful and good-natured, a typical Rheinländer, who had something that she found reassuring; a father figure.

Since she didn't care about the Nazis and the past, she would probably not have been able to understand that Holger was forced to become a father figure to himself because he had lost his own.

In the summer vacation Holger drove a milk delivery truck and Ingrid took on an extra job as chambermaid at the hotel. They worked in the mornings and met Jason for lunch at the university

canteen. It seemed there was somebody looking after Jason. He said
he was staying with a friend of his father's. But he didn't show much
sign of being looked after, and what he told them about his host
made them purse their lips and frown. Jason looked diminutive and
forlorn, so they appointed themselves his guardians. They accompanied him to the zoo and the KDW, to the best jazz clubs in town,
to their favourite cafés along the Kurfürstendamm.

Ingrid took him across the sector border to East Berlin. The ride
in the tram to Pankow left a deep impression on Jason, the layers of
greyness and decay on the houses, the hostility that he felt rising like
a chill off everything in the Soviet half of the city.

Her younger sister greeted them outside a door on a dark landing.
She appeared to be wearing white gloves. The whiteness of the gloves
stood out in the darkness of the landing where she said, 'Hello, my
name is Katje,' and reached out to shake his hand. Jason waited for
her to take off the gloves, but she didn't, and only after he had taken
her hand in his did he see that what he had thought must be gloves
was something bleached and white that was wrong with her hands.

Katje sat at the kitchen table beside her mother, shaking her
head in disbelief while she smoothed the silk stockings Jason had
brought them as a gift. The gratitude of the women made him feel
uncomfortable.

In the bedroom cupboard at Botho's house there were at least a
dozen pairs of stockings that Magnus had bought for his son,
because he had read an article in *The Times* about the scarcity of con-
sumer goods behind the Iron Curtain, especially jeans and stockings.
Jason was instructed to take silk stockings along in the event of vis-
iting East Berlin. But now that they were lying on a kitchen table in
Pankow being stroked by this girl, it was as if the hidden purpose of
bringing them all the way here had been to draw attention to Katje's
bleached hands, making Jason wonder about the cauldron of boiling
water in which they'd been plunged or whatever terrible thing it was
that had been done to them to turn them white.

On the walk back to the tram stop Ingrid told him what had happened to Katje's hands. Her mother had been pregnant with Katje in
Dresden the night the city was bombed. When she heard the air-raid

sirens she ran down into a cellar. The house above was flattened. She had no way of getting out. For three days she remained trapped under the rubble of the bombed house, terrified that she was never going to get out and would be buried there alive. Then she heard voices, and she screamed, and after three days they dug her out.

The shock changed the chemistry in her body. It affected the pigmentation. When the baby was born she had no colour in her skin. Katje came out of her mother an albino.

They had no way of treating Katje's condition in the east. They had sent her to West Berlin for radiation therapy for years, ever since she was a little child. They put her under a machine and toasted her from top to toe. Slowly her skin acquired colour. But in those places where it was spanned taut over the bone, on her feet and her hands and a streak across her forehead that she hid under her fringe, the colour wouldn't take. On those parts of her body Katje would probably remain streaked with white for the rest of her life.

Katje's *Schicksal*, as Ingrid called it, Katje's fate, had left an even deeper impression on Jason than the scars he saw on his way through East Berlin. He was appalled. For days they followed him around, Katje's white hands. With horror he thought of what had been favourite comic books only a few years ago. He thought of Battler Britain unloading bombs over Dresden and giving his crew the thumbs-up. Take that, Kraut! To be continued next week. A pair of white hands turned the page.

He sat on a wall under a tree in a leafy street off the Kurfürstendamm, half listening to the drone of traffic, half waiting for something to happen as he read Dylan's poem 'A Refusal to Mourn the Death, by Fire, of a Child in London'. When he came to the line 'The majesty and burning of the child's death', it was as if the air suddenly ran out of the coloured balloon on which the poem floated and it fell to the ground. Jason looked at it lying there on the page and felt a kind of disgust.

What was this nonsense about refusing to mourn the child's death? He felt betrayed by the facile sounds of the poem's words. He felt anger and then sadness because of what he could sense irrecoverably slipping away from him. He had tried to write a poem himself about Katje's hands, but the language died under him.

There was no such thing as the majesty and burning of a child's death. These were vain, empty words. The words about Katje's hands did not belong in a poem. Keenly, almost desperately he felt his utter lack of experience.

What, immediately, was there to be done to remedy the situation, and blaze a trail in the world?

Jason set off in the direction of the Kurfürstendamm. He thought of poorly paid but extremely useful (and indeed heroic) work as an orderly in a hospital. He would get on a tram and go to the university clinic, where he would present his case passionately and beg to be taken on. He thought ecstatically of Albert Schweitzer and his leper colony in Lambaréné. Africa! Jason immediately turned round and hurried back to the house.

Botho was sitting at the table in the alcove, eating peaches, when Jason burst in. He listened with complete seriousness to what the boy had to say, and when Jason was finished he rinsed his hands in the bowl of water at his side and suggested they send a telegram to Dr Schweitzer. Their chances of this telegram reaching Dr Schweitzer would, he thought, be very much improved if they could obtain an exact cable address for the leper colony in Lambaréné. The baron said he would telephone around to see if something could be arranged. And in the meantime . . .

In the meantime, while waiting to go to Africa, Jason met Elena.

8

E lena had already been in touch with Botho before Jason arrived
in Berlin, suggesting that he come out to Grunewald and stay
with her and Jens for a few days. Jason jumped at the opportunity.
He was coming to view Botho's kind attentiveness as increasingly
intrusive, even a little sinister. Since his encounter with Katje's white
hands, and Botho's most recent airing of the subject of *Deutschtum*,
the relationship with his new friend had turned a corner. Evidently
there was another side to Botho. Evidently there was some sort of
connection between the picture with the caption about the God
whose hand let iron grow and the shocking thing that had happened to Katje's hands. Jason no longer felt the thrill at these words
which they had occasioned in him only a few weeks earlier.

He packed his case and got on the train. He was so preoccupied
that he hardly registered the scenery passing by. In his mind, the land
en route for the outskirts of Berlin was gradually turning into equatorial Africa, and he was on his way to Dr Schweitzer's leper colony
in Lambaréné. Throughout the journey Jason was somewhere else, to
all intents and purposes living an alternative life. He was in fact living an alternative life for much of the time anyway (with practice he
had learned to do this effortlessly), because the present in which he
found himself trapped was so often uninviting. He had soon entirely
forgotten that he was sitting on the train to Grunewald.

He was walking along a terrace in the African dusk, feeling heat
rise off the ground. A woman walked beside him, apparently a nurse.
The nurse turned to him and said with a smile, 'I'll show you to your
quarters, Dr Gould,' and to his surprise he saw that it was Ingrid.
Jason was so entranced that he remained sitting in the stationary

train, staring out of the window at a sign reading 'Grunewald'. A man standing on the platform blew a whistle, recalling Jason to the present in the nick of time.

Flustered, he flung open the door and jumped down, pulling his suitcase out after him as the train lurched into motion. This was how Elena first saw Jason, flustered, the colour rising to his cheeks as he straightened up and walked towards her along the platform. Jason saw a woman in a hat, with a sense of brightness, and a man behind her who seemed to merge with the shadow she cast.

9

The moment Jason straightens up and Elena sees him, flustered, the colour in his cheeks, an accord is struck inside her. All the thirty-two years of her life and the sixteen of his (not to mention the history of the universe leading up to this moment), appear to have been orchestrated merely in order for quivering arrangements of atoms to be able to brush one another as they pass, setting in motion the accord that is the sound of Elena's destiny.

For Jason, on the other hand, no such sound is audible. Still in a state of confusion, Jason is likely to hear (if anything at all) echoes of the stationmaster's whistle that has plucked him out of his daydream. Jason's role in this encounter, as the relevant object of Elena's recognition under the auspices of the Attraction of Affinities, is to be passive. Floating past on his independent orbit, Jason is to be taken or left exactly as found, including the daydream that almost carried him past Grunewald station, for without daydream, whistle and hurried descent from train at the last minute, there would have been no evidence of the particular feature to which Elena responded the instant she saw Jason straighten up.

There would not have been the colour rising vividly to his cheeks, sounding the accord in Elena that she heard with a profound and joyful sense of recognition.

10

Elena remembered Jason's father clearly. She saw him sitting with her mother on one of the linen chests in the corridor of the house at Holm. She saw Sophie and Magnus smiling at each other. They were sitting on the chest 'just in case', to prevent unpleasant things from coming out in the night, only they didn't say so, because Elena had forbidden them to do so. Her Uncle Dietrich sat on one of the chests, too. The grown-ups pretended to be serious, but they weren't. They pretended so hard it was all they could do to keep themselves from laughing. They had seemed old to Elena then, but when she remembered that scene later she realised that Sophie had been a young woman, the same age as herself now.

Holm was still happiness – not just in her memory, she had known it was at the time, because unlike Jason Elena had always lived in the present. Sophie stood watching over her at the four corners of the day, her mother was everywhere, everything. Her father did not come, nor was he missed. She became her mother's child entirely. They were accomplices. Sophie had already whispered confidences to her as a baby. She talked to her, unburdened herself to Elena, and the daughter shared the mother's heaviness unquestioningly, as if it had been imposed on her by the law of gravity, almost from the day she was born.

When Elena turned eight, Sophie married again and they left Holm. This was the first time Elena lost her mother. In the new household, her mother disappeared behind her stepfather and the clutch of children that were born in the wake of his appearance. The confidences Sophie needed to share were shared with her husband now. Not unkindly, but heedlessly, adjusting to the changes required by life without a second glance back, the mother hollowed out her daughter's trust. Where she had once been strongest, she was now vulnerable. Elena felt abandoned.

She reacted by withholding herself. The two of them were so close that she knew that even the slightest neglect or oversight would be felt by her mother as cruelty. She could hurt her just by being less there for her. Off she went. Leaving home to go to boarding school in Weimar was Elena's way of punishing her mother. But she was not someone to bear a grudge for long. She came home for the holidays and, in time, mother and daughter grew together again. Elena had been born with her face turned to the light, compensating for her share of *Schwermut*, the heaviness that she had absorbed from Sophie when she was a child. Plant-like, reaching for what she needed, she grew up in brightness, sturdy and self-possessed. But she had a scar. Deep inside her wounded trust, on the surface long since healed, she was still vulnerable. A fragility remained.

War gained ground and spread itself out between them. It became difficult to get across the divide. In the end it was impossible. They didn't see each other any more. When bombs fell on Berlin just weeks before the end of the war, Elena lost her mother a second and final time. A sense of unused opportunities lingered with her, regret for the times when, out of thwarted love, she had been cruel to her mother. Her mother remained around her and inside her, a part of herself, and she mourned her for a long time.

Twenty or thirty people were living in the house in Grunewald in 1946. Elena shared a room with her brother and two sisters, throughout the years of black market before the currency reform, the airlift that kept the city afloat during the Soviet blockade of Berlin, the hunger and cold, the hunger to be alive. People would queue longer for a newspaper than for a loaf of bread. Her stepfather appeared, ghostlike, from imprisonment in Siberia, where he had spent five years. Gradually the refugees dispersed. The hard times began to soften, dark times to brighten.

The Christmas photographs of this period showed large numbers of people sitting down to festive meals with smiling faces. They

were people who had worked hard to earn their *Freude*, and did not
intend it to be disturbed by any intrusions from the past. Elena
would be somewhere in the crowd, also smiling, but with an absent
look on her face, as if still waiting for the party to begin. In all the
photograph albums from this period the people were small because
there were so many of them still living in the house, all crowded
into the picture. One had to look at Elena's face with a magnifying
glass to be able to detect her absent look, the look of a woman still
waiting, a woman who has not yet arrived.

In the course of the 1950s, the house that belonged to Jens' family reverted to its role as home to its owners. A few longstanding
tenants remained in the basement and the attic. As people wandered off to resume their lives elsewhere the faces that had to fit into
the picture became fewer, and correspondingly larger. Jens began to
figure in the foreground now, perhaps less (it seemed to her at first)
through any distinction of his own than through a lack of distinction
in others. In fact what set Jens apart were his sense of balance, his
constancy, an equable temperament that was never ruffled. These
qualities, by their nature unobtrusive, only showed their worth over
a longer time, as Elena often had cause to remind herself when she
had already been married to Jens for several years.

In the complete extinction of her home and family tradition,
continuity mattered, and Jens provided it. Elena did not look back
full of resentment, as did others, at homelands that had disappeared
behind a hostile border. She did look inside herself, however, and felt
sharply an absence of any material proof establishing who she was.
She felt an erosion of her identity, worn away not only by the greater
losses she had suffered – the home, the family, a whole landscape
which had disappeared – but by the irreplaceable hoard of smaller
losses, all the detail that had been woven in and around them. Not so
much as a photograph, an old toy or a piece of jewellery, not a single
souvenir of Holm, remained as proof of Elena's previous existence
there.

In this loss is hidden the significance of Jason's hasty descent from
the train. The impact on Elena when he lifts his suitcase and straightens up – flustered, the colour in his cheeks, his whole complexion,

reminding her instantly of her mother – is to restore that happy past. Jason's likeness to her mother is so unexpected it shines straight into her heart. No shade or filter is there as protection – it pours in! And on her heart is burned a double image of Jason/mother that she will never be able to eradicate. Past and future are instantaneously linked in this image.

On the surface there appears to be a lot of activity generated by Jason when he clambers in disarray from the train on its arrival at the station, shining a cosmic beam at Elena that resurrects so many memories. But relative to the speed with which Elena experiences the moment of their first encounter, Jason is virtually motionless. Jason sees a woman in a hat, with a sense of brightness. In fact it is not Jason but Elena, travelling forward from Holm at a velocity far beyond the speed of light, who arrives at Grunewald station.

11

Jason naturally knew nothing of the journey that Elena had behind her, nor could she know of his. (Not the train journey through the outskirts of Berlin to Grunewald, the one through French equatorial Africa to Lambaréné, where the prospect – which excited Jason – of Dr Gould being shown to his quarters by a beautiful nurse, looking just like Ingrid, was obliged to recede in favour of a beige Volkswagen, driving away from Grunewald station with Jason and his luggage inside it.)

Jens got out of the car to welcome him and shake his hand once more before driving back into town. Elena and Jason stood on the gravel path looking up at the house. It was a *Jugendstil* building with enclosed balconies and ornamental turrets. The summer morning, with cool eddies of air and a clear scent of pine from the surrounding woods, seemed to be waiting around them in expectant silence. Jason was at once in sympathy with the house and environs, the morning's coolness and scents, all of which he felt were echoed in Elena's presence.

'Let's have some breakfast,' she said, and taking his arm she went with him into the house.

Within a few days Jason knew most of the important events in Elena's life. To recapitulate what had happened to Elena before he knew her and to learn the score of her life by heart – this was why he had come. Sixteen years of it, from Holm to Berlin at the end of the war, had piled up before Jason had even arrived in the world.

The thought made Elena uncomfortable. There was so much he had to catch up on! She felt she had to bring Jason as soon as possible into possession of the years during which he had not even been born, spanning a bridge between Holm and Grunewald station and locking them in place before they crumbled away. There was now a beginning and an end to that avenue she recognised as the destiny for which she had always been waiting.

'I have arrived. Do you know what it means to have arrived, Jason? *Wissen vielleicht nicht, aber du ahnst es.*' Jason did not know what it meant, because knowing came from experience, which he lacked. But he could know it intuitively, by a process called *ahnen*, because he was a poet (even if he had failed to put Katje's white hands into verse). *Ahnen* was indispensable if Jason hoped to catch up on the many things of which Elena spoke to him that he could not know by experience. He closed his eyes and stretched his face towards her to absorb Elena's being by this osmosis she called *ahnen*.

Expectant, full of instinctive knowing: *ahnungsvoll*. It was a favourite word of Goethe's and of the German Romantic poets, a fact which Jason encountered with surprise. On the far side of this efficient, tidy, at first sight pedestrian people, Jason could glimpse those disorderly, emotionally charged mystics (perhaps lurking somewhere in Botho von Strehlitz's forest) who claimed instinctive knowing as their guiding light.

12

Jens was a writer, and the early Grunewald days in Jason's biography
became the first chapter of a *Bildungsroman* heavily influenced by
Jens. Sixteen years after the end of the war (concurrent with the span
of Jason's life), the Third Reich still constituted an inescapable
bottleneck through which everything in German history, culture and
life had to pass. You could choose to ignore it, to defend it tacitly or
damn it loudly, but you had to pass through it, if only by default.
Even, in retrospect, for Goethe and his contemporaries, *ahnungsvoll*
in the fever that burned nationalism ineradicably into the German
consciousness during the Napoleonic Wars, there was no way round
it. Even Goethe and his fellow poets had to squeeze through the
bottleneck in order to emerge in the second half of the twentieth
century, only to be greeted by Adorno's remark that after Auschwitz
there was no poetry to be written any more. German culture in its
entirety called to be reappraised.

On a mild evening Jason sat out on the terrace behind the house
with Elena and Jens and a friend who was a professor at the *Freie
Universität*. Little green blobs, luminous fireflies, floated around
them in the dark, sailing blithely, colliding, switching their lights on
and off. During a lull in the conversation, when they sat admiring
the display of the fireflies, Jason heard for the first time an inde-
scribable sound that came flowing out of the forest, just a few
moments before Elena began speaking of it. At the time Jason did
not know that he could communicate with Elena by telepathy.

On her last visit to Holm, in 1944, she said, she had accompanied
the estate gamekeeper on a deer hunt in the forest. For a long time
they waited silently in a tree for the deer to come. Then, she said,

'Below the level of the sounds that were in the forest, the sound *of* the forest gradually became audible. It was as if it opened up to us – waiting in the thickets, isolated in the stillness – pathways down which the noise of the outside world flowed into the forest. Both of us must have had a premonition of what had happened. The conversation suddenly turned to what would happen if Hitler were assassinated – by communists, I said to the gamekeeper. More likely by a bunch of aristocratic officers, I remember him saying scornfully. Which is exactly what happened. When we got back to the gamekeeper's house we learned from his wife that there had been an attempt on the Führer's life. I was reminded of that scene when I read in this evening's paper about the anniversary of Stauffenberg's attempt on Hitler's life.'

This started up a discussion about the Stauffenberg Conspiracy, to which Jason listened with the same excited and somewhat impressionable interest that seized him when he attended the meetings in Botho's house. Why, the professor with communist leanings wanted to know, had an extremely able military organiser on the general staff perpetrated one elementary blunder after another? Why had Stauffenberg spent months drawing up complicated contingency plans for handling the situation after the assassination while he still didn't have a reliable assassin to do the job, or what Stauffenberg revealingly called 'the dirty work'? Why, in effect, had Stauffenberg and his fellow conspirators taken a whole year *to fail to kill Hitler*? Because they were former admirers who were still in two minds. Their actions were the actions of sleepwalkers, performed as if under anaesthetic. They were hindered by idealism and an anachronistic officers' code of honour. And they were too close to him. For many of them, in the early 1930s, the Führer had represented everything it was desirable for a German patriot to be, and his death would mean the death of that ideal, murdered by their own hands.

Jens shuffled his feet for a while, a sign that he was getting ready to intervene. Jason, a tongue-tied spectator on a hill overlooking the battlefield, rubbed his hands in anticipation. This was the recognised procedure for discussions taking place in German – not jumping back and forth in a medley of close combat, but by due disposition of the heavy artillery, taking it in turns to fire from a distance. *Boom, boom* from one side; a pause while one waited for the shells to land, and then the same thing again from the other. It was considered rude to interrupt before the enemy was ready.

But Jens did not have any big guns to fire like the professor. He only wished to mention that it had once been remarked to him, by someone who had known them both at first hand, how there was a certain similarity between the would-be assassin and his victim.

The professor asked incredulously, 'You mean there was an actual physical resemblance? Between Hitler and Stauffenberg?'

'Not so much that. Sometimes the same fanatical gaze, perhaps, but . . . both had flair, even a touch of genius, a consuming interest in history, stubbornly independent judgement, histrionic talent, obsession with certain notions that after a certain point take off into mysticism . . .'

'What notions?'

'*Vorsehung*. They both believed Providence had brought them into the world to fulfil their missions, which may be why both left it with their missions unfulfilled.'

The professor fell silent, thinking about this.

'The similarity is not so unusual,' said Jens, 'because the assassin identifies with his victim. You see, the assassin and his victim have an undertaking in common. You might even call it a bond, a deed in which they are drawn together.'

The professor rejected this, because in the end Stauffenberg had not been Hitler's assassin. This was why the commemoration of 20 July, Stauffenberg's elevation to a hero's pedestal after the war, was so absurd. Stauffenberg qualified for official approval as the German resistance hero on account of having failed to kill Hitler, or, in other words, for *having saved the Führer's life*.

Both these remarks lodged with Jason, the sharp projectile Jens had fired at the professor and the even sharper one his adversary had fired back in reply. He would be reminded of them in a crucial discussion he was to have with Holger many years later.

13

Ach, wie vergänglich, the people who passed in and out of the house, the summer evenings spent talking on the terrace, the scents and the coolness and the little white flowers on the climbing hydrangea along the wall – Elena in the grip of *Schwermut* sat paralysed in the conservatory where the birds fluted and trilled, crushed by the specific gravity of gossamer, the dead weight of an airy spume of life.

She had a Slavic face, and Jens said she had the seven-layered Slavic soul, seven souls over which a Prussian conscience sat in judgement. Jens smiled as he said this. Behind these proper nouns Jens visualised entire landscapes, rich in memories and associations of which Jason could have no *Ahnung.* He tried to walk round the Prussian conscience that sat in judgement over Elena's seven souls, to view it from all sides. What was that, Prussian? Something at the same time rather fearsome and unprepossessing, like the bald eagle he saw on that great stone building in Berlin, reminding him of portraits of an ageing Frederick the Great?

Elena was mindful of her mother's sayings, recipes and house rules, mottos for life, quotations from Kant, Schiller and Goethe, a thread she held between her fingers to help her find her way through the labyrinth. The force of habit was strong. She liked directives. She liked to be given a goal, and was responsive to any moral support. She was highly organised. She was neat and tidy in her mental habits, which Jason appreciated every time he saw the perfect arrangement inside her cupboards. It was not just the order: it was the fact that discipline was to be expected, even when it was behind the scenes and not on view. This was Prussian, but there was much more to Elena than her Prussian arrangement. There was the Slav landscape: a vast reservoir of feeling.

Elena felt for people, deeply, all the time. Feeling, she seemed to seek out their contours and instinctively put them together. Her sympathy was something that could be felt glowing inside her, giving off a warmth and brightness. Jason was aware of a warmth emanating from Elena in waves in very much the way he felt heat emerge from the tiled stove which they lit on chilly evenings. From the moment she took his arm and went with Jason into the house he felt completely at ease with her; more than that, it was as if he was somehow not separate from Elena. He did not feel distinct from her. It was as if they had at once become a single person.

Jason told Elena about the picture of the Expulsion from Paradise on the wall of the missionary school in Africa, about the words he had overheard betraying the plan to send him away to school in England, and how the words turned into a caption that joined the picture. Picture and caption converged to a point that was arbitrary and at the same time inescapable, a doom in which he knew he would remain trapped for the rest of his life.

Elena told him about a process called *Anziehung des Bezüglichen*, for which she did not know an English word. Whatever belonged together would come together, she said, and she taught him another word: *Wahlverwandtschaften*. They looked it up in the dictionary and found 'elective affinities'. What was that? Blood was not thicker than water, oh no, said Elena; the only relations that count in life are those you choose for yourself. Did she feel any bond between herself and her father, merely because he was her parent? No! She had not freely chosen him. There could be belonging only by free choice. Jason was impressed. Yes, he told himself excitedly, free choice! Thoughts are free. Tarrah! Shake off the yoke!

He felt an aftermath of warmth when he sat in his room and tried to let his mind go blank as Elena said he must do. Now and then a word or an image took shape, which he wrote down, with a note of the time in the margin. After half an hour he reversed the process, trying to think of an image and concentrating on it as hard as he could. A very clear picture formed in his imagination. It showed a landing upstairs in a house. A small boy with fair hair stood at the top of the stairs. Over the child's head dangled a cut-out paper star on a piece of string attached to the ceiling. In his hand he held a wand. Jason wrote down a description of this image, too, and then he went downstairs to compare notes with Elena.

Jason had not been able to receive any of Elena's images, but Elena had recorded, in every detail, the picture of the boy with the star hanging over his head.

Who was this little boy with the star over his head, whom Jason imagined and Elena saw, perhaps simultaneously saw by herself, not as a second-hand image passed on to her by Jason? Was it Jason? Or was it some other figure, the embodiment of the destiny they shared, appearing at the end of the avenue where Elena had arrived? Was the boy with the wand their guiding spirit? Was that the significance of his wand?

It was certainly nothing Prussian in Elena that had wanted to try the experiment in telepathy. Definitely not. And the image of the golden child at the head of the stairs could only have been received in the innermost of her seven souls, where the Prussian who sat in judgement had no powers of jurisdiction over her.

'*Schau, wie schön!*' she exclaimed, pointing out a new cluster of buds that had opened on the climbing hydrangea.

But Jason did not want to look, to be told where to find beauty, and always to agree with Elena. He was stubborn. He resisted becoming one person with Elena. They were, after all, completely different from each other.

'*Nein, nicht schön!*'

He turned his back on her beauty and pretended to inspect a spot on the lawn. Elena was aghast. They exchanged heated words about the hydrangea. Jason said she should not enlist people in her own appreciation of beauty. In return she mocked his prickliness, his childish flares of temper and withdrew, hurt, into the house.

14

In the mornings they had German lessons. They sat outside in the garden on the forest's edge and began to read Goethe's *Werther*. At the outset came one of the most memorable passages in the book, an extraordinary lyrical outpouring in Werther's letter of 10 May. '*Eine wunderbare Heiterkeit hat meine ganze Seele eingenommen . . . ich bin so glücklich, mein Bester, so ganz in dem Gefühle von ruhigem Dasein versunken, daß meine Kunst darunter leidet.*' Jason made a simple mistake as they went through the passage, translating it together, and Elena corrected him.

'To be happy is *glücklich sein*. To be fortunate, to be lucky, is *Glück haben*. I am fortunate to be happy . . . please repeat after me, *Ich habe Glück, glücklich zu sein.*'

'*Ich habe Glück, glücklich zu sein.*'

'Good!'

Later, when he came into the house for lunch, Jason heard Elena singing to herself in the house.

La, la, la, la, la! In the hall downstairs she did a little skip and a jump when she thought no one was looking.

She lived on the crest of moments, the morning scents and coolness and the crackling of little white flowers as they unwrinkled on the climbing hydrangea around the house. Riding the crest of the wave, abreast of the spume that rose from the breaking wave, Elena was blissfully happy.

She lived through the first days Jason spent in the house without being aware of anything else. All her thoughts and sensations dissolved in time with the dissolving spray of each moment as it vanished. She felt herself surrounded by a warm fluid, until no hollow place remained in which the old ache could lodge. It made her invulnerable to ambush by some item she might chance to read in a newspaper, or when she heard of friends moving to another city, or saw flowers that had withered on the hydrangea overnight and lay scattered on the lawn the next morning, and she was overcome by an inexplicable sadness.

But now—

Eine wunderbare Heiterkeit hat meine ganze Seele eingenommen!

Jens was not jealous in the least. That was not in his nature. Entranced by Elena's happiness, he was delighted. The older and the younger man linked arms as spectators around the arena that was Elena's happiness. It was a glow that warmed them both. And it was a beacon, a reminder to both of them to watch over Elena's happiness.

Jason became aware for the first time of the power of a woman's feelings, and according to the mythology of his life he could sense what was beginning to converge at a point that would be both arbitrary and inescapable. If he embodied Elena's destiny, her destiny also became irresistibly his. *Ich habe Glück, glücklich zu sein.* I am lucky to be happy. It was both encouragement and admonition, woven into the thread that would show him his way through the labyrinth. However unrelated they might seem to Jason, all the events of his life still hung together. By a process of *Ahnung* he perceived his destiny before he was ready for it, or had any need of it.

The youthful Jason in Grunewald reminds one of the figure in Caspar David Friedrich's mysterious picture of the chalk cliffs on the island of Rügen. He stands by the tree on the cliff with his arms folded and his back turned towards the viewer, looking out to sea at the white sail on the horizon.

Aloof, a little defiant in his aloofness, he is a typically romantic figure. Lost in contemplation of the distant view, he seems wholly unaware of the clifftop drama in the foreground, where a gentle- man risks his life and peers over the cliff, perhaps to retrieve something, while a young lady gives directions. A bit lower! A bit more to the right! The young man looking out to sea with folded arms doesn't seem to be part of this other picture at all. Like the young Jason, he is deaf and dumb to the drama of experience in the foreground, because his soul is entirely absorbed with *Ahnungen* about the destination of that white sail on the horizon.

15

Elena has arrived, but Jason is still on his way to Dr Schweitzer's leper colony at Lambaréné. Heat is rising off the terrace he is walking along with the nurse resembling Ingrid, who turns to him and says with a blush (or so it seems in the African dusk), 'Let me show you to your quarters, Dr Gould.' This is the journey that Jason is anxious to resume after the few days in Grunewald have run on into several weeks and Botho Strehlitz rings up to inquire, a little sarcastically, if Jason entertains notions of ever coming back. According to Elena's timetable, Grunewald is where the train ends, because Grunewald is Jason's destination. According to Jason's timetable, Grunewald is the station where he changes trains and from which he will eventually resume the journey to Africa. He does set out with a smaller bag, however, leaving his suitcase upstairs in the turret room as a pledge that he will one day return.

This time he is wearing the talisman he has received from Jens and Elena, to keep him from coming to harm in the house of the old Nazi soldier, Oberst a.D. von Strehlitz, about whose gatherings Jason has told Jens and Jens has duly warned Jason. The talisman is the critical spirit of inquiry, of taking nothing on trust, which Jason has learned from the discussions in the open house in Grunewald. Jens is confident that the talisman will protect Jason from the malevolence of those emotional massages to which he has been submitted in the closed house in the leafy street with deep shadows off the Kurfürstendamm. For young Jason is susceptible to the old magician and his murky rituals. This time, on the advice of Jens, he goes into the room with the banners and the sabres in daylight to take a cold look at the square-jawed soldier whose picture he had thrilled at only a month or so ago, and it is Jens' voice he now hears asking quietly inside his head: 'What sort of a God is that, who has no love of slaves?'

Thus the pendulum lurched violently back in the opposite direction. Everything that had seemed elegant in Botho Strehlitz now struck Jason as exaggeratedly camp, the colonel's evenings a boyish masquerade. Even the dignity of Tiedke, gonging in the hallway and chasing away the shadows, had suffered since Jason noticed a smear of what appeared to be powder on his cheeks. Repugnance transformed the solemn major-domo into a smooth-faced satyr, the colonel's catamite, with an unmistakable odour of corruption and a lecherous smile hovering at the corners of his mouth.

In his post-war adolescence, Jason could move with seven-league boots through the cycles of recent German history, because in order to arrive in 1961 he too had no choice but to squeeze through the bottleneck of the Third Reich.

But what if there had been no Jens with a word of caution in Jason's ear?

What if it had been in 1934 that Jason thrilled, with a burning-glass enthusiasm that through the green fuse drove the flower, to the God whose hand let iron grow, and the square-jawed soldier, taking him at his word, had suddenly come alive, stepping out of the picture on the wall to hand Jason a rifle?

What iron flower might then have grown?

16

Instead Jason went swimming with the two sisters in Pankow. They knew the hole in the fence where you could slip across the wasteland and swim in the gravel pit on the far side of the Soviet barracks. It was forbidden, but lots of kids did it. Katje's boyfriend was late and Holger hadn't wanted to come, so Jason went on ahead with Ingrid. It was a hot day. They swam and sunbathed and still the others didn't arrive. Jason was fascinated by Ingrid's large breasts. He longed to touch them. She lay on her front and undid the top and asked him to put some stuff on her back. Then she fell asleep. Jason felt a pulse knocking inside his body like a hammer knocking inside a cave. Then the others came and Ingrid woke up and they all went swimming again.

It was true about Katje. She was toasted all over, only her hands and feet were white. It looked as if she was going swimming in socks and gloves. When they came out of the water Jason waited for Ingrid to undo her top again, but she didn't. To impress her, he told a true story about the beach in Africa where the Goulds' neighbour had watched his wife being eaten by a shark. Everyone wanted to hear more stories about wild animals and people in danger, so he told them more, and said they were all true, but only the one about the woman being eaten by a shark was true. All the others were invented. Perhaps they guessed, but they didn't care.

When the others went swimming again Jason asked Ingrid if she wanted more stuff on her back, and she said yes, and undid the top. He knelt beside her, his heart knocking inside his body like a hammer inside a cave as his fingers slid across her shoulders and down her sides. For a moment, perhaps unintentionally, she raised herself a little, and when he passed his hands underneath her he touched her breasts. It was such a brief contact that maybe Ingrid hadn't noticed it. Katje came out of the gravel pit and shook herself, showering them with drops of water, and they jumped up and chased her back in. In the evening they crossed the sector border and went to a youth club in Reinickendorf. Ingrid was on duty the next morning at the hotel, so she left early. Her tram was just leaving as they came out of the youth club and she ran to get it. Come out and see us again on Sunday, she called. Come early. Come for breakfast! And she waved as the tram went round the corner, heading back for East Berlin.

17

That was Friday. It was only two days to go till Sunday, but Jason could hardly endure the wait. All day he walked around the town and saw nothing. All his thoughts, his whole being shrank into his fingertips and became the sensation they had experienced when they fleetingly touched the nipples of Ingrid's breasts.

On Sunday morning he woke at five o'clock. He heard the birds singing in the tree by the window. Then they fell silent and he felt a tremor, an inaudible rumble, as if something was shaking under the house. An earthquake, in Berlin? He leaped out of bed and stared at the floor. Hearing a shout outside, he looked out of the window. A man went running down the street. What was a man doing running down the street at half-past five on a Sunday morning?

He crept downstairs through the shadows of the house. Again they gave him an uncomfortable feeling, as they had when he first arrived there, and he brushed his arms to get rid of the feeling. He drank coffee in the kitchen, burning his tongue, and slipped out of the house. He didn't want to run into Botho.

Jason waited for twenty minutes at the tram stop on the corner of the main road. At half-past six, long after the trams should have started but still no tram had come, he set out on foot for the nearest underground station. A man passed him on a moped, followed by another man who was running. More people appeared, all running. Jason, involuntarily, began to run too.

He went sprinting round the corner after the man and dashed out on to Ernst-Reuter-Platz. Cars had stopped in the middle of the road and a crowd of people stood talking and pointing in the direction of the Soviet sector. From the square there was a view clear down the

Strasse des 17ten Juni. A flow of cars, bicycles and pedestrians could be seen pouring into the avenue at intersections all the way down the avenue. Everything seemed to be sucked into this mile-long conduit, the city's main artery, flowing west–east and ending in the watershed at the Brandenburger Tor. The crowd of people standing talking on the square were sucked in too. Jason climbed into the back of one of the cars and the driver didn't even seem to notice he was there. He was listening to a RIAS bulletin on the car radio, shaking his head and muttering to himself. The bulletin said that at half-past three that morning the People's Army of the German Democratic Republic had begun to erect roadblocks and barbed wire along the forty-five-kilometre sector border between East and West Berlin.

The driver pulled up on the side of the road two hundred yards in front of the Brandenburger Tor, jumped out and ran in the direction of Unter den Linden. Hundreds of empty cars stood in the road where they had come to a halt. Jason could feel underfoot the same peculiar tremor he had noticed early that morning. Beyond the cars a dense throng of people packed the avenue this side of the Brandenburger Tor, blocking the view. Jason slipped through to the head of the crowd so that he could see what was happening.

Fifty yards away he could see coils of barbed wire attached to cross-beams piled in the middle of the road. Beyond the barbed wire stood a line of soldiers with machine-guns. Behind the soldiers were the tanks, rumbling into position to form a cordon across Unter den Linden, a line of gun barrels pointing at the crowd on the far side of the Brandenburger Tor.

Jason thought a war had begun. He waited for someone to fire at him. He stood there with a bag containing towel and swimming trunks, expecting at any moment to become the first front-line casualty of the Third World War. But the soldiers did not fire. They stood impassively behind the barbed wire, facing down the excited crowd who shouted insults at them and threw stones. He asked the man beside him if it was a war, and the man said he didn't know, but whatever it was, he had a job to do in Friedrichshain at eight o'clock, and by the look of things he was going to be late.

What was happening? Why was the People's Army closing the

border? Was this what it looked like when they closed the Iron Curtain? No one could tell him. Jason couldn't believe it: it was impossible to put up a fence right across a city to stop people going back and forth if they wanted to. It just was not possible.

For the first time since he had left the tram stop, Jason remembered that he was on his way to Pankow to go swimming with the two sisters. He dodged back out of the crowd and headed north along the sector border. He remembered Jens having mentioned that there were something like a hundred places in the city where you could get across the border to the Soviet sector. Perhaps they had decided to reduce the number? Surely there would be checkpoints open here and there to let people in from West Berlin? He was walking past the Reichstag when the other half of the thought occurred to him: and to let people out of East Berlin.

Jason began to run.

He ran all the way to Invalidenstrasse, turned right and saw barbed wire and armed soldiers right ahead of him. He ran on, all the way along the sector boundary into Wedding. Everywhere it was the same thing – barbed wire, soldiers with machine-guns, people coming out of houses, stirred up like ants and running confusedly to and fro in all directions.

Jason was desperate. He didn't understand; he didn't believe it. Should he go back? Where to? Was he already trapped? Was there barbed wire all around him? Realising that he must now be close to where Holger lived, he decided to press on.

At the corner of Ackermannstrasse–Bernauerstrasse he came across a large, hostile crowd on either side of the border. On the north side stood people in West Berlin, on the south side their neighbours in the East. Between them was a row of soldiers, keeping both groups at bay. Both crowds were yelling furiously at the soldiers. Normally you could just keep on walking down Ackermannstrasse and cross the border into East Berlin, but now Jason could see armoured cars stationed at the south end of the street. There was no question of getting through here, either.

He turned down Bernauerstrasse in the direction of the house where Holger lived. People hung out of the windows on either side and shouted across the street. Soldiers ran in and out of the doorways on the south side of the street, barking orders at the inhabitants, it seemed with the intention of evacuating them.

People leaned out of the windows of the houses on the south side of Bernauerstrasse, many of them still in their pyjamas, looking down incomprehendingly at the soldiers yelling at them to pack up their belongings and leave their houses immediately, as they were not allowed to live there any more. Orders were orders! *Befehl ist Befehl!*

It was ten o'clock on a Sunday morning, 13 August.

18

The houses on the north side of Bernauerstrasse, the road itself and the two pavements on either side belonged to West Berlin. But the houses on the south side of the street belonged to East Berlin.

When the occupants of these houses had been chased away, people still came pouring out of them in their hundreds. For a short while Bernauerstrasse remained one of the routes open to East Berliners escaping to the West. Refugees swam through canals, rivers and lakes, arriving dripping, with nothing but the clothes on their backs, to begin another life. They drove at speed through road-blocks. They made a dash for it through the barbed wire. And they entered the row of houses on the south side of Bernauerstrasse, stepping out into freedom on the north side.

After a few days, masons arrived under military guard and began to brick up all the ground-floor doors and windows of the houses on the south side of the street.

Jason witnessed these events from Holger's room on the north side of Bernauerstrasse. After days spent arguing in the streets with the soldiers of the People's Army who were doing these terrible things, arguments that achieved absolutely nothing, he and Holger were appalled when walking along the sector border in Wedding to find wall-building pioneers of the People's Army being protected from the anger of the population by their own policemen, the police of West Berlin.

Jason was speechless that such violence could be not only be perpetrated but could receive official support from those who were being violated. He was speechless in the face of their own powerlessness to do anything about it. Above all, he was speechless in his discovery that innocence could be so easily duped by cynical experience.

Students jeered at the mayor of West Berlin, Willy Brandt, who intervened in the nick of time when they were threatening to storm the border of the Soviet sector. They did not care about or even recognise the broader issues that might have justified the mayor taking preventive action. They cared about the injustices that were being done before their very eyes.

'THE WEST DOES *NOTHING*!' taunted the headlines in Axel Springer's right-wing press, and for once the students snatched the despised newspapers out of each other's hands. President Kennedy was on board the cabin cruiser *Marlin* when the news reached him, communicating only briefly by telephone with the secretary of state before he resumed his vacation, while Dean Rusk went to a ball game. A ball game! De Gaulle was at his country house in Champagne, on holiday, as were his prime minister and foreign minister. Macmillan was on holiday in Scotland with the foreign secretary, Home. Adenauer castigated Brandt but otherwise did nothing. Nobody seemed to react to the events in Berlin on that August weekend beyond noting that they had taken place.

The status quo had been preserved between the four powers while at the same time the leakage of manpower to the West, which had kept the Berlin situation so volatile since the official termination of hostilities in 1945, had finally been sealed up. It was as if the building of the wall had been prearranged, to take place in circumstances that suited everyone, with as little fuss as possible.

Holger and Jason watched the windows being bricked up on the second, the third and finally the fourth floors of the houses on the south side of Bernauerstrasse. There were fewer and fewer people, but still they came, the would-be escapees, forming human chains of legs and arms wherever possible, and when it was no longer possible they jumped. Sheets, blankets, whatever was available at short notice was produced by the crowd below in the street and proffered as a dubious encouragement to the few who still occasionally showed up on the roof. Several of the escapees jumped to their deaths.

At first Jason waited as anxiously as Holger for Ingrid to come.

She lived not more than a quarter of an hour's cycle ride away. It was unbelievable that on a Friday Jason could have been swimming with Ingrid in Pankow and on a Sunday find his way barred by tanks and soldiers with machine-guns. It was unbelievable that, from one day to the next, she should just disappear from their lives. It was inadmissible. It was madness. It was a personal affront. It was a public wrong. It was Youth discovering Mortality. And they were powerless to do anything about it.

Of course, Ingrid was familiar with the border geography of Bernauerstrasse. She must have known that the door would be left open a crack, if only for a very short time. Ingrid and Katje, perhaps. But their invalid mother? What agonised discussions were taking place in the kitchen where Jason had given Katje the silk stockings, it seemed just days ago?

With dread he watched the people who showed up on the roof across the street, in case Ingrid was among them, fearing that she might jump to her death. It was almost a relief when people stopped coming at last.

Once all the doors and windows had been bricked up, the buildings opposite Holger's apartment on the north side of the street ceased to look like a row of houses. They looked, unsurprisingly, like a giant wall.

Arbitrarily, inescapably, Bernauerstrasse (south side) had become a part of the Berlin Wall.

19

When weeks passed and still Ingrid did not arrive, they knew that now she never would. She had chosen to stay with her mother. Holger was proud of her. He didn't seem to be sad; he admired the nobility of Ingrid's sacrifice for her mother. And he stopped waiting for her.

Jason didn't stop waiting for Ingrid, however. He was aghast. How quickly Holger gave up! Jason could not understand his cold-bloodedness. He shed many tears, Holger none at all. 'I can't cry,' Holger said. 'There aren't any tears inside me.' Probably some of Jason's tears were shed for himself, whereas Holger's tearless sorrow for Ingrid was entirely selfless.

Jason attended the student rallies. He protested against the wall. He threw a few cobblestones and hid, panting and dishevelled, in derelict buildings. He booed Brandt. He enrolled as one of the first members of the Escape Committee started up by students at the *Freie Universität*. He became as susceptible to the romance of left-wing agitation as he had once briefly been (so long ago, it seemed) to the picture of the soldier with the caption: 'The God whose hand let iron grow, he had no love of slaves.'

Holger took no part in any of these activities. He drove a milk truck to finance his studies. He continued to enjoy people's company, and booze, and talk. In the evenings he sat in student pubs and promulgated his theories, a lawyer at heart, his mind quick and penetrating, sceptical, but also whimsical and extravagantly learned; something of a *Privatdozent*, in the best tradition of those independent German scholars whom Holger loved and desired to emulate, although he had already decided to work at the bar.

He mockingly compared the reaction of the Allied powers to the Berlin Wall with that of Palmström, the man who refused to accept he had been killed by a car because cars were not allowed on the site where he was run over.

Nicht sein kann, was nicht sein darf!

Holger considered the shape that Germany had contributed to the destiny of the twentieth century to be the irrational form that was all its own. It had been perfectly diagnosed at the turn of the century by Christian Morgenstern in his poem '*Die Unmögliche Tatsache*'. The Berlin Wall was only the last in the long line of Impossible Facts making up the history of the century in which, for better or worse, as a German for worse, he was unfortunately required to live.

20

On a green island in Grunewald Jason withdrew (like Hölderlin) to a tower room to dedicate himself to poetry for the rest of his life. Had that improbable artefact, the Berlin Wall, not sprung up like a barrier of thorns between Jason's hands on one side and the sun lotion to be applied to Ingrid's body on the other, the cycle of poems celebrating the lovers separated by the Berlin Wall, or Wall Poems, as they became known, would never have been written. More sun lotion would have been applied, followed by gropings in the shrubbery the next day and feverish lovemaking the next night, the bubble of adolescent enthusiasm punctured by the next change of weather, the end of summer at the latest. Real-life experience was the enemy of the young lyric poet, but the Berlin Wall turned out to be his friend.

So here was a lyric poet, hardly seventeen, writing scrawny, vibrant verses which identified the brand of sun lotion, specified the streets and the numbers of the streetcars and the hole in the fence round the wasteland behind the Soviet barracks where the kids went to swim, who suddenly took on another voice, transforming, by the use of menacing correspondences, a city everyone knew into something strange and frightening, describing the overnight appearance of the wall as a Trojan horse with gun turrets on its flanks, standing in the suburbs reflecting the steely light of dawn. The scrawny (but vibrant) poet castigated the armoured might of the Soviet bloc, as if the sole purpose of its intervention had been to suppress his youthful love, and he did so in a tone of voice shifting from elegy to sarcasm which had not been heard before.

Written in the space of a few weeks and rushed out by a student press, the Wall Poems caused something of a local stir. The voice of Jason Gould was compared to both the velvet lightness of Rimbaud ('*Pendant les bleus soirs . . .*') and the dark urgency of Georg Trakl (no specimens were quoted). The radio station RIAS interviewed the poet for *Culture News*. His name was mentioned a couple of times in the *Berliner Morgenpost*.

To Jason, it seemed as if he had already become world famous. He felt as if the Warsaw Pact (the Russians were, after all, an emotional people) could not but be moved by his appeal. Might his poetry perhaps even help to bring about a change of heart? Move the Soviets sufficiently for them to consider dismantling the wall? For a few months he was heady with the sense of destiny.

But: *man arrangierte sich mit der Mauer.*

One came to terms with the wall, and much more quickly than anyone would have thought possible. Although the protests continued, and there were frequent skirmishes between students and police along the sector border, the population was already adapting its habits and beginning to settle down. The wall, after all, had been imposed from above. It was an administrative decision, officially endorsed as an 'anti-fascist bulwark' by at least one half of the municipality. And Germans had respect for such things, as Holger pointed out in parallels he drew with 1789. In the year of the French Revolution, the council of Weimar had seen fit to impose a fine of six thalers on persons caught climbing over the town wall during the hours of curfew. Germans were still refining feudal institutions while the French were busy throwing theirs out.

Ingrid's appropriation as the object of sun lotion and veneration in his young friend's Wall Poems came as a surprise to Holger. There appeared to have been developments in the relationship between Jason and Ingrid of which he had been unaware. If at first he allowed himself a few misgivings, he quickly brushed them aside as bourgeois pettiness (Holger was still a Marxist), of which he should feel ashamed. She was not, after all, anyone's property. Ingrid had been transformed into the icon of a *Zeitdokument*. The Wall Poems had given her to the world.

He was impressed by Jason's poems. They had given Ingrid to the world. Everyone feted his young friend, at least for the next few months, until they began to get used to the wall. Everyone wanted to meet him. So talented! So young! Everyone was impressed – everyone, that is, except Elena.

21

For Elena there was something embarrassing about the Wall Poems. There was something in them that made her feel uncomfortable. What was it? She turned it this way and that and looked at it from all sides.

'He hardly knew that girl,' she said at last to Jens.

'That may be why the poems are so good.'

Elena was infuriated to hear Jens blowing in the same horn as everyone else. How could the poems be good if he hardly knew the girl? What he wrote about in the Wall Poems was not based on experience. The thoughts and feelings attributed to the wall lovers had simply been made up.

But wasn't it Elena who had expected Jason to grasp intuitively by that process of *Ahnung* things he was not able to understand from experience?

Jens said that she was jealous, and naturally that was how it must seem. But what Elena felt most of all was disappointment. In the weeks that Jason had spent working on the Wall Poems she had taken meals up to the tower room, washed his socks and underpants, gone for walks with him in the forests of Grunewald. Sometimes Jason was playful, in high spirits, hiding behind trees and imitating owls. Sometimes he was depressed. Knowing another person in all the facets of their being – wasn't this the way you loved and were loved by another person?

Elena didn't like the poems. She didn't believe them. She sensed something fraudulent, even opportunistic, in the way Jason had exploited the building of the Berlin Wall to launch this paltry, made-up love affair. When she read the elegy that had been singled out for

praise by the reviewer in the *Berliner Morgenpost* she recalled Jason
hiding behind trees, hooting like an owl, the same day he had
written it. She snorted and hurled the poems across the room.

'Detestable!'

Jason didn't ask her opinion of the Wall Poems, and Elena didn't
volunteer one. Her absence from the ranks of his admirers was a
conspicuous omission, but as Jason wanted to see only the ranks, he
overlooked the omission.

But then people began to settle down and gradually got used to
the wall. Passionate outrage gave way to stoicism. Jason, whose name
had been associated with passionate outrage, not at all with stoicism, found his fame beginning to wear off. To his surprise, he
watched it ebb away as casually as it had come. His destiny no
longer looked as unsinkable as it had just a short time ago. Holger
said fame had to be maintained like anything else, like a house or a
car; and in a poet's case it was ideally maintained by death. Failing
that, he should bring out a follow-up collection, but since the
publication of the Wall Poems, Jason had not written a single line.

He had not been able to. He was not unhappy: on the contrary,
thanks to Elena (and in terms of an artist's productivity this could
only be a disaster, as Goethe already pointed out on page two of
Werther), Jason was much too content to feel like writing poetry.

When he was sixteen Jason had taken the high Romantic view
expressed by Werther's sufferings and Beethoven's knitted brow.
Durch Leiden Freude! For the creative person, nothing less than
suffering would do. But Elena didn't think much of *Durch Leiden
Freude*, and on Jason's arrival in Grunewald she took his sentimental
education in hand. It was easy to be unhappy. It was much harder to
be happy. One must strive for it. The caption to the picture of Jason's
life, the Expulsion from Paradise, should gradually give way to the
Will to Happiness that Elena wanted to be at the heart of her
relationship with Jason. She was the muse, but the thoughts and
feelings initiated by her had been attributed to another woman.
This was why Elena had hurled the Wall Poems across the room.

She might have hurled the book and her exclamation –
'Detestable!' – at Jason personally, but she didn't. And Jason might

have asked Elena her opinion of the Wall Poems, which she so studiously withheld, but he didn't. They both avoided this area. There was too much at stake. It was only when Jason's fame had begun to fade, and a letter from Magnus on his son's seventeenth birthday nudged the question of what he intended to do with his life after six months of hanging around in Berlin, that the issue became unavoidable.

It came to a head on a tram one autumn afternoon. Elena and Jason boarded the tram in the centre of Berlin, headed for Grunewald. At one point on their journey the tram tracks skirted the wall. It was by now much bigger, more solid than the first barrier that had gone up in the summer. Now it bordered a wasteland where everything had been demolished for about a hundred yards on the East Berlin side. When Elena saw Jason peering wistfully over the wall, even standing on tiptoe to get a better view, her frustration exploded in anger.

'You hardly knew that girl! That's why it doesn't ring true! How could it? You're only interested in yourself! You can't fool me. I know. You made it up that day we were in the forest and you were pretending to be an owl. You didn't care one little bit!'

Jason turned white. Mortally wounded, he sprang out of the tram and bounded down the street. Horrified by the harshness of the words she had flung at him, Elena jumped after him. There was no sign of him. Elena walked up and down the street. She walked round the block. She shook her head. She walked back the way she had come. She began to cry, but it was all to no good.

Jason had disappeared.

22

When Jason didn't return, Jens notified the police. Elena reproached herself and was mortified at what she had done. Happiness and unhappiness, in her seven souls she had a reservoir of both. Her whole being became a stage for her emotions, where the drama of catharsis was played out while Jens waited anxiously in the wings. In the first years of their marriage, her Prussian soul had sat in judgement over an affair with another man which threatened to run out of control. Stricken by a sense of duty, Elena obeyed. She cut the lover off, overnight, for the rest of her life. Years passed before he even saw her in the street again.

Jens remembered how paralysed she had been. Music had helped her to get over her unhappiness. She lay on the floor, listening to music, and then she got up and resumed her life without the man she had loved. But after Jason disappeared she just lay inert on the floor with her eyes closed, as if she were dead. 'My blood runs through his heart. I shall die without him,' she said to Jens, and he knew it was the truth.

She lay on the floor with her eyes closed, and for a long time it seemed as if she was looking into a dark tunnel. She fell asleep, dreaming on into the same darkness of this tunnel, and she knew that she was once more lost at sea, and that she would drown before she could reach the shore. But when she woke up she remembered she had arrived. The tunnel opened out into the avenue in which she had arrived. This was her destiny. She lay motionless on the floor with her eyes shut, because she knew that if she stayed in the avenue Jason would find her there.

When Jason came back after several days Elena put her arms round him and kissed him. Jason held her tight. For hours they sat folded into one another, embracing in a way they had never embraced before.

23

Magnus Gould imagined life as possible in a number of variations, like different versions of a musical composition or a painting. When Jason decided not to return to England and stayed in Berlin, his father resigned himself to the course of events which, for those many contradictory feelings that underlie our actions, he had himself helped to set in motion. Jason and Elena were embarked on the different course of life that Magnus had rejected (among a pile of others he filed away in a mental drawer. But he could still imagine he might have lived with Sophie Romberg).

The picture of three people overlooking the chalk cliffs on Rügen is only one among an infinite number of possible images. Jason at sixteen is like the figure on the right standing under the tree, his arms folded, his back turned to the viewer, looking out to sea at the white sail on the horizon. Preoccupied with *Ahnungen* about the destination of that white sail on the horizon, he seems deaf and dumb to the real-life drama of experience in the foreground. The other two figures have so little to do with the young man on the right that they do not seem part of the same picture.

In a later variation on the theme of these figures in a landscape, the mood has completely changed.

A different perspective (or perhaps a different landscape) shows the sea at the bottom of a gentle slope and a sailboat directly below, running up on to the shore. In the same instant the boat touches the shore, the figure under the tree turns to the woman in the foreground, his face lighting up with an expression of profound and joyful recognition.

The white sail on the horizon has gone.

1974

1

Holger had once asked a composer friend to describe what writing music was like, and the composer had said it was like opening a door on a sound that was already going on. Holger liked this description. He imagined this was what feelings were like. In the background, feelings were always there. You opened the door on to your feelings, and all of a sudden you heard them.

When Holger mythologised his life he imagined himself inside a labyrinth. He made his way along the passages of this labyrinth in silence. But behind the walls the sound of feelings must always be there. He conjectured this from observing other people, particularly his women friends. Opening a door on one's feelings must be like opening a door on a classroom where a noise was already going on. Suddenly you would hear them, the children who were making a noise, who were your feelings.

Without feelings, it was impossible to know what went on inside other people. He thought of people as living inside separate sound-proof chambers, each with its own labyrinth whose passages you walked in silence. Now and then you opened a door on to a noise of feelings that was always going on. These were the interconnecting doors, like doors in a hotel suite, by which people had access to one another.

In one of Holger's nightmares he is walking down the passages of the labyrinth, opening one door after another, but not hearing anything, opening doors and still hearing only silence. The nightmare is a motion picture of the still image that is the image of Holger's life. It shows a person whose feelings have been amputated.

Holger asked a lot of questions because he was a person whose feelings had been amputated, but who wanted to be able to give the impression he had them like everybody else. So he took an interest. Other people could be put together by guesswork and conjecture. He asked them about their feelings to find out what his own must be like. But he had no proof. Sometimes he imagined the people around him walking up and down the passages of their own labyrinth in the same silence.

'A person whose feelings have been amputated' is Holger's own description of himself. It just comes to his lips, he has no idea from where. Perhaps it is rather theatrical. The description suggests to him that he might once have had feelings but that somehow they were cut off. There is a logical procedure of inquiry here that Holger finds comforting.

Because he took comfort in logical procedures (and it gave him a professional alibi for asking as many questions as he liked, opening interconnecting doors on the sound, or the imputed sound, going on inside other people's lives), Holger became a lawyer. The courts were a stage for a drama to unfold in which the lawyer could take part, giving him access to all the feelings of which human beings are capable. He had no illusions about himself. He knew that he became a lawyer not primarily in order to earn money or because it particularly interested him, but because it opened interconnecting doors to feelings that would otherwise have remained silent. He became a lawyer because he was emotionally destitute, and thus of necessity a parasite living off the feelings of others.

Law seemed to make him invulnerable. There was a dividing line between those who worked from inside the fortress of the law, the mandarins of the law who administered it, and the common people who lived outside the castle walls. Holger knew from his own experience that this was the hidden, biographical text of Kafka's book *Das Schloss*. Kafka was a lawyer who worked for an insurance company. The Jew who lived in the ghetto in Prague (and perhaps looked up daily at the Hradin on his way to the insurance company) longed to be invulnerable inside the castle walls like everybody else. But Kafka's vision of invulnerability within the castle walls is a vision of something that *sui generis* will always remain outside the human condition, just as the hapless surveyor–hero in his book remains outside the castle walls.

Still, the lawyer had better chances of survival. When Holger opened his own legal practice twenty-five years after the war, not a single member of the legal profession, which had made itself an accomplice of the Third Reich by proclaiming evil to be right, had been punished for his part in the systematic abuse of justice. Lawyers were tried by lawyers; they were looked after by their own kind.

Gefühlsamputiert. In German it could be said in a single word. What a language!

It could take an abstraction, such as a condition of being numb in the aftermath of amputation, and turn it into something three-dimensional one could walk around and look at from all sides. Thus the abstraction came to exist in three-dimensional space, a condition of lacking feeling one could walk around and even, paradoxically, get a feeling for. *Gefühlsamputiert*: once the word was in place, so also was the condition it described.

Holger couldn't remember any one moment of shock, the severance itself. The feelings had been amputated by a process of slow freezing. He was a bookish child and he made the discoveries himself. He was a child reading secretively under the covers that had been drawn over the 1950s, and his reading was complicated by a thrilling element accompanying the fact that it took place in secrecy. From the beginning he knew that his mother and father had been on the other side. He could tell it from their silence. They would not have approved of what he was reading, and discovering.

Here and there, on the young tree that Holger was in the 1950s, the shoots stunted. The avenues of trust and affection closed. There was never any such thing as family feeling. Rather, from the age of nine or ten, there was a sort of repugnance on Holger's part at having to live in undesirable intimacy with the strangers who masqueraded as his parents.

In other circumstances, Holger might have been recognised as a victim. The atrophy of his emotional life and the retreat into autism would have been diagnosed. Measures, if only the human measures of sympathy and understanding, would have been taken to alleviate his condition. But there were too many victims. Compared with all the others, Holger was not a real one.

Because no feelings seemed to him adequate for what had happened, Holger ceased to have feelings at all. Any awareness of inadequacy, first of his feelings and then of the rest of himself, was the symptom of that slow freezing that led to the condition of *gefühlsamputiert*. Naturally, Holger still had feelings, but because he did not admit them it was as if they were no longer there. Perhaps the sound of his feelings did go on, like music, behind the silent corridors of the labyrinth in which he found himself, but he would never know, because he never opened the communicating door.

2

Petra was not the first girl with whom Holger slept, but she was the first with whom he spent the night. In 1963, such intimacy still had a future in marriage, which Petra expected and with which Holger complied. They had a big wedding in Cologne, and perhaps because the bride and groom and all their guests were Rheinländers, with a reputation for good humour and good living to keep up, it was a very festive, even brilliant, occasion, with lots of champagne and lots of *Freude*.

Three years later Petra left Berlin with her two babies and returned to her parents' home. She hated that town with the wall, which had become the symbol of everything that was wrong with her marriage. She was only telling her friends in Cologne what she had already told her husband in Berlin: that her marriage had been the biggest swindle of her life. Behind her husband's jovial, good-natured façade was a man unable to express any feelings, with whom Petra had lived in silence for three years.

In fact Holger *was* jovial and good-natured. Those qualities only took on the appearance of a façade in comparison with his apparent lack of personal emotion. Where social feelings were concerned, Holger could deliver the goods. But when Petra tried to extract a personal feeling from Holger, he would stammer and look away. Nothing infuriated her more than a man who stammered and turned away when she tried to pin him down.

'Holger's sick,' she said, and her mouth curled in contempt.

He was popular with women nonetheless, and until he set eyes on Colette his relationships with all of them would at some time reach the point where Holger stammered and looked away.

Nothing could have been further from Holger's idea of the truth about himself than the perception that he was a victim. As a lawyer, defending his clients in court, he had staged his life in such a way that other people were the victims and he was the person who came to their aid. As a husband, however, and with all his women friends after his marriage, Holger found himself up against people who wanted to see *him* as the victim and come to *his* aid. This bordered dangerously on the zone where the nerve ends of amputated feelings began to twitch, and he felt bound to turn away because he couldn't face it.

Colette was different from the motherly women who wanted to come to his aid. After a succession of motherly women, Holger, with a cry of joy, discovered the *putain*.

She slept around, she peddled her arse, she was a drunk, she was destitute, she had whatever was going and didn't complain. On the surface of it, Colette was so much sicker than Holger that by comparison he took on a positive glow of health. The roles were clear and he could relax. She was the victim, he was the one who came to her aid.

In this perfect balance of their mutual requirements, despite the quarrels and the lies and the squalor that accompanied Colette, Holger achieved a sort of contentment. He could never have admitted as much, however, because he never spoke of personal feelings. Life with Colette was enhanced by sexual refinements whose pleasure was rooted in a truth it suited both of them to ignore: that the rescuer can be moved to rescue others out of an awareness of himself as victim, and the victim can wish to punish the rescuer in revenge for all the humiliations that in her role as victim she has had to endure. Thus it was with groans approaching ecstasy, as Colette administered to his body its ration of pain, that Holger gratefully received the hurt as a gift in which he perceived a rare feeling that flashed all the way down into the numbness at the core. He was a successful, even distinguished defence lawyer, aged only thirty-four, crouching naked on all fours in a cage in the playroom of a penthouse in Berlin, being prodded through the bars by an emaciated woman armed with a toasting fork, both partners groaning in expectation of the ecstasy imminently approaching, when the buzzer sounded angrily through the apartment, on and on, and didn't stop. Somebody down in the street was pressing the bell and didn't stop until Holger, in exasperation, finally opened the door.

3

When Holger spent the New Year with Jason in Frankfurt, and met the two sisters again after more than ten years, he didn't recognise Katje. Perhaps he had never looked at her properly before. She did not resemble the schoolgirl who always stood waiting on the landing of the apartment block in Pankow when visitors arrived. Nor did her appearance have any connection with the quite different woman whose photograph, not much bigger than a large postage stamp, was among the two dozen terrorists on the wanted poster on display a few months later. In the photograph she had her hair cut very short and dyed blonde. She wore dark glasses. She was tall and slender, even frail-looking. But when Holger bumped against her in the kitchen, he felt a muscular body that was surprisingly hard.

Somebody had spotted her, identified her in a restaurant in Hamburg and notified the police. She got out by the skin of her teeth, and an hour later she was on the train to Berlin. She came to Holger like a hunted animal, making the same kind of desperate appeal that ambushed his heart even as he sensed the still unwavering hardness inside her and knew that she was going to use him. For weeks she didn't take a step out of the house. She let her hair grow again. She took off her dark glasses and showed him her pale, beautiful face. She put the metronome on top of the piano and sat there for most of the day, practising Bach and Mozart, mechanically, like a schoolgirl; unwaveringly, like a terrorist who had taken it upon herself to assassinate the music.

Holger recognised her hands. They were just as described on the Wanted poster. Strips of white ran down the backs from the wrists to the finger joints. He watched them marching up and down the keys, stifling the music, herding the notes back into the keyboard every time they began to sing and tried to run out. Katje's white scars were a brand mark. Her hands gave her away.

How could he refuse her shelter? Holger couldn't refuse anything to anyone. He was a defence lawyer whose clients were all long since dead. It was neurotic, it might even be lunacy, but never again did Holger want to be held accountable as a result of having refused to do something for someone, however trivial, however remote the connection (perhaps he had once turned down a request for a loan or been too lazy to answer the door) for anything that might have happened to the Jews in the course of the last two thousand years.

Soon Colette found Holger preoccupied, insufficiently attentive to her. She complained, and he lent her some money. She flew to Sicily, to escape the never-ending winter in Berlin, she said. She had an admirer who lived in a *palazzo* in the old part of Palermo.

Holger and Katje became lovers from the day Colette left. In the corridors of the criminal courts the lawyer felt a thrill when he walked past the poster with Katje's picture in the gallery of wanted terrorists and thought of the hard, muscular body of the woman he had just been holding in his arms. She made love in the hard, dry way he expected of her body, but when she came she murmured his name with a tenderness that took him by surprise.

Pausing in the corridors of the criminal courts to look at Katje's picture one day, Holger ran his eye down the other faces and names. He stopped with a jolt when he reached the name beneath one of the faces, which had been inked over with a cross. Holger Meins had been arrested with Jan-Carl Raspe and Andreas Baader, joint leader of the Baader–Meinhof gang, after a shoot-out in Frankfurt almost eighteen months earlier. Instinctively he knew that Katje and Holger Meins had been lovers, and that it was this other Holger, his name-sake, not he, whose name she murmured during their lovemaking with such unexpected tenderness.

Holger had long ago ceased to be a Marxist, because any claim to be the sole representative of the truth, of communism or whatever, had seemed to him to be untenable. He had spent too many ragged hours at student meetings in Berlin, where people shouted at each other and banged their fists on the table. To have to live with a dogma allowing no room for compromise was bad for people, and especially bad for Germans. After the shouting and the banging of fists came the knives and guns and the liquidation of opponents. It would be the same with the Baader–Meinhof gang, now masquerading as urban revolutionaries under the theatrical name RAF. There was a lot of noise and theatrical effects, but in the end the blood was real.

The lawyer argued with the terrorist. He wanted to prove to her the wrongness of her ways. Whether you called yourself an urban guerilla or an SA stormtrooper, he said, made no difference in the end. Once you started minding other people's business for them you went on to take control of their lives, and eventually of their deaths. It was always the same. It had been a mistake to set fire to a department store. The moment Baader struck the match the fuse of reprisals had already been lit, the state hunt for the terrorists, the shoot-outs with cops, the spiral of killings and counter-killings that were to come. All because someone had fooled around with matches in a department store.

Katje replied that the store was a symbol of capitalism. It was a symbol of the imperialist domination of the working masses. The violence of the state must be met with violence. Holger said it wasn't a symbol of anything, but a place where people went shopping.

The difference between a department store as a symbol of capitalism and as a place where people went shopping was at the core of another German argument dividing East and West. The argument was about substituting ideas for things. Katje substituted imperial domination for government by a coalition of liberals and social democrats, the violence of the state for men and women in uniform, and in making these substitutions she also made moral judgements. Holger could see that in Baader's mind it was indeed a symbol of capitalism, not a department store, which he was setting on fire, and that in Meinhof's mind, when her comrades stormed the reading-room of the Central Institute for Social Questions in Berlin to liberate Baader, it was indeed imperial domination, not men and women in uniforms, at whom the members of the RAF commando were shooting.

These were the ghostly battles being fought by the RAF on behalf of a *Volk* that was not there. In Germany there were no impoverished South American villagers, no Basque separatists, no feuding Irish Protestants and Catholics to support the revolutionaries or espouse their cause. There was nobody there. A past was there. Holger could understand better than anyone that the RAF was trying to exorcise the ghosts of the Nazi murderers, returning to the scene of the crime where they had amputated their victims' feelings.

Holger's own father and mother, his uncles, the shopkeeper on the corner, the priest and the local mayor – none of them had been there. Nobody had been there a generation ago either. A generation ago the national socialists had fought a war and committed crimes on behalf of a people that wasn't there, including Holger's own father and mother, the shopkeeper, the priest and the local mayor, but almost none of them had names, which was why, among their successors, a generation later, there could not be any victims, only people with amputated feelings. No feelings (as Holger eloquently explained) could be an adequate response to the crimes that had been committed. Documentaries could be made, but not feature films about individuals with whom you could identify, with whom you lived and with whom you died. You kept on substituting one thing for another, ideas for things, paper work for dirty work, a final solution for a genocide, and no one was there except the ghosts who kept on returning to the scene of the crime.

Holger could sympathise with Katje, not with himself, because it was surely not he but she who was entitled to the role of the victim. Almost in passing, he observed the way in which for the terrorist, who was a doer, he began to substitute a victim, who was done to; a victim he liked to envisage in the same state of passivity as her sister Ingrid a decade ago (with those indispensable props of his pornographic bourgeois imagination, a tight black skirt and a starched white blouse, worn by a waitress for what other purpose than to be dishevelled by the intruder he saw raping her in the pantry of a hotel on the Kurfürstendamm?).

What went on inside his head? This was the question that would often occur to Holger on formal occasions, in court, at meetings of the Bar Association, at receptions in City Hall given by the mayor. The captions that ran inside his head accompanying the images he saw were obscene and unprintable. A few involuntary movements of his lips, giving voice to the captions that were inside his head, were all that divided him from betraying himself and falling irrecoverably from grace.

This discrepancy between his private thoughts and his social position grew more extreme as the years went on, and Holger became an eminent member of the legal profession. In his private thoughts, the kind of idling, erotic thoughts that filled spare moments while waiting at traffic lights or during tedious summaries in court, it became Holger's habit to imagine himself in the position of power that, as an eminent member of the legal profession, he might have enjoyed at the time of the Third Reich.

Inside Holger's head there was more material on the Third Reich than on any other subject. He had begun assembling his private archive in his early teens, and in his twenties he began adding motion pictures to the collection. Perhaps he had known the Third Reich in more detail, across a broader span of experience, than most people who had lived at the time. In the retrospective, summarising position of historian rather than actor in the contemporary world, judge rather than eye-witness, he had perhaps been more exposed to its impact, and across a wider range of its horrors. This was how the captions had begun, in the 1950s, as a running commentary in Holger's head, a sceptical *hinterfragen*, the habit of asking what might be behind the appearance of his countrymen prospering in the years of the 'Economic Miracle'. Where had she been? What had he done? And later, increasingly often as time went by: what would you, Holger, have done?

Mentally he turned himself into a customs inspector, always on the look out for suitcases with false bottoms. People with double standards, past standards and present, led double lives. Involuntarily Holger began to live by double standards himself.

His unconscious was not unconscious any more. The old archetypes and what they stood for – sexual desire, immortality, superhuman power – had been usurped by specific images that followed him through adolescence and formed his sexuality. Perversion was Hitler lying on the floor being urinated on by his niece. Promiscuity, once impersonated by a limping, rather endearing village god in the rural setting of Olympus, was now personified by Goebbels with a club foot in Berlin, seen standing in multiple mirror reflections in polished boots and britches, bending rows of secretaries over rows of desks. And worse, more brutal, more explicit, the scenes he found himself imagining without desire. The images of the Third Reich stored in Holger's head became the garish playground of a fantasy that was floodlit all the time, and had lost the capacity to lose itself in unconsciousness. An unshaded lightbulb burned night and day in the cell of his mind.

These preoccupations had worn Holger out and made him old when outwardly he was still a young man. On the surface he was the perfect team player, endowed with social skills and a prepossessing personal manner that persuaded his colleagues to nominate him as president of the Bar Association in Berlin.

'Fascist pig,' Katje called him, called everyone, and in a way she was right, because even in the act of repudiating their parents' fascist generation they became contaminated themselves. Katje tried to run away from it and found herself in a hall of mirrors, pointing her finger, levelling her accusations at something she saw in front of her which in reality was behind her, pointing at herself. Holger, who tried to face it, watched it overwhelm him from inside. There was nowhere to go. There was no escape. The feelings were amputated, it was only the nerve ends that still sometimes twitched when they clung to each other, knowing they were each other's kind and shared each other's destiny.

4

When Ingrid's mother died the only reason her daughters had for staying on in East Berlin was that they were not allowed to leave. Ingrid and Katje waited another two years, watching and planning, until they had plucked up enough courage to risk the swim across the Spree to West Berlin one summer night. Of course, they had amazing luck. Ingrid knew the risks and how lucky they had been. But afterwards it seemed to have been so easy that she was angry with herself for having waited, and lost those two years.

She had forgotten how different it was in the West. Many years had passed since she had last been on the other side. She couldn't remember if there had always been such a difference, or if she had just been used to it because she saw it every day. It wasn't easy for Ingrid to get started in the West. In East Berlin she had worked at an institute specialising in tropical diseases. There didn't seem to be any such institute in West Berlin, or none dealing with the particular tropical disease that had been Ingrid's speciality. She received financial assistance while they tried to find her a job. For Katje it was easier. Her younger sister had still been studying at the Humboldt University. Now she went to the *Freie Universität* instead.

Ingrid had to move from Berlin to Frankfurt because of her work. There was no help for it. Something about her training, or approach, or her particular discipline in the field of tropical medicine in which she worked, seemed to be slightly out of line with orthodoxy in the West. She found herself separated from Katje for the first time in her life, living alone in a city where she felt even more at a loss than she had in West Berlin.

For the first few days in Frankfurt Ingrid stayed in a hotel. She didn't know how to make a phone call from her room or how the shower worked, and she felt ashamed. The unfamiliar luxury made her feel inadequate.

Moving into an apartment and beginning her new life in Frankfurt, she found herself missing things that she had never realised she cared for. She missed the institute where she had worked and the old house where she had lived with Katje in Pankow, the shabbiness, the homeliness, the shortage of things and the need for improvisation. She missed having guidelines in her life. Life in the East had been limited but secure. Now it didn't seem to have any boundaries at all. The availability of everything, instantly and in unlimited supply, made a mockery of her previous values. There was freedom in surplus everywhere, undermining the sense of what was scarce, and therefore precious, that had been the core of her pleasures. She thought a little wistfully of the sugar buns which had been available only in a particular store at the end of the week, and how she used to make a ritual of eating them with Katje at breakfast on Saturday mornings.

It would have to get worse before it could get better – the phrase had often been on the lips of the invalid who was her mother, and Ingrid found herself repeating it when she got up in the mornings. It was not just her job where Ingrid felt slightly out of line with the way things were done. Listening to the way people talked, she would feel just slightly out of line with life. She sat and thought to herself: it's another country over there, they don't have the slightest idea what it's like. Sometimes she felt like a foreigner in disguise. She felt like a spy.

At first she used to spend a weekend with Katje in Berlin every month. They shared the narrow bed in the women's hall of residence where Katje lived, and ate in the student canteen. They had fun together. For Ingrid there was even a sense of wellbeing in the institutional atmosphere of her sister's life, the sparseness, the regimentation that was familiar from her past life. But then Katje moved out of the hall and went to live in a commune. Ingrid saw less of her sister. Months now passed without them meeting at all.

Katje's lifestyle changed radically. She had got involved with the circle of students who took their lead from anarchists like Fritz Teufel and Langhans. She was arrested for demonstrating in the nude at a sit-in outside the City Hall. She became a political activist, always to the fore when students took to the streets and engaged in running battles with the police. The atmosphere that had at first been provocative and exuberant became increasingly hostile. It escalated from one injury to the next, one court appearance after another, until both sides regarded the other with mistrust and hatred. Out of the blue came a telephone call from Katje telling Ingrid she was going underground, and then her sister's picture appeared on a poster of wanted terrorists that hung by the counter in the local post office. How could this have happened?

Ingrid began to imagine that she was being kept under observation. She suspected her telephone was being tapped. She got into the habit of scrutinising the street before she left her apartment. Without wanting any such thing, she felt she had become her sister's accomplice.

Already Ingrid was thirty-one. She celebrated her birthday with friends in Frankfurt, only they weren't so much friends as colleagues from the institute where she worked. When she got home she sat and thought about her life. Somewhere she must have taken a wrong turning, but when she went back and looked she couldn't find one.

When Ingrid mythologised her own life, it took on the appearance of one of those striking socialist posters that had fascinated her as a child. Propaganda could be so memorable. The poster showed workers, farmers, groups of men and women with clean-cut features, forever about to march forward, forever about to set out into the future with confident strides. As a child she would turn round in the street, her eyes following the direction in which the poster people with the clean-cut features were gazing, and wonder what it was about the view that inspired in them such confidence.

They inspired her to her own poster nonetheless, fashioned in the same forthright style, like a topographical map, showing the salient features in bold relief. The heroic death of her father when she was only two years old, the bands and marching on state occasions when schoolchildren were sent out to line the streets of East Berlin, the invalid mother for whom she had sacrificed the chance of a career in the West, the swim to freedom across the Spree – on the map of her life there were pronounced features with strong lines, like the Berlin Wall, so striking that they showed up on satellite pictures taken far away in space. But then the topographical map had flattened and lost all its contours. The forthright, marching lines had petered out. It was not until Ingrid reached Frankfurt, the point where the lines seemed to peter out, that she suddenly realised the main elements on this map of her life had not been of her own doing. True, she had taken her destiny in her hands when she swam across the river to West Berlin, but that again had been in response to circumstances beyond her control. She had always been a figure acting against a background, but there seemed to be more drama in the background than in anything the figure was doing.

In Frankfurt, the background had receded and Ingrid, at the age of thirty-one, could clearly see herself waiting to be given directions for her life. Something must happen to which she would be required to respond. The background against which she had been moving all her life was stronger than she was. She saw that this was a pattern she would not change. Her destiny could never be something of her own determination, but of that stronger background to which she was inescapably bound.

It was a couple of months after her thirty-first birthday, a few months before Katje went underground, when Ingrid took the usual short-cut through Frankfurt station on her way back home, that she once more had the unpleasant feeling she was being observed. Someone in the crowd was following her with his eyes. She hurried round a corner and waited to see if she was being followed.

A few moments later a man came past, walking fast, in fact almost running. He did not see Ingrid hiding, but when he saw that she was no longer in front of him he immediately turned round. Ingrid was not in the least afraid. The man *was* following her, and she had caught him red-handed, but even as she walked towards him to confront him with her accusation, something made her hesitate. It was a troubled sense of familiarity. Ingrid did not instantly recognise him, but with every step forward it was as if she was moving backwards, and by the time she came up to him the ten intervening years had shrunk to nothing, revealing the gravel pit behind the Soviet barracks in East Berlin on an August afternoon, and Ingrid had remembered Jason even before he spoke her name.

5

Jason still lived with Jens and Elena in the house in Berlin-Grunewald, but he rented a small apartment in Frankfurt where he stayed when he was covering stories in West Germany. At the time he was writing a series about terrorism, and he commuted between Stuttgart, Frankfurt and Bonn. The leading RAF terrorists were awaiting trial in the high-security prison building that had been specially built for them in Stuttgart-Stammheim.

Holger was coming from Berlin to spend a couple of days with Jason over the New Year, and Katje was staying in Frankfurt at Ingrid's apartment. The four of them met up at Jason's place on New Year's Eve. It was smaller than Ingrid's apartment, but it was at the top of a high-rise building, giving them a better view of the fireworks bursting all over the city. It was the first time they had all been together in thirteen years.

Holger talked a lot, as he always did in company. Jason moved round the table where his friends were sitting, clearing the dishes and carrying them into the kitchen. He walked round Holger, who talked without respite, and it was as if he could visualise the curtain of words that poured out of Holger's mouth, screening him off from the rest of the room. It was Jason's image of Holger's life. Surrounded by people, he sat alone behind a curtain of words. It was difficult to interrupt or dodge under the curtain to get at Holger. He communicated in order to ward people off.

Jason knew him well, and because he was interested in what Holger had to say he did not object to the word-curtain. The word-curtain was the way the kind-hearted but standoffish Holger, who avoided confrontation in private to the same extent that he sought it publicly in court, exhibited his will to dominate. Holger was a cultured German for whom culture provided the legitimate means to intimidate intellectual inferiors.

Jason was familiar with Holger's technique. The theme would be introduced by a rhetorical question, unanswerable except by Holger himself. Then came the elucidation in the form of an epigram or a paradox, followed by further explanation in more general terms. He kept a tight grip on his subject. Nobody else could get in.

'What alternative is there to the two basic types of relationship between men and women? Is there one? I challenge you to name it. The woman is either a motherly type or she is a *putain*. And no man will want to have to do with the same type of woman in succession. After he has had the motherly type, he will choose the *putain*. Or vice versa . . .'

Katje sat in silence as Holger talked, her white-streaked hands resting on the table.

Holger disguised his most intimate thoughts on life as formal propositions, which were usually expressed as laws. Inside the generalisations there would often lurk a personal confession.

All of this was curiously rigid. Probably he had developed the habit from pleading cases in court, where you tried to invalidate the premise of what your opponent was saying. It was not a question of agreeing or disagreeing with this or that point. You had to accept or jettison a system, the entire structure of Holger's case.

Katje had made up her mind to jettison it.

'That's the most complacent, male-chauvinist bourgeois drivel I've ever heard.'

Jason thought of the *putain* Colette, her succession to the motherly Petra, and smiled to himself in the kitchen.

The evening was taken up by this running battle between Holger and Katje, which Holger did not take too seriously and seemed to enjoy. It was a meeting between a cactus and a cushion. Plump, puffing a cigar, the cushion looked comfortable. The cactus, by contrast, was so brittle one expected pieces of her to break off at any minute.

Jason had observed this at his meeting with Katje at Ingrid's

place, where he listened to her talk about the Red Army organisation, RAF, and its aims. He knew she was a sympathiser on the
fringe of the group, but not how deeply she was involved. The first
impression of Katje (thirteen years after Jason had first seen her
coming towards him with white hands on a dark landing in Pankow,
almost thirty years after her mother crawled out of the rubble of a
bombed house in Dresden) was her complete lack of humour and a
stubbornness, brittle and cactus-like, that reminded him of Michael
Kohlhaas.

At the time he met Katje, Jason was working on an article about a new
breed of political extremists which had emerged in Germany over the
previous few years. He sought to place these extremists (in those days
he still avoided the word terrorists) in a tradition of agitatory
Protestant reformism that had begun with Luther. Psychologically,
they had features in common with a type of German, an anti-hero
who had become a prototype, described by Kleist in his novella
Michael Kohlhaas.
    In the sixteenth century, the horse-dealer Kohlhaas had set out on
a journey from Brandenburg to Saxony in order to sell his animals.
On reaching the border between the two principalities, he was
informed by the servants of the junker whose lands he had to cross
that he would need a passport to do so. Kohlhaas assured the junker's
men there must be a mistake. He had crossed this border by the Elbe
River seventeen times in his life, and never yet been asked to show a
passport. The junker's servants told him that in future he would be,
because a new regulation had become law. Kohlhaas appealed to
the junker in person, to no avail. He was obliged to leave half of the
horses he had been hoping to sell in Saxony as a pledge before being
allowed to continue his journey.
    In Dresden Kohlhaas made inquiries with the authorities and
confirmed, as he had known from the beginning, that no such regulation existed. The junker had made arbitrary use of his powers and
had cost Kohlhaas dearly. On the return journey to Brandenburg he
found the horses he had left with the junker half starved and in an
atrocious condition; the stableboy he left behind to look after them

had been beaten and driven away by the junker's lawless men. Kohlhaas demanded full restitution: the horses must be returned to him in exactly the same condition in which he had left them, and the junker punished for what he had done.

The quarrel dragged on and on. Various compromises were suggested, but Kohlhaas, who had a keen sense of justice, 'as fine as a set of scales for measuring gold', in the striking phrase that Kleist places as a mark of his intentions, would not budge an inch. Unable to get satisfaction from the authorities, he took the law into his own hands. The man who had been the model of a good citizen became an outlaw and a rebel, and the relatively minor incident of the maltreatment of his horses, for which he had demanded full restitution but not received it in a form he considered acceptable, led the country to the brink of civil war. 'His sense of justice turned him into a murderer and a robber.'

The figure of Kohlhaas became part of the national mythology in the way that literary characters like Robinson Crusoe or Huckleberry Finn had become part of the national mythologies in Britain and America. *Michael Kohlhaas* was a cautionary tale, but Jason's reading of the story (its author had written his novella against the background of national liberation struggles during the Napoleonic Wars) was that Kleist had been more inclined to sympathise with Kohlhaas in his struggle against arbitrary abuses of power than to damn him for taking the law into his own hands. The author went out of his way to characterise him as *rechtschaffen*, a fair man who remains decent despite the terrible revenge he takes. Important details in the story, such as the maltreatment of Kohlhaas's pregnant wife at the instigation of the spiteful authorities, and her subsequent death as a result of the shock she has sustained, reinforced Jason's impression that the author felt sympathy for his character. It is his wife's death, in effect her murder, that is the last straw for Kohlhaas. Thereafter he becomes implacable. An eye for an eye, a tooth for a tooth. The Judaic law was as much quoted as misunderstood, for it was by no means an incitement to a cruel revenge. It was quite specifically an admonition *not* to exact revenge, but to punish in kind.

To Jason it seemed remarkable that the Germans should have

reserved a place in their national mythology for a story that exemplified, alongside that familiar characteristic of *Rechthaberei*, or argumentative self-righteousness, the very un-German quality of civil disobedience. Kohlhaas was the anti-hero in the national pantheon because his name stood for extremism, for self-righteousness and obstinacy that went too far, causing right to deteriorate into wrong. He was kept there as a warning. Perhaps because, at bottom, they considered civil disobedience a questionable virtue at the best of times, Germans did not regard Kohlhaas as a tragic figure, a hero of civil disobedience gone wrong. They did not approve of Kohlhaas, let alone like him.

Another hero of civil disobedience whom the Germans installed in the national pantheon was Luther (although his elevation was due less to such disobedience than to outstanding cultural achievements as the Bible translator and master mason of the language). In Kleist's version of the Kohlhaas story, a meeting takes place between Luther and Kohlhaas, between the hero of civil disobedience whom the Germans liked and the anti-hero whom they didn't. Despite his distaste for Kohlhaas, Luther sees enough right in his cause to allow himself to be persuaded to intercede with the state on his behalf (to no avail – at the end of the tale Kohlhaas is put to death). At their meeting, the great reformer and moral leader cannot be faulted in his damnation of Kohlhaas's ungodliness, but as a character he fails to come to life. From a modern point of view (and probably Kleist's), Luther's arguments sound like a rearguard action in defence of a doomed feudalism. Kohlhaas emerges from the encounter the winner on points. He is the more human, the more sympathetic of the two, and he is the one with whom the modern world identifies more easily, even though Kleist cunningly appears to condemn him.

Jason had the story of Kohlhaas very much in mind when he began to write about the wave of terrorism that broke over Germany with the Baader–Meinhof burning of the department store in Frankfurt. Here was a new Kohlhaas, or a whole bunch of them, whose problem was that nobody had maltreated their horses. They lacked a grievance. Lacking a grievance, they had no choice but to provoke one. They set fire to the store and robbed banks. They

goaded the state into taking hostile counter-measures, justifying
further and more extreme acts of civil disobedience. Baader, Meinhof
and their henchmen and henchwomen went to jail. They were held
captive by a hostile state power. This became the grievance on which
the RAF could build, and in which it had its apparent *raison d'être*.

The lack of a reason for their actions distinguished German terrorists from the revolutionaries in South America, the Basque
terrorists in Spanish cities and all the other urban guerillas at the time
(except, significantly, the Japanese, with whom the German terrorists
briefly made common cause). What they lacked in grievance they
made up for in a hunger for civil disobedience

To Jason it was understandable. In the aftermath of the Second
World War, Kohlhaasian principle had never been riding so high.
After the mass demonstration of civil obedience by their parents'
generation, making that generation the accomplices of a regime that
had plunged the world into death and disaster, opposition by way of
a change did not appear to be such a bad thing. The terrorists
emerged from nowhere to exorcise the ghosts of obedience that had
sanctioned the lack of resistance resulting in the inaction that had
made possible the barbarism of the Third Reich.

In Jason's mind, the German terrorists evinced an interest in civil
disobedience for its own sake, as an end in itself. They never articu-
lated it in this way but to him this is what is was. It was an attempt
to rearrange the priorities in the Germans' national mythology, to
make them less dutiful in their respect for law and more open-
minded in their distaste for rebellion, because this was a desirable
shift of emphasis within the national character.

Kleist's description of Kohlhaas's sense of justice, 'as fine as a set
of scales for measuring gold', has connotations of something more
than precise measurement. It suggests over-exactness and a lack of
flexibility. There is insufficient give and take, too little tolerance
around the borders where things have to fit together.

One of those borders was the frontier between Brandenburg and
Saxony. When Kohlhaas was travelling to market to sell his horses in
the sixteenth century (and to a lesser extent at the time Kleist's story
was published in 1810), these German principalities still regarded one

another as sovereign *foreign* states. Crossing the Elbe, one travelled *abroad*. Von Knigge, in an essay published at around the time Kleist was writing, thought that it was in the differences of customs and manners, varying substantially within the many states making up the Reich, that one had to seek the cause of their mutual intolerance (and with it of German intolerance as such), because travellers who expected to find differences when travelling abroad were unprepared for them inside their common German nation. It is human nature to scrutinise and judge most sharply those to whom one feels closest, to criticise in others the faults that one recognises in oneself.

Intolerance accompanied the shrill expectations that Jason encountered in Katje, emerging white-handed from the shadows of the landing thirteen years on, a sound that was already going on, like the scream of someone who has spent a lifetime in silence, before the door was opened. It was the old German idealism, with its unhappy gift of rendering abstractions with such plasticity that they seemed like three-dimensional objects you could reach out and touch. You could reach out and kill imperialism because it was there, wearing the uniform of the state. You could set fire to symbols, and department stores went up in flames. It was the old German idealism with its demands for impossibly exalted aims, the backlash of disappointment already forming on the rebound from the goals it had inevitably failed to reach. It was the old German idealism recoiling from its encounter with the Impossible Fact, an angel repulsed from the battlements of heaven and falling in a never-ending spiral downwards.

6

When Ingrid resurfaces in Jason's life a ragbag of submerged associations come floating up with her, as if tied to a string of corks. Memories of adolescence, embedded in the phrases Jason had once used to describe her in a book of poems that has long been out of print, are revived when he meets her again. What seemed to have disappeared with Ingrid forever behind the Berlin Wall – an alternative version of his life in which he continued to write poetry, made a journey to Africa, and fell in love with a nurse at Dr Schweitzer's leper colony in Lambaréné – pops back up into view the moment she appears again.

It is as if he is unravelling the fabric of the life he has been living for the past ten years, back to that Sunday morning in August, when he was on his way to East Berlin to go swimming with Ingrid in the gravel pit behind the Soviet barracks and the Berlin Wall intervened. Now he can set out on a different track. There are no soldiers barring his way in the other script of his life. The moment he crosses the sector border he begins to follow this alternative version.

A brand-new adolescent longing, almost never used and put away in 1961, flares up inside Jason the moment he sets eyes on Ingrid again. It comes out of the freezer into the oven and instantly burgeons.

They spend evenings together. They meet at weekends. Soon he does not bother to go home to his own apartment, but stays over the weekend at Ingrid's place. There have been other periods when work has kept Jason in Frankfurt, but never for more than two or three weekends at a stretch. Almost always, when Jason stays in Frankfurt during the week, he returns to Berlin to spend the weekend in Grunewald.

Soon he was unable to extricate himself from his involvement with Ingrid. Soon he was going to have to tell Elena, as they had long ago agreed, in the event of something like this happening. Elena would know even if Jason said nothing. But he put it off, hoping that Ingrid would somehow dissolve. At last he called Elena and told her he had fallen in love with Ingrid after meeting her at Frankfurt station, 'entirely by chance', he added, as if chance were an extenuating circumstance of which Elena would somehow approve. But Elena said nothing. She withdrew into silence. Jason was shocked that for the first time in a telephone conversation with Elena there were silences between them, when he could think of nothing to say. It would be better if he stayed in Frankfurt for the time being and didn't come home at all, he said. Yes, it would be better, Elena agreed, and at once hung up without even saying goodbye.

Jason remained in a state of shock for several weeks after this conversation. He couldn't believe what he had told Elena, or that she had accepted it, or that she had hung up without saying goodbye.

He dreamed he was standing on a cliff with Elena and Jens, looking out to sea. Both of them were upset. They had lost something and were trying to retrieve it, but the cliff where they stood was too steep to climb down. All Jens could do was go down on his hands and knees and try to reach over the edge, but his attempts were useless. Whatever Jens was trying to reach, Jason had an uneasy feeling that it was he, Jason, who had thrown it there, and he should be helping Jens to get it back. But he waited on one side and looked out to sea. Standing outside the picture, he could see it as a whole, but the Jason standing inside the picture couldn't even turn his head to watch what the others were doing. He was paralysed.

Ingrid watches Jason standing in her apartment looking out of the window, framed against the evening sky between a lamp and a giant cactus. Compared with the picture of which this is a pastiche, it is a ludicrous image, suggesting that Jason is already sinking into middle-class domesticity. Here there is no trace of the romantic hero intent on his destiny. But Ingrid would not recognise this. She would be hurt by such an interpretation, and feel bound to protest.

Fortunately for Ingrid, she cannot see Jason's face. He is looking out of the window, and his back is turned towards her. Already she is getting to know his habits, and this makes her happy. In the late afternoon, at the blue hour when the light begins to go, Jason likes to stand and look out of the window as he smokes a cigarette. She relishes the silence between them, a bond of silence she can feel holding them together, and at such moments it seems to Ingrid that she has been living with Jason all her life.

7

On the far side of the grey sky over Frankfurt Jason saw the blue. At some time he must have turned round to make a suggestion to Ingrid, for she had been thinking of changing her job in any case, and they locked up her apartment and headed south. South of the Alps it was already as warm as in early summer. They slept with the windows wide open. In the mornings, when the cool air scudded in, she put her arms round him to get warm, and Jason, still learning the moves in this other version of his life, put his arms around her too, and held her tight.

The lakes with the little hunched houses, looking down from the steep shore, where they stayed a night before passing on, the twisting roads with the scent of pines, the sudden noise of a city, the piazza where they drank coffee and read the newspapers, it was all a stage for their own choreography, a *pas de deux* for two lovers. This was the image of them reflected in the landscape with its swiftly changing moods from soft evening shadows to the fierce brightness of noon. They arrived somewhere to occupy a room, a table or just a chair, forming part of an orchestra of brief impressions that just as quickly dispersed when they got back into the car and drove on – not merely forgotten already but never registered by the indifference of the landscape through which they passed. For this, too, was part of the image, human in its fragility and its *Vergänglichkeit*.

For her part, Ingrid cannot have felt this. Flush with the landscape, immersed in the experience, she was happy in their self-containment. In an empty street in a small town she stood looking into a shop window because she saw something there that interested her. Nothing challenged her immediate curiosity, nothing interfered, no shadowy contours of an awareness of anything else. Jason stood in front of the window beside her, but he was looking down the street. He saw the empty chairs in the café where they had just been sitting and which left no imprint of their having been there.

Jason's receptivity on this journey with Ingrid was so acute that it recorded impressions which were not there, like the feeling of vacancy left behind on a chair by someone who had previously been sitting on it. He moved with a sense of wondering and newness through this alternative version of his life. Moving around freely inside it, inhabiting and taking full possession of it, he still saw it from a distance, as if he was living in a house that did not belong to him.

They took the ferry from Livorno, hopping islands through the Mediterranean to the Aegean, and when Jason saw the white walls and the white roofs under the exact shade of blue he had imagined on the far side of the sky he had been looking at from her Frankfurt apartment, he felt able to settle down with Ingrid in a house that did not belong to him, with cool stone floors and a well, bougainvillaea inhabited by drowsy bees, a line of cypress trees on the horizon and the sea at the bottom of the hill.

All these things were there, but not as part of the view that Jason saw. The view that Jason saw corresponded to the view on the poster in his imagination. The poster view was made up of elements, each of which resembled the real view perfectly, but not when put together as a whole, because the poster view in Jason's imagination was a cliché with a commercial message. It was kitsch. It wasn't the real thing at all. It was the view that hung on the walls of the house in which Jason lived but which did not belong to him.

Life with Ingrid on an Aegean island, in the house with the poster view, was like living on a set where an advertisement was being made. Everything was effortless. Everywhere was light and space. Always the floor was perfectly swept. In the clean light space of their poster life Ingrid moved effortlessly, barefoot across swept stone floors, with her long blonde hair bounding in slow motion around her beautifully shaped body. She was perfectly at home in their rented house.

Ich bin so glücklich, she said, reminding Jason of German lessons with Elena on the lawn behind the house in Grunewald. *Ich habe Glück, glücklich zu sein.* Ingrid was lucky to be happy. Undeterred by the threat of mines and bullets, she had swum across the Spree straight into poster land, where Jason was waiting.

Who was the woman in the background, whom Ingrid knew of but Jason did not talk about, as if her existence was a secret? Jason didn't talk about Elena, and Ingrid didn't ask, but she could sometimes feel her presence in the room.

Jason stood silently with his back turned to Ingrid, looking out of the window. Then he turned round, and they headed south.

They left the car in the ferry harbour and steamed up to the Bosporus on an old Turkish freighter. In Istanbul, in the papers at all the news-stands, it was the lead story. Brandt and Guillaume: the German chancellor and the spy who had betrayed him. Jason was stunned. He recognised the photograph of the spy: he had met him once at a party conference in Berlin. He spent all day at the main station, drinking sweet coffee and reading newspapers. At the station in Istanbul, intruded on by all the strange smells and sounds, the story of Brandt's betrayal by Guillaume did not seem real. Jason couldn't believe it. Apparently the spy had even accompanied his master on holiday in Norway, handling all his private and confidential papers, secrets it must be assumed he had passed on to the German Democratic Republic. There was a strong likelihood that the case would prove to be the downfall of Willy Brandt.

While Jason had been living his alternative life on a poster island he had missed one of the espionage coups of the century and a crucial political story, but it was not his own bad luck that troubled him. He felt the stab of Guillaume's betrayal of Brandt, the iniquity of his deed, as keenly as if he had done the deed himself. It was the story of deep personal betrayal which made Jason smart with shame.

Ingrid lay naked, asleep in the heat of the stuffy hotel room. Jason sat on the edge of the bed and looked down at her, the object of desire, her arms behind her head on the pillow, her golden hair still bounding in her sleep, her body striped with bars of sunlight that came slanting through the shutters. But he felt no desire for

Ingrid. He felt her beauty as a curse. An ache throbbed inside him. He was aware of a gradually broadening, inexplicable sense of dread. It was stifling in the room. He got up to open the shutters, and went out on to the balcony.

· The balcony looked out over the busy port on the Black Sea. The ships came and went, just as they had in Malmö harbour on that summer night Magnus Gould spent sitting on the harbour wall forty years before. The son saw what his father had seen. Here was the turntable swinging each vessel round in the direction it had been assigned, the dial pointing to the place that would become its destination.

Ingrid called him in from the balcony and began to read aloud from a guidebook. According to Greek mythology, the guidebook said, the Black Sea was the sea which Jason and the Argonauts had crossed to fetch the Golden Fleece that hung in a grove on the far side. There were ships parting daily from Istanbul for Colchis, the El Dorado on the eastern shore where the River Rioni ran into the Black Sea, carrying nuggets of gold, which local prospectors still washed out of the stream with the help of a fleece, just as they had been doing thousands of years ago. Boarding one of the ships for a cruise across the Black Sea to Colchis before returning to Frankfurt had been Ingrid's idea, but the spy Guillaume had intervened.

The Brandt story was too important, Jason told her. He would have to cut short the extended holiday they had planned. He suggested to Ingrid that she visit Colchis by herself, and he flew back alone to Berlin the next morning.

8

Jason stepped out of the elevator and walked across the brightly lit foyer to the glass door. He pressed the bell. Through the door he looked into the lawyers' offices, waiting for Holger to appear from the far end of the corridor he was facing.

At half-past seven in the evening the daylight had almost faded. Jason looked past the empty chairs for clients whom he could imagine waiting at the near end of the corridor, on past the shadowy reception area lit by a single spotlight, the bookshelves lining the walls, into the gloom at the far end where Holger would soon appear. He saw first the glimmer of his shirt, white in the darkness. Holger leaned over the reception desk for the keys to unlock the door, and advanced down the corridor with an unhurried, almost stately tread. He peered out, raising a hand, acknowledging Jason's presence outside the door, only when he was already quite near. The procedure was always the same. Perhaps there were reflections in the glass, and Holger couldn't see him clearly on the other of the door.

To Jason, the image of Holger advancing down the corridor with the keys to let him into the office after hours reminded him of someone who did not realise he was in a prison, whom he had come to free. To Holger, the image of Jason waiting outside the door reminded him of someone entreating for asylum, whom he was admitting to a safe place.

Jason handed Holger a cigarette, and they walked up and down the corridor smoking, exchanging the latest news.

'I was in Bonn,' said Jason, 'for an interview with Brandt. He was moving into a new office. People kept on coming in with boxes and files, arranging them in piles on the floor. Brandt said he didn't know what to do with them, because there was so much less space than in the chancellor's office. He put a cheerful enough face on it, but naturally it must hurt, having to recognise he has less space because his official stature has shrunk. From now on, office and power, everything he has lived for, will begin to shrink.'

He stopped and turned to Holger.

'I find it difficult to imagine this is where it ends. Was this the culmination point for him, or something else that we don't know about in his life? Was Brandt's decline irreversible from the moment Guillaume fluttered past and he was fatally brushed by the spy's wings? Did he live sixty years for this betrayal? Was betrayal by Guillaume his destiny?'

'No, I don't think so, because Brandt is passive. He is the object of someone else's action. Brandt did not live to be betrayed by the spy. Guillaume lived for it, and it is his destiny. The person betrayed doesn't identify with the traitor, but the traitor *does* identify with the person he betrays. Brandt is passive, and yet . . . don't you feel that in some way Guillaume fits the spy?'

'Fits? In what way?'

'By the logic of the Attraction of Affinities. Where there is an ideal, there is also its betrayal. Doesn't the one accompany the other, like its shadow? Guillaume as Brandt's shadow. What do you say? In the photographs published in the papers Guillaume is always following his master, like his shadow. Where there is an ideal or an idealisation, of a thing or a person, whether communism or Christ, isn't there also its antithesis in readiness, its betrayal or the person who betrays? Hasn't that been your own experience?'

Jason stood rooted to the spot, as if Holger had been reading his most personal thoughts.

'You see, I have been thinking about what you wrote recently concerning the nature of German terrorism, an essay in an American journal, with reference to Michael Kohlhaas. I thought it was very interesting.'

'Ah, that.'

'Simplifying what you seemed to be saying, isn't German terrorism itself the ideal, there on its own behalf?'

'The exalted sense of justice of Michael Kohlhaas?'

'"As fine as a set of scales for measuring gold."'

They had reached the glass door again and now turned back.

Holger said, 'The man is a horse-dealer. Now, what does that suggest to you?'

Jason shrugged.

'What sort of a person might have been an itinerant horse-dealer in the sixteenth century, passing back and forth between Brandenburg and Saxony? Who might be likely to have had the connections and the capital to set himself up as a horse-dealer, and to have been familiar with the very fine scales required for weighing gold?'

'Does it matter?'

'Of course,' said Holger, 'because Kleist's story of Michael Kohlhaas takes on a quite different significance if one conjectures that the hero of his story was a Jew.'

Holger walked on down the corridor, humming softly, trailing his fingers along the bookcase while he took a long drag on his cigarette. Jason watched it glimmer and fade as he followed him into the darkness at the far end of the corridor.

9

When Jason called to see him after business hours in his office, often late at night, Holger could see Jason long before his friend could see him. Stepping from his room into the dark corridor, Holger was not visible to Jason, but Jason, outlined against the illuminated landing outside the glass door, was clearly visible to Holger.

The lawyer felt that this gave him a certain advantage, which both reassured and shamed him. How helplessly transparent his friend was, like an insect, in the brightly lit glass case behind the door! How easy it was to see through him! Every time he opened the door to let Jason into his office he went through the motions of pretending he had not seen him until he had almost reached the entrance, and every time he felt a flush of pleasure at the sense of shame this deviousness aroused in him.

Holger mythologised his working life in the office as the work entrusted to the administrators of a castle. He thought of the law as a castle, an impregnable fortress. His first brief, immediately after setting up in practice, was on behalf of an old woman who had been overcharged by the electricity board. The electricity board tried to resist Holger's instructions, but in the end they had to obey him. The old woman was reimbursed. She came to Holger and clasped his hands. He understood what power the people who lived inside the castle had over the people who lived outside it, just as his colleague Kafka had done, who did not live in the citadel but the lower town, in the Jewish ghetto in Prague, looking up at the Hradin.

When Holger mythologised his life as a child he imagined himself inside a labyrinth, but it was not until he chose his profession that he realised the labyrinth was inside the castle, and that it would never be anything but the castle, because there was only the one. After the war, not a single jurist was convicted for the miscarriages of justice which had been perpetrated during the Third Reich, because lawyers were looked after by their own kind. This monopoly of the people who lived inside the castle was the source of their power. The arbitrariness of justice accompanied the arbitrariness of power, like its shadow, like the shadow that it cast over the horse-dealer Michael Kohlhaas. Kleist's story does not begin with the Jewish horse-dealer's abuse of an ideal justice but with the junker's abuse of his feudal powers.

The walled medieval citadel is the image of the citadel of Christ, inhabited by the defenders of the faith. The junker's men come down from the castle, perhaps to announce a new levy on trafficking in horses between Brandenburg and Saxony, or perhaps a new dispensation absolving their lord's subjects of levies at all, because their powers are arbitrary. The Jew lives in the shadow of the citadel of Christ, or perhaps he is a traveller passing through, like Kohlhaas. He pays gold for the right to be where he is, to marry, to deal in horses, to appeal to the lord for protection and to be sheltered inside the castle walls when enemies invade the land. Sometimes these rights, which the Jew has paid for in gold, are granted him by his lord; sometimes they are not, and he is left to his fate outside the castle walls. Sometimes the whole community of Jews is put to the sword by the inhabitants of the castle themselves. So they live and die side by side, for a thousand years.

What has the Jew got to protect himself? Gold. Nothing but gold can help him, which is why Kohlhaas has a sense of justice as fine as a set of scales for measuring gold. Justice is measured in gold. Gold buys imperial patents and letters of safe conduct. Justice can be had (sometimes) for gold, but without gold there is no justice to be had at all. Jews must attend to the business of acquiring gold, or they will die.

The Jew living outside the castle is entirely at the mercy of the Christians living inside it. If necessary, they can do without his services as moneylender, but in his role as their victim the Jew is indispensable.

Holger believed that where there was an ideal there was also its betrayal. The neighbour whom the Christians loved by command-ment had another neighbour whom they tied up on a leash outside the castle walls. The Jew was the shadow of the Christian ideal, where love turned to hate, and could turn to hate with impunity, because the Jews were the murderers of Christ. The Jews became the victims of the Christians and the Christians became the scourge of the Jews.

Why didn't the Jews go?

In Kafka's book *Das Schloss*, the surveyor remains in the vicinity of the castle because there is nowhere else to go. Either we belong here, or we belong nowhere. Surrounding the castle is a snow-covered waste-land. For better or worse, the castle is the oasis, the community of life. Like the surveyor, the Jews hung around the castle, a band of pet-itioners in the diaspora, waiting for the coming of the Messiah, and they accepted the Christian scourge as a sign from God that they were still living in sinfulness, and they bore the scourge as a penance to hasten the Messiah's coming. When the Christians set fire to the ghettos, the Jewish martyrs joined hands and went dancing into the flames of the holocaust that virtually wiped out the Jews at the same time as Christians and Jews were being decimated by the Black Death.

This happened two hundred years before Luther's meeting with the Jewish horse-dealer Michael Kohlhaas. Luther was an old and bitter man when he met Kohlhaas. He had become a reactionary. Perhaps the moral leader of the Reformation was busy penning his denunciation of the Jews when the horse-dealer called on him in his chambers in Wittenberg, asking him to intercede with the authorities on his behalf. Twenty years earlier, Luther had written a humane, compassionate tract sympathising with the Jews – in an attempt to convert them to the true faith, it is true, but the Jews had appreciated it nonetheless.

What caused this change of heart? The steadfastness with which the Jews clung to their belief? A falling-off in Luther's own? Had Luther, his convictions failing him in his later years, perhaps been reading with a certain bitterness and envy of those Jews dancing in the flames, rejoicing on their way to martyrdom, when he was startled by the unannounced visit of the Jewish horse-dealer to his chambers?

Why did the privy councillor Goethe, three hundred years later, express reservations about a new-fangled dispensation permitting marriage between Gentiles and Jews, on the grounds that such intermarriage might undermine morality?

And why, half a century on again, did Wagner recant the revolutionary idealism of his youth, qualifying his championship of civil rights for Jews as having been for the *principle* of the cause of freedom rather than for the particular case, because (as was well known) he had always been involuntarily repelled by Jews?

But how, in the middle of the nineteenth century, was one able to identify a Jew? How could Wagner know with such accuracy when to be involuntarily repelled?

By a stigma – by a name, a profession, a belief, perhaps by a nose. But a nose was unreliable. The better to be recognised (for the safety of the Christians jeopardised by them) the Jews were required in the Middle Ages to wear marked clothes identifying them as such, and this imposition of a stigma by law would return with a vengeance a thousand years later.

It is not the Jew to whom the Christian is bound by fear and hate and whom he needs as victim. It is the stigma of the Jew.

The stigma of the Jew, the stigma of the strangeling, the changeling, the victim sought out and branded by society, is inescapable for both Jews and Christians. A century on again, Holger is as susceptible to it as any other German, with the same mid-twentieth-century mixture of guilt and curiosity. These feelings are already triggered off inside him by the name Gould, surely the stigma of a Jew, although Holger has never raised the subject with Jason, because it is still taboo.

The image of Jason in the illuminated glass case outside his office door, transparent in his helplessness, visible to Holger long before Holger is visible to Jason, reminds him of someone entreating for asylum whom he can choose to admit or not, according to his powers of discretion, to the safety of the castle walls, and this knowledge gives Holger a sense of power, which at the same time excites and shames him.

10

'And suddenly there is Kohlhaas, not the fawning Jew with gold nuggets up his sleeve, throwing himself on his Christian masters' mercy and ready to buy justice at any price, but a modern terrorist – self-possessed, relentless in his principles, ideologised to the core. Here is the Jew who *demands* justice, at first for himself and his maltreated horses, in the end for its own sake. Thwarted, his sense of justice turns him into a murderer.'

Jason followed Holger into his office and slumped on the sofa. Holger paced up and down.

'Kleist's story is still shocking. How did the writer achieve this effect? By an anachronism, superimposing on the feudal relationships of the sixteenth century the mentality of a nineteenth-century revolutionary. Did Kleist know he was writing a story about a Jew? Perhaps unconsciously he did, and this is the secret that gives the story its power. In the sixteenth century, Luther can still castigate Kohlhaas for his ungodliness, and be right, because for Kohlhaas there can only be eternal damnation. In the nineteenth century, however, ungodliness is no longer a charge that will stand up in court, and the horse-dealer, pleading extenuating circumstances that include the effective murder of his wife, already has something of a case.

'But let's suppose Luther's charge of ungodliness means just what it says, and the horse-dealer is ungodly because he is a Jew, for whom in the Christian scheme of things there could never be anything other than eternal damnation. Perhaps in the opening scene, when he first appears before Luther, standing with his petition in the chambers of the Reformation champion (who happens to be in the middle of penning his denunciation of the Jews, keeping alive the stigma of the Jew for coming generations of Christians), Kohlhaas has gold nuggets up his sleeves and at any moment will begin to fawn and throw himself on Luther's mercy, because this is the stigma of the Jew from which neither Jew nor Christian can escape. Perhaps this is what Luther expects – the servile act of Jewish obeisance before the Christian master. And the horse-dealer does indeed ask the favour of Luther's intercession, but as a free man, who is his equal. He does not offer gold. He will not budge from his principles. He does not offer to recant. Imagine the impact of this behaviour, coming from an upstart Jewish horse-dealer in the sixteenth century.

'What is it that so shocks Luther, provoking him to hurl out his charge of ungodliness? A Jew is no longer willing to honour his contract with the Christians. This is what shocks the ageing iconoclast Luther. A Jew is no longer prepared to play the role of victim to the Christian role of oppressor. He will no longer offer gold for letters of patent granting him protection in the lord's castle. He asserts his moral right. The land surveyor gets on a train that takes him away to a foreign country. The Jew leaves the castle behind him, because he has lost interest in it, and emigrates to America. Kafka's *Das Schloss* never gets written. When the Gestapo arrives at dawn in the ghettos of the twentieth century, the successors of Kohlhaas take machine-guns from under the bedcovers and open fire. The implications of the sequel to the story in which Kohlhaas is identified as a Jew are indeed stunning.'

'But it doesn't happen.'

'It doesn't happen – not yet. Only a few recognise racism for what it is, agree with Herzl that the Jewish question is a national question with only one solution – a national Jewish state – and take a ship from Europe for Palestine to begin a new life.'

Holger got up and opened the window in his office. The cool night air streamed in. Reclining on the sofa, Jason could feel it flow-ing over his body, and shivered. Holger swivelled back and forth on the chair at his desk, fiddling with a pencil. Then for a long time he sat perfectly still with his eyes closed, his elbows resting on the desk, fingers interlocked.

'I know how to prize my undeserved fortune that I am both a German and a Jew – yes, because born in slavery I love freedom more greatly than you; yes, because born with no fatherland I would love a fatherland more ardently than you; and because my place of birth was no larger than the *Judengasse*, the alley in the ghetto where the Jews lived, and just beyond the locked gates of the ghetto a foreign country began for me, I will not be satisfied with a town, a region, not even a province – no, nothing less will do for me than the great fatherland in its entirety, as far as its language reaches—'

'Who is this me and I?' interrupted Jason, astonished. Looking over, he saw that Holger had been reading from a book. Holger put the book on one side and said:

'This is the authentic voice of the assimilated Jew, the German Jew, who is tragically never allowed to become the Jewish German. This is how the Jews have come to see themselves, more *Deutschnational* than any German – but what can that mean, if it excludes them? – nationalist. The fatherland of the Reich may be incomparably larger, but it is still the same castle, and for the Christians the Jew is still the neighbour whom they do not love, still tied up on a leash outside the castle wall. After two thousand years of assimilation he is weary of the stigma that keeps him tied up on a leash, condemning him to the humiliation of outsidership. Naturally the Jew wants to come inside. To disguise his Jewishness he forswears his religion, is baptised a Christian, changes his name and moves to another city – anything to be admitted to the castle on equal terms.

'For Jews and Germans have become inseparable and indistinguishable. Living so long together, they have come to resemble one another. As the Germans approach the threshold of nationhood, one becomes aware of the narrowing convergence of that mystical entity the German *Volk* and the claim of the children of Israel to be God's chosen people. In the age of enlightenment, Germans have already discovered their destiny as the *Kulturvolk*, the cultural leaders of the world. Later, it will just be as leaders of the world. For both Jews and Germans believe in messianic roles for their people. Hitler, like Moses, will be right to trust in the irrational, in the power of this mystical belief, the appeal of a promised land. Germans, too, little loved by their neighbours, attracting the dislike of their neighbours, but also their respect, and their envy, acquire a stigma which, if only by virtue of analogy, and however arbitrarily, draws out a perception of the resemblances there are between Germans and Jews. Looking from the one to the other and back again, you find you can no longer tell which is which, and the warning of a great German historian who is also a righteous Gentile, Theodor Mommsen, that anti-semitism represents "a suicidal drift of national sentiment", takes on an ominous, extraordinarily prophetic significance.'

Holger paused and looked at Jason, and Jason thought: what court is Holger pleading at?

'What happens, fifty years after Mommsen delivers his prophetic warning? The Christians murder the Jew that has lodged in the body of the German nation. They hate the Jew who is in themselves. They long to be rid of the load of the Jew who is themselves, to rub out the witness who knows too much. In the Jew they murder a trinity, the victim, the witness, and the accomplice of two thousand years of oppression. One last time the Jew acquiesces in the Christian crime. The deed takes on the appearance of another genocide, like the holocaust six hundred years before, but this time the hearts of the Jews are beating inside the German national body. Germans are killing themselves. A *Volk* of lemmings rushes over the cliff. A *Volk* commits national suicide.'

'But not the *Volk*'s lawyers,' broke in Jason sarcastically. 'The lawyers see to it that they survive. They devise clever explanations. Things cannot be that are not allowed. *Nicht sein kann, was nicht sein darf.* Isn't that how it's done?'

Holger was taken aback by Jason's outburst. The attack came so personally and so unexpectedly that he was left speechless.

'It is easier to live with something one can understand,' Holger said.

'It is easier to live with something one can forgive,' echoed Jason brutally. 'There is nothing one can understand.'

He got up suddenly and stood in front of Holger's desk.

'What entitles you to live more easily? By what right? Patents of forgiveness from Jews, paid for with war compensation funds? Letters of safe conduct, declaring that it logically had to be so and couldn't have been otherwise? Words, words, words. Clever words, pious words, explanatory words, sorry words – none of them can change what is done. But you keep on doing it again with words. I'm disgusted by all these words. You are masturbating with words. You are a voyeur, jerking off every time you talk about it. Why can't you just leave it alone?'

Jason was not a Jew, but in Holger's mind the name Gould had a stigma, and he became one in Holger's mind. What Jason missed was that Holger gave no sign of being involved in the things he described, but Jason should have known better, because Holger never spoke, had never been able to speak, of his personal feelings.

11

Katje had been living with Holger for several months before she ventured outside for the first time. There was a bar a few blocks from the apartment house where Holger lived, shabby, dark, the rock music on full blast all the time. Deprived of noise after months of solitude and silence, Katje sat by the loudspeaker and soaked it up until her brain felt as if it would burst. When she walked home in the silence afterwards her head took off and she levitated, floating back through the streets.

She went out only at night, and only to this one bar. Restaurants were too great a risk, because of Katje's white hands. White hands on a table had already been identified at a restaurant in Hamburg. They were given a specific mention in the caption under Katje's picture on the wanted terrorists poster. Sometimes she walked out with Holger. Deprived of action, her body craved it. Sometimes she walked for hours until she was exhausted, walked all night and crawled into bed as it was getting light.

At heart she was old-fashioned, religious, a puritan crusader, scrupulous to a fault, ascetic in the demands on herself, pristine in her idealism, self-righteous and unforgiving when she was disappointed in the end. She lacked moisture. There was a lack of fluidity inside herself. Everything in Katje's life was counted and measured and weighed against something else. Holger took the metronome off the piano and hid it in a cupboard. Effortless in the kitchen, humming to himself, he cooked wonderful meals for a woman who was never hungry. He threw away the dark shirts he was sick of always seeing her wear, and gave her bright clothes to put on.

Apart from the nemesis he knew would surely come, because

nemesis was in her nature, part of a destiny in the idea of retribution that Katje craved for herself, it seemed to him that the solution to her life was at bottom a simple one. All she needed to learn was a measure of gratification, to accept instinctive, sensual pleasures. How naïve were his attempts at therapy, although for a while, at least, they seemed to work. He watched her get better, and waited for the nemesis he knew would come.

It came in the form of Ulrike Meinhof. In the summer she was brought from Stammheim to Berlin to face trial for her part in the violent liberation of Baader, almost four years to the day after it had taken place. On that day in August 1970, the warped idealism of a protest movement still lingering on from the student rebellion of the 1960s had ceased to be a reformist principle and became the prejudice of a terrorist organisation. Holger did not want to miss an opportunity to learn more about another woman terrorist, of whom there were strikingly many in the movement that Meinhof and Baader had initiated, and he went along with Jason to the courtroom in Moabit when she made her first appearance in the dock. He recognised that Katje was in the same mould as Meinhof, and had been formed by her.

She spoke for three-quarters of an hour about the goals of the anti-imperialist struggle of the RAF: annihilation, destruction, demolition of imperialist rule politically, economically and militarily. Holger observed the striking contrast between the violence of the language in the litany of charges brought by Meinhof and the apathy of her appearance. She spoke in a monotone, her voice at such a low ebb that at one point she interrupted her address to ask if the public could hear what she was saying.

In that contrast alone lay the surrealism of what she was saying. For a moment it struck Holger that it was not the people in the courtroom to whom she was appealing with that question but the ghosts who inhabited her mind, shreds of a phantom *Volk* that existed nowhere except in Ulrike Meinhof's brain. Behind her question quivered a different anxiety. She was worried she wasn't audible because there weren't any listeners.

When he heard Meinhof announce that from now on all the

RAF prisoners would be going on hunger strike until a long catalogue of their demands had been met, Holger sat up. He at once
foresaw the consequences this would have for Katje.

Among the terrorists awaiting trial in separate prisons was that
other Holger, his namesake who was now his enemy, reaching out to
destroy the pleasures Katje had gradually been learning to accept,
and to take her away from him. In solitary confinement in the
Wittlich jail, Holger Meins joined the others on hunger strike.

Katje heard the appeal for solidarity from the Wittlich jail, and
felt ashamed of the relative comfort of her life on the run. She, too,
stopped eating, not all at once, but by slow degrees throughout the
weeks that Holger Meins continued his hunger strike. She stopped
her night prowls. She no longer had sufficient strength. She turned
her face to the wall. She would not touch Holger in bed. Then she
would not lie in the same room.

In early October, the federal attorney brought official charges
against Baader, Meinhof, Ensslin, Raspe and Meins, the five founding members of RAF. They were collectively charged with five
murders, fifty-four attempted murders and numerous bomb attacks.
The concept of collective accountability had not previously been
implemented under German law. Holger noted with misgivings that
a degree of opportuneness had once again been required of the law,
and had once again been forthcoming.

After a month of fasting, the condition of the hunger-strikers
had become critical. When they still refused nourishment, prison
doctors began feeding them by force. Their lawyers brought charges
of cruelty against the prison administration.

Holger asked to see the testimony of one of the prisoners, and was
horrified by the moral and physical outrage that force-feeding
involved. He had never realised just what it meant. The prisoner was
shackled by the arms and legs, pinned down on a bed, the jaws
forcefully prised apart and an object inserted between the teeth so
that the mouth could be kept open to allow an inch-thick tube to be
inserted down the throat.

He watched Katje wasting away in his apartment, the double of
the hunger-striker in prison, her face extraordinarily hollowing out.

It was eerie to see her beginning to resemble the gaunt man in prison, hunger victims everywhere, victims of famine, victims with their faces pressed against the fences of concentration camps. Holger had looked at these images a hundred times in his life, but now, for the first time, he saw them.

He was sure he was watching her die in front of his eyes. She was burning right down to the stub. It was like the oldest of images he had read countless times in literature. Her vitality swelled in little gusts and sank, a flame in a draught, a guttering candle flame almost burned down to the wick. Holger was overcome by a weight of such sadness that he sank to his knees and crawled on the floor, begging Katje not to die. He wept for her and begged her not to die. He wept and begged her to live for him.

A doctor who was a trusted friend of Holger's came to the apartment to give Katje transfusions. Holger took a holiday until she was well. He even tried to pray. He felt he was taking part in an exorcism and had to muster all his strength to ban the powers of evil. And Katje recovered. Slowly, she seemed to be turning to him again.

These events were like forces of nature. They engulfed Holger so completely that there was no room for the alter ego at his side who was the dispassionate observer of his actions. Thus Holger was not aware of having cried for the first time since he was a child.

In the background, feelings were always there, but Holger was unaware that he had already opened the door on to them, and that at last he could hear them.

12

Holger was in Naples the day that Holger Meins died.

Colette had been caught with heroin in her possession when she stepped off the boat from Sicily, and was being held in jail. He flew down at the weekend, in response to an urgent call from the German consul in Naples. He met the consul and the firm's associate lawyers, to whom he entrusted her defence, and tried to arrange bail, without success. He wasn't even able to see Colette. Throughout a warm November afternoon he sat with the consul in the magnificent chambers of the Neapolitan lawyers, listening to them weigh the pros and cons of Colette's case in a language he didn't understand, accompanied by floridly expressive gestures which he found increasingly irritating. They told him they would do what they could, and if that wasn't enough – well, the women's prison in Naples was considered one of the most beautiful in Italy, and the young lady could do worse than spend a year or two as their guest. Holger stayed overnight and flew back to Berlin on the Sunday morning.

Katje was not in the apartment when he returned. He knew that something must be wrong. He called a friend who was one of the associates of Siegfried Haag, the lawyer representing Holger Meins, and learned the details of the terrorist's death the previous afternoon.

Haag had gone to Wittlich jail in response to an urgent summons from Meins. After two months of hunger strike the prisoner was so weak he had to be carried down on a stretcher for the meeting with his lawyer. He knew he was dying, and appealed to Haag for help. But it was too late. Within hours of the lawyer's departure Meins was dead. The news was made public the same evening and caused a wave of protest actions across the country. *'Macht kaputt, was euch kaputt macht!'* Do as you would be done by. It was what Jason had called the Kohlhaas syndrome.

Holger now knew why Katje had gone. The death was like a doom, an irreversible judgement from a final court of appeal.

On the day Holger flew back from Naples the bell rang in an apartment in Berlin Neu–Westend shortly before nine o'clock in the evening. Over the intercom the caller announced he was from Fleurop and had brought flowers for Günter von Drenkmann. The city's highest-ranking judge had celebrated his sixty-fourth birthday the previous day, and unsuspectingly admitted the caller. The moment he opened the door the apartment was stormed by a commando of masked terrorists. Three shots were fired. Drenkmann collapsed, bleeding profusely, and the terrorists disappeared into the night. Within minutes the judge was taken to hospital, where he died.

Holger was appalled by what had been done. He knew Drenkmann slightly from meetings of the Bar Association. The judge had nothing to do with the terrorist trials. Revenge had been taken, but they had killed the wrong man. Holger knew that this was not how Katje saw the matter. Katje would not have acknowledged Drenkmann as a man. She saw the president of the Berlin court of appeal as a symbol to be liquidated, just as Baader had seen the department store as a symbol to be set on fire. In the mind of Katje, Drenkmann existed only as an idea.

The RAF prisoners in Stammheim issued a statement about the murder of the court of appeal judge. 'We shed no tears for the dead Drenkmann. We are pleased by such an execution. This act was necessary, because it has made clear to the pigs of the police and justice departments that any one of them, at any time, right now, can be held responsible for their actions.'

Against the will of the federal attorney's office, Jean-Paul Sartre was granted permission by the regional court in Stuttgart to visit Baader in jail. Jason came to Holger's office to discuss these events. The squabbles over questions of competence reminded Jason once again of the dispute between Brandenburg and Saxony over the right of trial in the Kohlhaas case four hundred years before. The idea had begun to obsess him.

At the press conference after his visit, Sartre criticised the intolerable prison conditions to which the RAF prisoners were subjected. The charges caused an uproar, but they were probably no more or less substantiated than anything else in the proceedings. Sartre was accused of having taken up the terrorists' cause, although he had expressly distanced himself from it and spoke of the damage they inflicted on the political left. Holger was unimpressed by the intervention of the old magician. He regarded Sartre as a self-serving manipulator and opportunist. It depressed him to watch the familiar process of the substitution of ideas for things take its course. Suspicion and hatefulness, polarising the German public, would be all that was stirred up in the wake of these events.

Holger went through the worst days of his life. He knew there was more to come, and when it did there would be no escape for him.

The call from Katje came through one morning a few days before Christmas, just as Holger was leaving the office on his way to court. The conversation was short and to the point. Katje needed money. She asked Holger to come that evening to the bar near his apartment with ten thousand dollars in cash. Before he could say anything she had hung up.

There had never been any question of Holger not helping Katje. This was their pattern. She was the victim and he her helper. He immediately sent one of the secretaries to the bank to pick up the ten thousand dollars in cash. But when he returned from court that afternoon, and stood at the window looking down into the street, he felt a profound contempt for himself and what he was doing. He realised he must make up his mind one way or the other. He was no better than the lawyers who had been the Nazi's whores and changed their principles with their masters. He must forego the safety of the castle and take his chance outside. Katje was still the victim, but it was the wrong way of trying to help her. She must be stopped before she killed herself or others. He knew there was no way she could be persuaded. It would have to be done by force. Either way he would lose her.

Holger called the police. He said he knew of the whereabouts of a wanted terrorist. The conditions he demanded in exchange for his information were that he would lead them there himself and no firearms were to be used in making the arrest. The police must remain in the background. He would overpower the person himself and then hand her over. The police said they could not guarantee his safety. He was asked to sign a declaration absolving them of responsibility in the event that something happened to him.

There was a light surface of snow on the ground when Holger left his apartment that evening. Shoppers crowded the pavement. He stepped out into the road. The stores were still open, and Christmas carols blared out under the awnings of lights along the street. He reached the corner and looked back. But why stop? Was there somebody behind him? He turned the corner and saw Katje standing on the doorstep of the bar fifty yards away. The sight of her was unexpected. It came too soon.

As Holger walked towards her, the words rose involuntarily in his mind. Where there is an ideal, there is also its betrayal. Those were his own words. They described what both of them were doing. Faithful to one another in betrayal, they were in this together to the end. Katje stepped out of the doorway on to the pavement. The long coat she was wearing swung open as she moved towards him.

How pale her face looked under the streetlamp. How thin she was. Treacherously Holger raised a hand in greeting. But Katje wasn't looking at him. She was looking past him. He saw her frown, and that was all. That was the only sign she gave that she realised something was wrong. She frowned, and already she was pushing back her coat and raising the machine-gun to open fire.

There was a shout. Holger heard a single shot. Katje spun round. The gun dropped from her hands. He ran towards her and caught her just as she was falling.

Her head slumped in his arms. Blood came pouring out of the wound. He knelt down in the road and propped her head against his chest. He looked down and saw her blood staining his chest. He felt a pain there. In the background he heard the blaring Christmas carols. He became aware of the sound of music.

You opened the door on to your feelings and all of a sudden you heard them. With bowed head Holger listened, watching the stain spreading slowly across his shirt front, and it seemed to him as if the blood was flowing from his own wound.

1983

1

E lena didn't want to cross the border. She hadn't been back since 1945, she had got all that behind her, she reminded Jens. This was her instinctive reaction when the letter came. But Jens said he wouldn't go unless she went with him. He didn't raise the issue of whether it was right to be going, as Elena had expected him to do. It was a late honour, and it was a dubious honour, coming from the ministry of culture of the German Democratic Republic. Had the GDR writers' congress been taking place anywhere else, she assumed that Jens would have turned it down. But an invitation to Rügen, just as Jens was beginning his novella about Friedrich's picture – this symmetry was irresistible.

Why shouldn't he accept a prize for the 'contribution to the struggle against imperialism' that had been his life's work? Jens knew perfectly well why. No writer could accept a prize from a government that had a record of gagging, censoring and imprisoning authors of whom it didn't approve. But Jens wanted the prize. He was weary of offering himself as a hostage in the war of principles that had gone on all his life, and he wanted to be rewarded for his idealism. He wanted a prize. He was tired of voicing ideals on someone else's behalf, of his own and others' high-mindedness, which so often turned out to be a blind for guilt or self-importance or whatever self-seeking motivation it was that camouflaged itself behind the masquerade of idealism. He would go to Rügen, and Elena would accompany him.

They crossed the border to East Berlin and caught the train to Stralsund. It was the flatness and emptiness of the countryside in Mecklenburg, pushing back the horizon and opening up enormous skies, which Elena remembered from her childhood. She didn't remember the decay, the faded, fumbling houses, the exhausted villages, eroded by decades of neglect. She had told herself to expect it. Perhaps it was a more just reflection of the past than what you saw in the West, where the scars had been painted over, but still she looked out of the train window with dismay, a sense of helplessness at what was left in the junkyard of the landscape. After all, it *was* the past. Life moved on, or died.

It was an extremely hot day. Shortly after noon they reached the dam and passed from the mainland to the island. A diffuse brightness, an almost palpable coil of light, settled along the Baltic coast. Elena looked back and watched the spires of Stralsund receding in the haze.

Jens had notified the East German authorities that he didn't want to go directly to Binz, and they had approved the itinerary he was asked to submit. They changed trains at Bergen, waiting for an hour for their connection down to Putbus on the south coast. It was said to be Europe's last *Residenzstadt*, planned under delusions of grandeur by the Prince of Putbus a hundred and fifty years before.

Elena and Jens wandered round the abortive capital on a humid afternoon. The town was a wreck. It wasn't even real. It resembled a disused film set that had been left out in the rain. On the downs overlooking the Baltic stood the circus that was to have been the centrepiece of the Putbus capital, but no more than the circus ever got built. The ring of deserted houses in the Classical style, their roofs capsized, the façades blistering, was still waiting for the rest of the city to join it. In the gaps between the single row of houses Jens could just make out the blue-grey sea in the distance, merging almost indistinguishably with the sky.

They crossed the road and sat in the shade of a huge tree spreading over the orangery at the entrance to a park. The heat fatigued Jens. He rested while Elena walked along the terrace of the orangery, trying to get a look inside. The glass was broken, the windows boarded up. Jens had a vision of her at successive stages of her life – Elena walked away from him and he saw her grow younger, then she turned, growing older again as he watched her coming back towards him.

There was something else there, he felt, which would enable him to begin writing his novella. Jens didn't know quite what it was. He couldn't find it out. He had to wait for it to come to him.

From the crest of the hill where the orangery stood there should have been a view of the palace the Prince of Putbus had built at the centre of the park. Jens tried to orientate himself. He remembered it from a school outing to Rügen before the war. He walked with Elena down the sloping lawn, looking around for the building. It had gone. Jens became agitated. Surely he couldn't be mistaken. He stopped a man on his way through the park, and asked him where it was. Right here, said the man. Jens was actually standing on the spot where the palace had been until twenty years ago. It had become too expensive to maintain, so the authorities had blown it up. Not a stone was left standing. The debris had been used for mending roads. Jens was so disillusioned by this needless act of destruction that he lost his appetite for the rest of Putbus, and they trudged back to the station.

The engine on the narrow-gauge railway from Putbus to Binz was still running under steam. The cars were pre-war, with benches, leather straps for opening the windows and a platform at either end, where Elena stood outside and let the wind blow into her face. The track ran through the bracken, winding across a hilly, densely wooded landscape without any views of the sea, but she could sense it just behind the next line of trees. The air was soft and had a transparent quality, full of the brightness rebounding off the sea, an invisible coil that lay all around her.

Jens was dozing inside, the only passenger in the car, or, as far as she could see, on the train. Train and landscape alike seemed to be empty of any other human life. It was an island without people. She saw no cars on the road, but whenever the engine approached a crossing it sounded its whistle – to Elena's ears a mournful sound. She felt homesick for Jason, which was nothing unusual, but also for Jens, whom she could see through the glass door of the car where he was sitting, jolted in his sleep. How could she have the feeling of missing him when he was there?

She went into the car and sat down opposite him. It was very warm inside. She took out a handkerchief and wiped her throat and chest. The train had stopped, for no apparent reason, somewhere out in the country. Elena listened to the hiss of escaping steam and the sound of Jens breathing heavily in his sleep. When the train jerked into motion his head slumped. She laid a hand on his knee. He lifted his head and opened his eyes. Are you all right, she asked, as the train released another of its drawn-out whistles. She glanced up a dark tunnel, a cobbled road in the deep shade of overarching trees. They were crossing another avenue. There had been avenues of trees all the way from Putbus, reminding her of Holm. Just tired, replied Jens, is there anything the matter? Elena took his hand. I think we've arrived, she said.

There were no taxis at the station. It was still some way into town. A man driving past saw them standing with their luggage at the side of the road and offered them a lift. He wanted to change some money. Elena suggested that if he took them to the Kurhaus she would give him the cab fare in West marks. The man said his name was Heinz and asked her if they were interested in purchasing amber. She said they weren't. They drove through the streets of a derelict spa, crowded with holidaymakers. Heinz said there wasn't enough accommodation for all the people who wanted to come. The workers from the industrial centres in the south, people with lung trouble on account of the coal dust, were sent up to Rügen for a holiday once every seven years. They wanted to come more often, but there wasn't room. He asked if Brandt and Schmidt had made a better job of socialism in the West. Jens said yes, he thought that on the whole they had. Elena noticed the dead wood here and there along the avenue of plane trees down which they were driving. The dead trees hadn't been replaced. Nobody had even bothered to remove them.

They arrived at the Kurhaus in Binz. The avenue petered out in the sand. Beyond lay the sea.

2

When Jens conceived the idea of his Rügen novella he had already celebrated his seventy-third birthday. To arrive at Rügen, he had to travel back to a landscape he had last visited before the war, in the novels and poems every educated German read at school. It was the landscape invented by Romantic idealists in the late eighteenth century. Friedrich and Runge, who painted the landscape the poets wrote about, had a circle of admirers, patrons and friends, including Goethe and Kleist, Ernst Moritz Arndt, the physician–painter Carl Gustav Carus, a close friend of Friedrich's, and the poet Kosegarten, who was his fellow countryman from Pomerania. Friedrich spent most of his life in Dresden, but he was born in Greifswald. The flat landscape of northern Germany under the broad skies along the Baltic coast was the one to which he always returned, in his life and in his paintings.

There was still restricted access to that landscape – in Mecklenburg, on the other side of the mined border sealing off the German Democratic Republic. But the other one, the spiritual landscape, about which Friedrich and his friends enthused, the landscape idealised by sentiment and appealing to the *Gemüth des Beschauers* – it was less easy for the twentieth-century visitor to make his way back there. Jens re-encountered the Romantic ideal of landscape with a sense of strangeness. It no longer seemed relevant. It had ceased to be a subject of art. He thought the disappearance of landscape from art was a loss that deeply mattered, although he could not have said why.

'*Schliesse dein leibliches Auge . . .*' (such was Friedrich's credo). 'Close your bodily eye, so that you first see the image with your spiritual eye. Then bring to the light what you have seen by the dark, in order for it to exert its influence on the viewer the other way round, from the outside inwards.'

Closing their bodily eyes, the poets and painters invented blind a landscape that arose out of thoughts and feelings. Nature became their accomplice, serving as manifestation of the ideal.

Their urgency and enthusiasm seemed to have been driven by a sexually charged, masochistic awareness of death. Kosegarten, Friedrich's mentor, required the closeness of death to be palpable in all manifestations of art, always hovering in the wings. The quality in the artist from which that sense of death originated he called *Jenseitsbezogenheit* – mindfulness of the world to come.

Looking further back, to the German roots of Protestantism, the twentieth-century visitor to these Romantic landscapes could already detect the spirit of *Jenseitsbezogenheit* in Martin Luther's *Mitten wir im Leben sind, mit dem Tod umfangen* – 'In the midst of life we are surrounded by death.' This was the tradition in which the painter had been brought up, and Jens saw its influence in Friedrich's pictures.

'Nothing can be gloomier and less appealing than such a position in the world: to be the sole spark of life in the wide domain of death, at the solitary centre of a solitary circle,' wrote Kleist a year before he committed suicide. He was reviewing Friedrich's picture 'The Monk by the Sea' for a Berlin newspaper. Four-fifths of the picture were taken up by sky, above a narrow strip of sea and a barren shore on which the monk was standing. There was nothing else in the painting. This narrow strip was the border situation between life and death that figured in so many of Friedrich's paintings, empowered as they were by symbols of *Vergänglichkeit*, the spirit of *Jenseitsbezogenheit*.

This was a very German view of landscape. It was not how a Frenchman saw it. The sculptor David d'Angers visited Friedrich's studio in Dresden, and on seeing his pictures exclaimed (according to Carus, who was present at the scene): '*Voilà un homme qui a découvert la tragédie du paysage!*'

Obviously, d'Angers could not have spoken of the *Vergänglichkeit* or the *Jenseitsbezogenheit* in Friedrich's landscape, because such words did not exist in his language. Instead, he spoke of the tragedy there, and in this gesture there seemed to Jens to be something that was just as inimitably French.

Vergänglichkeit and *Jenseitsbezogenheit* were inimitably German concepts. He could explain their meaning but he could not show the invisible web in which such concepts hung together, forming the base sensibility at the core of the language. These words lived in the German language, and in the words lived thoughts. They lived here and nowhere else.

But did they still?

The discomfort Jens felt with the Romantics when he began researching his novella was their high-mindedness. They believed their spirituality. They believed in the significance and rightness of what they were doing. He envied them a capacity he no longer had, and here was the reason for his discomfort. It was himself he found implausible.

To celebrate his birthday, Jason and Elena had arranged a reading at a local bookshop, where Jens read from a collection of stories which had been published just after the war. The title story had recently been made into a television film and the book reissued, thirty years after it had gone out of print. The reading was attended by a lot of young people, in their twenties, even in their teens, who had seen the TV film. They stayed on for the birthday party that was held for Jens in the bookshop afterwards. Jens got a little drunk and made a speech, thanking everyone for coming and telling them how happy he was. He was no longer used to such attention.

After the party he fell into a deep depression. The small success made clear to him how large the failure had been.

At the general election that spring a conservative coalition had come to power. For the first time in almost twenty years the Social Democratic party would not be participating in the government. Already people began to speak of *die Wende*, a turning point in post-war German history To some extent Jens felt that it was his own as well. Much of his writing had been generated by the war and the aftermath of war. He had originally made his name with stories about his experiences as a soldier on the eastern front. He was already in his late thirties when he had written them. Dictatorship and war had used up his youth. Berlin after the war, the devastation, the occupation, survival and recovery – these were the subjects that fuelled the books he was writing throughout the 1950s and into the 1960s.

He was a socialist, and it was as a social critic that he saw his function as a writer. Almost the same age as Willy Brandt, Jens had supported him throughout his years as mayor of Berlin, and when Brandt took the Social Democratic party into the grand coalition in 1966 Jens felt almost as if it was a part of himself which had arrived in Bonn, a part of himself which felt betrayed when Brandt was compromised by the spy affair and resigned from office seven years later. By then the treaties with Moscow setting the seal on the *Ostpolitik* had already been signed and passed into history. The détente with the Soviet Union seemed to Jens to supply something like a moral justification for Germany's continued existence after the war, just as Brandt's spontaneous gesture of kneeling at the tomb of the unknown soldier in Poland restored his faith in its moral leadership. That era was already beginning to fade during Schmidt's chancellorship after Brandt's demise, and by the time of the conservative victory that brought the *Wende* it had become extinct.

Brandt's gesture derived its moral power from the sincerity of his feelings, and Brandt, like Jens, could only have those feelings because he belonged to the generation that had been personally affected. No chancellor would ever be able to make such a gesture again. The time for such an expression of sorrow had passed, and the personal involvement had gone with it. Commemorative acts remained, rituals expressing decency and goodwill, but not conviction. The time for even such acts, for anything more than the formalities required of an anniversary, would eventually pass too. Within a few generations the wound would have closed, only a scar would remain. Nothing resisted time.

The decline in Jens' personal fortunes seemed to be synchronised with these larger cycles. His subject matter and his idiom gradually became passé. Jens was unable to exist as a writer without the trauma of war and holocaust as the implicit source of his creative power. It was larger than himself. It was larger than his art, a subject matter from which he could not escape. As a writer he had lived with a sense of moral coercion. The moral attitude infused everything he wrote. So long as it coincided with a vital need, embedded in the personal experiences from which conscience and moral consciousness were inseparable, his writing had remained fresh, because it was necessary. But when the moral attitude lingered on after the need had gone, as it was bound to, if those experiences had been told well, and the need became superfluous, the writing turned lifeless. By the age of sixty he realised he had nothing more to say, while the books he wrote a quarter of a century before had in the meantime been forgotten.

For the previous ten years, forgotten as an author, he had survived precariously as a translator of *samizdat* literature smuggled out of Russia. Even in his capacity as a translator, the choice of language and the gesture of solidarity with a suppressed literature betrayed the extent of the moral claims that were still exerted on Jens by the past. He no longer wrote his own books, but he could continue to serve the books of others.

Meanwhile, during these years of self-imposed silence, his creative self mysteriously regenerated.

It was at about this time that he went to Switzerland to discuss the translation of a work by a Russian writer who was living there in exile. His car broke down on the outskirts of Winterthur, where Jens encountered Friedrich's painting face to face in a museum. It was snowing. He had a few hours to kill while the garage repaired the car, and he wandered into the museum, where he found the picture waiting for him. Of course he had seen the reproduction many times, but here it was, the real thing, hanging on a wall in front of him, 'Chalk Cliffs on Rügen'.

Curiously, the picture stirred a longing inside him. He felt a desire to be there, inside the picture with the three people on the clifftop, to share their lives and disentangle the riddle that the picture posed. What were the figures doing? If he could find an answer, surely it would also show the nature of their relationship with one another? To resolve the question that pinned them down on the clifftop, to release them from the quandary in which the painter had confined them – if only he could do that! For this was the other feeling the picture aroused in him: embarrassment, mingled with pity. He longed to walk out of the picture with them into other scenes of their lives, where they would be invisible to the museum visitors.

Jens had seen the picture so many times, and yet he had never been moved in this way. He considered why. He noticed the uneven brushwork on the canvas, what seemed to be a crack in the painting of the sea. This was the original. *This was the picture Friedrich painted.* It was a relic of the painter, like a hair or a piece of skin.

> Leaves, like the things of man,
> You with your fresh thoughts care for, can you?

Everything was perishable – *wie vergänglich.* The painter's imagination had left three people stranded on the clifftop forever, and Jens' heart warmed to their plight. Standing at the window and looking down into the snow-covered street, he was inexplicably moved.

It was a case of Attraction of Affinities. He was the other half of the torn banknote. The painting engrossed him, because there was something about it corresponding to what was already inside himself. The hard edge of Friedrich's *Jenseitsbezogenheit,* his unwavering view of the ultimate reality, which came stabbing through even his lightest work – Jens could sympathise with that. There was a mood in the picture which seemed familiar, the levity besides the starkness, the frivolity of the red dress on the brink of a precipice, in the background the sea rising and rising until it seemed to be flooding the sky. Something like this mood of levity-on-the-brink he recognised in himself.

Jens began to collect the evidence of contemporaries who had known Caspar David Friedrich, and found himself putting together a German portrait.

The painter and writer Louise Seidler, who met Friedrich in Dresden, described him with his blue eyes, ash-blond hair, bushy whiskers and clear-cut features as a classic representative of an old Teutonic type. Carus, the physician, spoke of Friedrich's striking appearance, the large-boned frame, his childlike candour, the melancholy expression, his pallor, his distinctive north German character. There were many others who shared the view that in the seriousness and simplicity of his nature Friedrich was an exemplary German figure.

This would have coincided with Friedrich's own perception of himself. A Protestant and a patriot, he was a young man during the wars of liberation to rid Europe of Napoleon's occupying army, when Germans were discovering themselves as a unified modern nation.

For Jens, there was an uncomfortable synthesis of the Protestant *Jenseitsbezogenheit* and patriotism in Friedrich's art. The lone chasseur at the edge of the forest, symbolising Napoleon's army about to be swallowed up in the Russian winter, could be seen making his way into a forest of fir trees more suggestive of Germany than Russia. The fir tree, being an evergreen, was also the tree representing Christianity in his paintings, sometimes at odds with a nearby oak which symbolised the heathen, Germanic past. Runic stones, marking ancient Hun graves (one of the painter's favourite subjects), were often surrounded by blasted oaks.

These apparently innocuous landscapes were political paintings. After the Restoration, following Napoleon's defeat at Waterloo, the nationalist sentiments they expressed would have been regarded as seditious. Friedrich made a point of wearing the *Teutsche Kleidertracht*. This so-called German costume, consisting of a shirt with a broad collar, a long coat and a beret, had been propagated in 1814 by the radical nationalist Ernst Moritz Arndt as a sign of resistance to foreign interference, and of solidarity with patriotic, democratic ideals.

Jens' discomfort with Friedrich lay here. German nationalists in 1814 were progressive liberals in favour of a free press, free speech and abolition of aristocratic privilege. After the defeat of Napoleon and the conference in Karlsbad in 1819, they were pursued as demagogues and many of them were thrown into prison. The reactionaries were on the other side. Jens appreciated all that. These early-nineteenth-century German nationalists still embarrassed him, however, because he was too used to seeing it the other way round – to the *Teutsche Kleidertracht* being appropriated by the reactionary patriots who were their successors.

A picture such as 'Two Men Looking at the Moon' exemplified the discomfort Jens felt. It was painted in 1819, the year of the Karlsbad conference, when the *Teutsche Kleidertracht* had been forbidden. The two men looking at the moon in this picture were standing under a blasted oak, and both were wearing the German costume propagated by Arndt. 'They are up to demagogic tricks,' was Friedrich's sardonic comment on the picture.

He had painted it as a protest, in the same spirit that he painted the chasseur being swallowed up in the German forest, or his visions of neo-Gothic cathedrals, recalling the triumphant architecture of German medievalism as an exhortation to build a new German nation and the city of God. Friedrich had his own Blakean vision of a Jerusalem on Germany's pleasant pastures green, but one isolating itself from the larger European community, suspicious of what lay on the other side of its borders, and stigmatising that attitude for all the world to see in the self-consciously theatrical costume of the *Teutsche Tracht*. It was cramped by the spirit of small-town, provincial Germany.

Stubbornly retained throughout the artist's life, almost as a signature, a prop of Friedrich's identity, these symbols weighed down some soaring paintings with their heavy-footed German message. The man in the extraordinary picture 'The Wanderer Above the Sea of Mist', painted in 1818, was wearing an abbreviated version of the *Teutsche Tracht*, as was the man observed from the rear in full regalia, walking down to the shore in 'The Steps of Life' twenty years later, shortly before Friedrich's death

In 'Chalk Cliffs on Rügen', the rear-view figure standing under the tree to the right, his arms folded, paying no attention to the clifftop drama unfolding right beside him, was another of Friedrich's theme signatures. This man, too, wore the German costume.

It was the *Teutsche Tracht* that alerted Jens to the allegorical nature of the scene at the top of the chalk cliff on Rügen. The view of the cliffs purported to be a view of Rügen, but in fact it was a synthesis of several views, notably at the Wissower Klinken and Stubbenkammer, with the foreground foliage borrowed from elsewhere. The landscape in the painting had not been copied from nature, only the parts had. The artist had reassembled them in his imagination, and the landscape he thus invented existed nowhere but in his painting.

Friedrich did not paint scenes he saw in nature, but scenes he saw inside himself. The most solid objects reflected the most abstract processes of thought, the most natural landscape the most artificial arrangement of its elements. The younger man to the right wearing the *Teutsche Tracht*, fraught with Friedrich's personal symbolism, preserved his idealistic integrity at the risk of his practical exclusion from the action in the picture. The young woman on the left and the older man in the middle wore early Biedermeier fashion, suggesting post-Restoration bourgeois ambitions with which the young man in the beret could not have sympathised. Perhaps it was just a coincidence that they had arrived on the cliff at the same time, and the young man had nothing to do with the couple.

The whole scene, with the narrow strip animated by the three figures in the foreground threatening to crumble away under their feet and slide down the sheer cliff, belonged on one of Friedrich's allegorical stages exemplifying the Lutheran *Mitten wir im Leben sind, mit dem Tod umfangen*. The actors in the clifftop scene were poised between life and death, symbolised by the white barren cliffs on which nothing grew, with the ocean and the drifting sails in the background, representing unearthly *Jenseitsbezogenheit*.

3

In 1818, at the age of forty-four, Caspar David Friedrich married Caroline Bommer, nineteen years his junior. His brothers and sisters in Greifswald, to whom Friedrich communicated everything in a correspondence that continued all his life, were not notified until a week after the wedding. For Friedrich's friends, the marriage came without any forewarning. They were completely surprised by the step the middle-aged artist seemed to have taken at very short notice, 'in the interval between ordering a desk while still a bachelor and taking delivery of it as a married man'. This detail emerged casually from Friedrich's remarks on the expense of getting married. He was a frugal man, whose frugality was sometimes indistinguishable from stinginess, notably towards his young wife.

Why had the painter wooed and wedded the Dresden merchant's daughter so suddenly?

Evidently because he had already formed a deep attachment to Líne before he met her. This attachment had long ago been formed to someone else, perhaps the mother who died when the boy was six, and Friedrich had rediscovered that person, with all the accompanying feelings, in the resemblance he found in Líne. Jens had been stricken by Elena the moment he saw her because he recognised in her (at the time not consciously) a much-loved woman who had taught him the piano when he was a child. Elena was stricken by Jason the moment she saw him because Jason resembled her mother. By the end of his life Jens had come to believe that patterns of recognition underlay all strong emotional relationships in people's lives.

The objects of such sudden attachments were taken by storm and bowled off their feet. How grateful Elena had been, a homeless refugee, desirable to men but at the time not wanting desirability, grateful above all for being taken care of and given back a sense of belonging. How surprised, flattered and soon convinced of her own worth by the famous painter's attentions the pencil merchant's daughter must have been (even if he was a bit on the old side and his linen not absolutely clean).

To be wanted with such urgency by another person gave one a self-assurance that was naturally irresistible. When passion encountered common sense there was a trade-off between the two. Friedrich and Jens had had no reason, but every instinct, to marry Caroline and Elena; and the two women had had no instinct, but every reason, to marry men who were almost twice their age. So they still had scope in their emotions to form sudden, powerful attachments themselves. The scope was there in them and had to be filled. At some time Líne would fall in love with someone else. It was a matter of chance.

The chance became greater the more the elderly husband was insufficiently attentive to his wife and gave her the feeling of being left alone. This had already happened in Friedrich and Líne's case. The warning of what to expect was there in the letter he wrote a week after getting married. 'Only in the room that I need in order to pursue my occupation has everything remained as it was.' The artist craved continuity and solitude, not merely in the room in the house that Líne could not enter and change with her meddling housewifely hands, but the room inside himself.

Even in the letters he wrote her when they were separated he described to her his relish of solitude. The cloud-walking, penny-pinching absentee husband did not lavish on Líne either his company or his money. The Romantic was not the man for romantic gestures. Absent on her birthday, he wrote his wife a dour Protestant letter instead, telling her she would not be getting the birthday cake she had hoped for.

'So as you are not left empty-handed and without any joy on your birthday, give a thaler to someone needy whom you see passing by, and let their joy be your joy. That may be a pleasure to which the palate is insensitive, but it is a gain for the spirit within.'

Thanks!

The threesome in which the couple found themselves involved had come about with Friedrich's connivance, perhaps even his encouragement. Jens felt confident about that, from his own experience of a *ménage à trois*. The same relationship was at the core of his novella, in which Elena inevitably became Líne, and Jason impersonated a Norwegian painter by the name of Johan Christian Clausen Dahl.

Dahl had first met the Friedrichs in the year they married, and in Jens' scenario it was Dahl, not Friedrich's brother, who accompanied the newly wedded couple to Rügen in August of that year. Dahl was thirty-five years old when he took up residence on the floor below the Friedrichs' apartment in 1823. Líne was twenty-nine and Friedrich forty-eight.

Friedrich's star was already beginning to decline. His subjectivism and private allegories, his landscapes as membranes of intense personal experience, grew less and less accessible to a public that was becoming accustomed to the style of a younger generation of Romantics. Their paintings looked back to the traditions of a religious art that was more objective, more conventional, and more easily comprehensible. The Romantic *Weltanschauung* (the word itself had made its first appearance with Kant in 1790, and was already the intellectual prop of a previous generation) had been superseded by the realism of Biedermeier, the precise representations of scenes from bourgeois life.

Painters such as Dahl could appeal with their realistic and dramatic representations of landscape. When the professorship for landscape painting at the Dresden Academy became vacant in 1824, it was not Friedrich but Dahl, the younger man who lived on the floor below, who was chosen. The art of C.D. Friedrich and P.O. Runge went out of fashion and reached a dead end. During the last twenty years of his life, Friedrich had already slipped into obscurity.

Carus, physician and family friend, left an account of Friedrich's last days after the painter's death in 1840.

'Certain ineradicable obsessions, manifestly the first indications of a sickness of the brain, which was indeed the subsequent cause of his death, had developed in the dark, often harsh sensibility that was peculiar to him, and began to undermine completely the life of his household. Suspicious, as was his manner, he tormented himself and those close to him with representations of his wife's infidelity, which were quite without substance, and yet which still managed to preoccupy him entirely. Fits of cruel harshness towards those around him were not an exception, and I had serious words with him about this, attempting to influence him in my capacity as a physician, all to no avail.'

It was at about this time, between the stroke he suffered in 1835 and his death in 1840, that Friedrich painted a watercolour variation of his much earlier work, 'Chalk Cliffs on Rügen'. It must have been one of his last pictures. The view down over the white cliffs to the Baltic rising up and out below showed the view from the Wissower Klinken on the east coast of the island. Although marginally different from the synthesis of views which had been fused in the earlier painting, it was unquestionably intended to echo that picture.

This explained Jens' sense of shock when he first saw the watercolour version. For the tree that once framed the three figures on the clifftop in a warm, dark enclosure (miraculously lit up, made almost joyous, by the red dress the woman in that earlier picture was wearing), had now been taken out of the landscape. Nothing was left but a stump. The three figures in the animated clifftop scene had gone, the foreground emptied of all signs of life. By the time Jens was ready to begin his novella, he understood why.

4

In Jens' first outline it was the bright, vivacious Líne who suggested that Dahl joined the couple on their honeymoon on Rügen, but gradually he came to realise that it could only have been Friedrich. In fact, Dahl joined the newly wedded couple there expressly against Líne's wishes. Seeing by the dark, as it were, Jens made this change unaware at first of the implications it would have for the rest of the story. A detail adjusted changed a life. For the moment, however, he was more concerned with the itinerary that would bring Dahl into the novella.

The impoverished young artist crossed his native Norway on foot from Trondheim to Oslo, by all accounts, where an uncle paid his sea passage to Copenhagen. He spent a few days with friends in Sweden before continuing his journey. Embarking on the packet from Malmö, Dahl reached Sassnitz on the east coast of the island on an August evening in 1818, and travelled the same night the few miles down to Binz, where the Friedrichs were staying.

Binz was not yet the fashionable spa it later became. It was still a fishing village, and the accommodation Dahl shared with the Friedrichs was extremely simple. This didn't deter the two men in the least, but the young lady from Dresden, used to the conveniences of city life, was less than enthusiastic about the rustic simplicity of the island. She also had to come to terms with the unexpected degree of intimacy in which she found herself living with the two men. Alternatively, and even worse, her husband would set off with the young Norwegian on walking tours across the island, leaving her on her own for days at a time. They came back with their knapsacks full of sketches, and a growing friendship of which Líne began to feel jealous. This expressed itself in shows of animosity against Dahl, which rather amused her husband. He cast himself in the role of 'Dahl's advocate at the court of my wife', as he jocularly called it, doing everything he could to win her favour for his young friend. That Dahl, on the contrary, had already found far too much favour in Líne's eyes, from the moment they had been blessed with the sight of him in Dresden earlier that year, and that her shows of animosity towards him were an attempt to disembarrass herself of quite opposite feelings – this inter-pretation would surely never have occurred to Friedrich, whose childlike nature was straightforward and without guile. Such, at any rate, was the verdict of her husband's friends, men of experience, like the family physician Dr Carus, and who was young Caroline Bommer to disagree with men of experience, who had moreover known Friedrich far longer than she?

How could she know? How could she compare, when such things were not mentionable even in front of her own mother? That her husband fell on her body like a ravenous old wolf, short, sharp and brutal in his needs, and that there could never be any pleasure for herself in such an act, this apparently was a woman's lot, to be borne in silence. But there was worse. In shame she submitted to those bestial practices her husband also required of her because she wished to please, even though she found it impossible to reconcile them with the duties of a Christian wife. This still did not seem to her to impinge on Friedrich's character, however, whereas in the question of their association with Johan Dahl there was something that did.

Was it that she had a guilty conscience? For wouldn't it have been an absurdly simple matter for a painter whom all the world described as a visionary to look into a young woman's heart and read her thoughts? Why then, if Friedrich had recognised her secret, did he subsequently arrange for her to see even more of the young Norwegian painter in Dresden than she already had on Rügen? Too often, when Friedrich knew he would be going away, he asked Dahl to come and play cards with his wife, 'to distract her from melancholy thoughts' during her pregnancy. If Friedrich placed temptation deliberately in her path, it could only be his intention to test her loyalty and the steadfastness of her will. Outwardly, nothing ever passed between Líne and Dahl that gave her cause to reproach herself, and yet all those hours spent innocently with him during her husband's absence necessarily became times of a wholly unnatural self-scrutiny – a conscious reserve when greeting or taking leave of Dahl, or when she sat beside him on the sofa – and Líne would be left not at all with the feeling of her honour having triumphed but rather of having acquiesced in some furtive conspiracy.

She gave birth to a daughter, whom they called Emma Johanna. After her worries that she was becoming estranged from her husband, Líne was reconciled by the tenderness and consideration he showed her throughout her confinement. Her situation was also eased by Dahl's prolonged absence from Dresden at this time. Friedrich showed his best side as a father, the cheerful, playful side of his nature that was sparked by the love he could show his child. The winter evenings Líne spent with Friedrich and little Emma at the house An der Elbe, before family circumstances made it necessary for them to move to larger accommodation further down the street, were among the happiest in her life.

At this time Friedrich was in the process of completing a landscape of Rügen, which would be 'a profane work no doubt more to his wife's taste than the religious paintings', he said with a laugh. The painting would celebrate the themes of youth and age, of friendship, idealism and love, in overlapping scenes from life that were shown in a single instant. He reminded Líne of the walk they had taken with Dahl the previous summer from Sassnitz along the cliffs to the Stubbenkammer, and how, at the sight of the chalk cliffs, she had exclaimed she was so happy she wished she could have that view in front of her

forever. Well, she now could, for he had painted it. Líne was
touched by this token of Friedrich's affection. But when she saw
the picture it so astonished her that she found it difficult to conceal her disappointment. Friedrich asked her, in the direct
manner he had, if she liked it. They stood in his studio, looking
at the painting on the easel, and for a long time Líne remained
silent. Then she said that 'like' was a poor word to express the
feelings which were always aroused in her by his paintings, but
that they were not the easiest to interpret, and they had never
failed to benefit from whatever explanations the artist might be
gracious enough to offer on their behalf. The deviousness of this
reply was audible: to herself it was as if she had shouted out a
lie, but Friedrich only smiled.

'Explanations? Well, now, this old fool here for example,' he
said, pointing at the figure on his knees at the edge of the cliff
(the artist was not in the least pretentious when talking about
his work – he seemed rather to enjoy using blunt language and
poking fun at it, but Líne could never tell if this was a screen
to protect himself). 'An old man must do anything to please a
young wife, even make a fool of himself, if he wants to keep
her for himself.' Líne could not fail to hear the allusion to
Dahl in this peculiar remark, as it seemed to her, and said that
his explanation surprised her considerably. Her own understanding of the picture was that the young lady to the left
must have dropped something over the cliff, a handkerchief
perhaps, which a breeze had snatched out of her hands, and
that the gentleman in the frock coat was being gracious enough
to try to retrieve it for her. She now turned to her husband and
asked him if this assumption was mistaken.

A very different expression, thoughtful and serious, came
over Friedrich's face as he took her hands in his and said, 'Líne,
in the old man who has married a young wife lives the young
man who would like to have shared with her his youth. His
youth, his hopes, his longings and ideals – the young man on
the right embodies all this, but he is in a different time. They
stand in the same picture and can never see each other. She can

see only the older man he has since become, who has lost his youth. This is why we show him in such an indignified position, risking his life as he reaches over the cliff's edge in an attempt to recover his lost youth.' Líne was so touched by this wholly unexpected interpretation of the picture that she burst into tears. She felt ashamed at the imputation of a rivalry with Dahl she had construed in her husband's words. She could not help noticing, however, that although Friedrich mentioned Dahl as having been with them on the walk to the Stubbenkammer which had inspired the painting intended to commemorate love, idealism, friendship etcetera, there was no trace of him in the picture. For the figure in *Ieutscher Tracht* representing the idealism of youth was manifestly not the Norwegian Dahl, but Friedrich himself.

Dahl remained a frequent visitor to the house, and Friedrich took a benign, fatherly interest in the young man's career, which he did much to advance; ironically, in the light of later events. This state of affairs had now continued for two years, and despite the firmness of Líne's moral character under these conditions of inescapable intimacy with a young man whom she found very prepossessing, it was inevitable that nature should demand its own course. The child she lost in the fourth month had been Dahl's. The loss of a child that resulted from a union so passionate on her side and so chivalrous on his was especially painful to Líne, who with Dahl had experienced the true pleasure of physical love for the first time. However, she recognised that it was better so, and soon became reconciled to it. Not long afterwards she became pregnant again, this time with her husband's child, and the child was born at the larger house An der Elbe 33, to which it became necessary to move on account of an ever-growing family. But the child died at birth.

At thirty she was no longer a young woman in the eyes of the world but a settled wife with a famous husband whom she respected, treasured, but did not love from her heart. That

Líne in her own eyes still felt herself to be young was thanks
to Johan Dahl. Whenever he came to the house her spirits
soared, although she took pains to conceal this from her husband in order not to hurt him. The couple had never spoken
with one another about Dahl's position in the household, but
that he was her lover was always implicit. Without any doubt,
Friedrich was genuinely fond of the young painter. Sometimes
it seemed to Líne that it gave him pleasure to share with his
friend the woman they both loved. She was their bond, and
her position between them required her to preserve a delicate
balance.

As painters, both men were accustomed to retreating into
their own worlds, and living undisturbed in the imagination.
When they emerged, it was as if Líne were the threshold over
which they passed on their way back to the other world. It was
she whom they both sought out first when they were tired of
themselves and wanted company. One man must not be
favoured more than the other, and this was only possible
because one was favoured differently from the other. She
played cards with Dahl, she laughed with Dahl, Dahl entertained her. She loved him because of his lightness, but in that
lightness she recognised something which would not be tied
down. Dahl was not entirely reliable, and in that lay part of his
charm. She understood that the man whom she loved was not
necessarily the man whom, had she been free, she would have
chosen as her husband. It was less easy to get along with
Friedrich. She remained a little afraid of him. But she knew he
would never desert her, and that he would always provide for
his wife and children.

The ambivalence of feeling that characterised her situation
was well caught, it seemed to Líne, in 'Woman at the
Window', which Friedrich painted at this time. A figure in a
closed interior was such an unusual subject for the artist that it
betrayed to Líne how much she had occupied her husband's
thoughts, and how clearly he had seen her situation. The
woman stands inside, looking out. The room in which she

stands is bare and dark. It is Friedrich's studio. This is the
house in which the woman is confined, but standing at the
window and looking out she turns her back on it. The world
outside is bright, full of life. She looks out at this world
longingly, but she belongs inside and cannot escape. She is
afraid to escape. She is a prisoner, but this is the prison she
would choose if she had her freedom.

What could she do but wait? She stood at the window and
looked out, waiting for him to come. She had lost Dahl's attention. His visits became less frequent. There was someone else,
Líne could feel it. Her unhappiness was exacerbated by her
passivity. Lacking scope, unable to move, her imagination ran
wild. Friedrich had seen this, too, and put it in his picture. He
felt pity for his wife and was, he said, 'disappointed at the
fickleness of Dahl'. She was pregnant again, and did not know
with whose child. The alliances changed. Now the husband
and wife were allied against the lover who was fickle. They
showed a moral indignation, with Dahl as the object, which
was an emotional need that had been long overdue. They had
made an investment in Dahl, so to speak, and felt short-
changed. They shunned him. For Dahl, this was much too
strong a reaction to an affair he had been having in town that
was not serious at all. During the five years he had spent in
Dresden, the house An der Elbe had become a second home.
He did not want to jeopardise his relationship with the
Friedrichs, however complicated it had become. It was in these
circumstances, the return of a prodigal son and lover, that
Friedrich and Líne suggested Dahl should move into the floor
below, which had become vacant. Dahl moved in, and a
daughter, Agnes, was born.

On the year following Dahl's move into the house a third
surviving child was born. If there had been any doubt as to the
father, his signature was written in the boy's face. Friedrich
called him Gustav Adolf, after the Swedish conqueror, which
was a jibe at the Norwegian who was his father. Friedrich's
humour was difficult to make out. There was usually irony in

it, and sometimes malice. He tolerated Líne's relationship with Dahl, but only in exchange for his right to take them to task for it whenever he pleased. There was a coarse side to his nature an outsider who knew only Friedrich's ethereal paintings would never have guessed at. Líne was not spared allusions to her sexual relations with Dahl, of which the child who so resembled him was a daily reminder. Here there was a rare hint of jealousy, a suggestion that Gustav Adolf stood not merely for the Swedish conqueror (Greifswald, where Friedrich was born, had remained a Swedish possession for two centuries after the Thirty Years War, and had only recently been returned to German sovereignty), but for an intruder and a usurper. This found expression in his mocking remark that Friedrich had been only good enough for daughters, whereas Dahl had done better and bequeathed him an heir.

Issues of title and legitimacy were particularly sensitive at this time, when Friedrich had just been passed over for the professorship of landscape painting at the academy in Dresden in favour of the younger man, making both Dahl's and Líne's position extremely difficult. It would have been hypocritical, or impertinent, or both, to have attempted to console Friedrich, who was in any case too proud to let anyone regard him with pity. The alliances changed again, this time with Líne and Dahl united by a commiseration for the jilted painter which they were not allowed to express. If the purpose of their collusion was for Friedrich's benefit (Dahl accepted the post only after a secret agreement that Friedrich would be offered an honorary professorship as compensation), the means by which they achieved it had the contrary effect, for in the end Friedrich felt himself isolated on the opposite side. But Líne waited for this disappointment to pass, knowing that everything passes and is forgotten in the end.

Friedrich was sixty-one years old when he suffered a stroke that for a while immobilised him completely and much reduced the scope of his activities for the remaining years of his life. As a painter he had slipped into oblivion and effectively lived off alms, dependent on the kindness of friends who purchased his pictures or arranged for their purchase by others. Dahl's fortunes had risen as Friedrich's had fallen in the ten years that had passed.

The three-sided relationship between Líne, Friedrich and Dahl, the balance shifting now this way, now that as it adjusted to subtle, invisible fluctuations, subsisted for over twenty years. During the last few years, when Friedrich was semi-paralysed, the Friedrich–Líne alliance became dominant, because it was he who now most needed her. Dahl's success and Friedrich's failure consolidated it, a final expression of that implicit sense of their moral superiority over Dahl which had always made itself felt whenever Dahl, by his youth, or his charm, or the fact that it was he whom Líne instinctively loved, was felt to have too much of an advantage, and jeopardised the balance of the life they shared.

What was Líne to make of those last pictures, which her husband must have intended to represent some kind of retrospective view of his life? The painting called 'The Steps of Life', showing an old man seen from the rear in *Ieutscher Tracht* walking down to the sea, where he is greeted by a younger man and three children on the shore, was clearly a valediction to his family life. It was the painting on which Friedrich had been working at the time of his stroke. Almost no picture of Friedrich's united so many figures within a single canvas. But where was his wife? Where was Líne? She was hurt to the quick when she saw the painting from which she had been excised.

Friedrich had presented her with nothing but riddles, all his life. Throughout their marriage she had always guessed about, never known the man who was at her side. The human being with whom she had been more familiar than with any other remained the greatest stranger. This seemed to her at last to be the barren core of Friedrich's vision. There was no certainty in anything. Nothing could be known. There were only illusions.

The hard, real substance of all experience, Líne's married life, ran away between her fingers like water.

And where was Dahl, anywhere in the two or three hundred paintings that Friedrich left? 'He did not paint people but enigmas, his private symbols of people,' said Dahl, pointing at the stereotypes which appeared again and again in pictures from all periods of Friedrich's life. Friedrich used this convention because in fact he was embarrassed by his incompetence, having no talent for representing the human figure. Could the younger man in 'The Steps of Life' have been Dahl? Dahl had flattered himself that this might have been so, in recognition of his lifelong friendship with Friedrich, until he saw the final version of an old theme, 'Chalk Cliffs on Rügen', perhaps the last picture that Friedrich ever painted. It echoed the earlier, brighter, happier painting that Friedrich had interpreted as a declaration of his love for Líne, and echoed it terrifyingly. All the figures had been excised from the landscape. It was a pitiless destruction. To Dahl and Líne the picture seemed like a deliberate act of vandalism, a negation of their life together, of life itself.

At the end of Friedrich's life Dahl held a different view of art from his former mentor and became, after his death, one of his most perceptive but also severest critics. He took his revenge for what Friedrich had done to himself and Líne in his last pictures.

'Friedrich often seemed to have crossed the boundary between painting and poetry. In his opinions and his needs he would suffer no one,' said Dahl in the summary of his friend. 'C.D. Friedrich was hardly what one would call a child of fortune. His destiny was the destiny of all waters that flow deep, to be understood by a few and misunderstood by many. The age saw in his pictures contrived ideas that were not true to nature. Many thus bought his pictures as mere curiosities, or because, during the time of the wars of liberation, they sought and found their own political–prophetical meaning in them. Artists and art-lovers saw in Friedrich only the mystic, because the mystical was what they were seeking themselves. Friedrich knew that one paints and can paint not nature itself but one's own feelings – which must be natural feelings, however. Friedrich saw this in a tragic manner all his own, which cannot quite be called contrived, but which presumed too much in what it is possible for art to show.'

5

Elena went down to meet Klopfenstein, the man from the local reception committee, in the Kurhaus lounge. She excused her husband's absence. Jens was upstairs in their room, resting. It had been a long day.

Klopfenstein was sympathetic and polite. Politeness was unusual in this country. Everything was done grudgingly, as if people resented having to do it. She could feel resentment in the air. She wondered whether people resented her because she came from the West. But Klopfenstein was different, relaxed and friendly. Perhaps it had to do with living in a backwater where there seemed to be less evidence of an omnipresent centralist state. So when he told Elena that delegates from Dresden and Leipzig had also arrived, and asked her if she and her husband would like to join them for dinner, she was reluctant to refuse. He might get the impression they looked down on his hospitality. If Jens felt up to it, she said, they would be pleased to. Could they leave it open? Klopfenstein seemed extremely happy to be able to assure her they could. He left a pile of brochures on the table with information about the island, and Elena wandered out for a stroll round Binz.

The town was derelict, and perhaps that was its charm. She liked the clapboard houses along the seafront with their closed balconies and filigree woodwork. She remembered them from the holidays she had spent in the 1930s further up the coast, in the direction of Stettin. Everything here seemed familiar. It was the same Baltic, with the same soft, mild air, the murmuring ocean, a soft rumble that sounded as if it came out of a shell. She turned away from the sea and walked through a campsite among the pines. She found herself on the outskirts of Binz, surrounded by high-rise hotels and ugly blocks of flats. In the vast dining-room of one of the hotels, tables with identical decorations and white paper napkins had been laid for several hundred guests. There were shopping arcades and an amusement park with a dolphin suspended in mid-air over the entrance. The paint had come off the dolphin. His tail was broken. A sign said 'Out of Order'. The amusement park was closed. Elena walked through the shopping arcade on her way back to the seafront. It was all so meagre and shabby because no one was responsible. No one cared about the dolphin's broken tail. Elena began to feel depressed, and turned back to the hotel.

A party of Swedish tourists was waiting outside the Kurhaus. More tourists kept on emerging from the nearby liquor store, carrying their purchases in plastic bags. Some had already started drinking them. The Swedes shouted and laughed. Elena watched them make their way down the pier to the ship that was moored at the end. It had a Swedish name. The tourists must have come on a day trip from Sweden, and were now on their way back home. East German holidaymakers looked on from the pier while the Swedes embarked, waving as the ship pulled away. Watching the onlookers left behind on the pier, Elena felt the poignancy of this scene. Rügen was as far as the workers sent up from the south for a holiday every seven years would ever be able to go. Whatever lay across the water belonged to a world they were forbidden to enter.

At the Kurhaus reception desk she picked up the brochures Klopfenstein had given her and called the number he had written on a piece of paper. He wasn't in. She left a message that she and Jens would not be joining the party for dinner, and went upstairs.

She found Jens lying on the bed, reading. The room they had been given in the Kurhaus didn't have a toilet or shower. It had a view of the sea. She stood at the window and took off her necklace, looking out at the sun going down. A breeze came in off the sea, making it pleasantly cool in the room. Jens was in good spirits. He had slept for an hour, he said, and felt refreshed. She told him about Klopfenstein's invitation to dinner, and that she had just cancelled. Perhaps it was a mistake. Jens laid aside the book he was reading and asked her where she'd been.

Elena walked up and down, taking off her clothes and talking at
the same time. She told Jens about the dolphin with the broken tail
at the entrance to the amusement park and the Swedes with their
plastic bags getting on to the boat at the pier, and suddenly she
understood why she could sometimes have the feeling of missing
Jens, as she had on the train that afternoon, even when he was there.
Unless she explained about the dolphin's tail and the hundreds of
identical tables laid for dinner in the enormous hotel room on the
seafront, Jens would not understand why she was telling him these
things, because he was unaware of the feelings they had released in
her. The sense of missing Jens that Elena also had when she read his
books was for the same reason, only the other way round: his books
described events in which nothing was left for the reader to guess.
This was one way of expressing the difference between Jens and
Jason. She never missed Jason when Jason was there. Elena put on a
dressing-gown and said she was going down the corridor to take a
shower, but her mind was on something else. She was thinking how
strange it was that Jens had had to wait until the end of his life to
write a book that ventured a guess, and how ironic it was that tomorrow he would be given a prize for a life's work which contained not
a single thing for the reader to guess, and which she always felt had
failed to come alive because it never took any risks.

Jens was beginning to die even as Elena left the room to take a
shower. Perhaps he'd been dying all day by slow degrees, through the
heat, the strain of the journey and the emotions it aroused. His
death didn't happen all at once. There was something in the organ-
ism setting a process in motion which had a beginning and an end.
He was already dying when they went downstairs and Elena
arranged to have the cocktails served in the lounge, although it was
closed, because she didn't feel able to face the crowds in the dining-
room. They sat there for an hour, chatting about this and that,
looking out over the Baltic as the sea changed from dark blue to
black between twilight and dark.

Dying is like destiny. It can only be seen in perspective, perhaps
seen at all, when it's past, which is why Elena subsequently read into
the last hours she spent with Jens emotional nuances that weren't

there at the time. In fact the evening was a continuation of the
thousands of others they had spent, and would become significant
later only because it turned out to be the last. This is the illusion that
death gives life as a parting gift, of there having been a course to run
between a beginning and an end, possessing an outline and perhaps
even a purpose – in retrospect, a destiny.

Jens was in bed and, unknown to Elena in the other bed beside
him, had already begun his gradual slide through layers of ever
deeper sleep while she was lying awake, looking through the
brochures that Klopfenstein had given her. The texts were propaganda; historical excursions into the imperial beginnings of Rügen's
resorts in the nineteenth century, their cultivation on a gigantic but
failed scale by the Nazis and now the socialist triumph; the island's
other industries, fisheries and chalk manufacture in Sassnitz. It was
only to illustrate the wealth of chalk as a local resource that
Friedrich's picture of the chalk cliffs was reproduced in the brochure.
Elena knew that Jens would be amused, and she put the brochure on
the bedside table for him to look at in the morning. Moths drawn in
through the open window by the bedside light careered erratically
around the room, casting enormous shadows, crashed into the lamp
and lay stunned on the brochure which Elena had placed on the
table. She turned out the light and was instantly asleep.

Friedrich's picture of the chalk cliffs, face up on a table beside the
bed in which Jens convulses and passes into a coma when the blood
vessel bursts, is the image etched on her retina the moment Elena
switches off the lamp, still decaying behind her eyelids while she is
falling asleep. It is a decaying image, a faint reproduction of the
original which Jens saw in a gallery in Winterthur and in which he
recognised the irresistible symmetry that brought him to Rügen, a
faint, fading light at the end of the tunnel. Dreaming of it, Elena can
sustain the flickering image little longer. Obscurely she sees the
clifftop scene, surrounded by encroaching dark, and she has to guess
it quickly in her sleep, crying out to Jens, to warn him of what he is
about to lose, stretching out her arm and pointing, but the words
won't form on her lips. She has a stark feeling. There is dread. Then
the light goes out, and the image is extinguished.

1990
January to
February

1

When at last he got through to the representative of the German Democratic Republic in Bonn, and asked if he would need a visa to get into the country, the man at the other end of the telephone said he didn't know, one should be prepared for all eventualities, because although the German Democratic Republic was still there in a formal sense, all the evidence suggested that it had effectively ceased to exist. Technically, however, a visa might still be required to enter a country that was no longer there.

Jason asked the man at the end of the line what he would advise him to do. There was a long pause, during which he listened to other telephones ringing unanswered in the background. He was reminded of a scene on television at the time the Berlin Wall had been breached two months before. When the first live TV link-up was established with East Berlin later that night, so that viewers in the West could be informed of the state of affairs by the persons responsible for them in the East, his screen showed a row of chairs on which no one was sitting. The studio in East Berlin remained empty all night. Persons responsible never appeared.

'Just go there,' said the voice at the end of the line. 'That's not official, only what I'd personally recommend.'

Elena drove Jason to Geneva airport, and two hours later he was on board a plane to Leipzig.

The formalities, or perhaps the lack of them, surrounding his departure for a country that in a sense was there and in a sense was not; his arrival at Leipzig airport, where he was met by guards with rifles but nobody to shoot at, who conducted him into the deserted lounge instead, reminding him of a law requiring visitors to change money on arrival in the country, even if there was no longer anywhere to do so: nothing about this journey seemed any more arbitrary than other journeys he had made in his life.

He walked across the lounge, noticing the sparse furniture standing on thin legs, lost in the emptiness, and emerged from the airport building into a forlorn, second-hand atmosphere extraordinarily reminiscent of the 1950s. Taking his bearings in the soon-to-be former German Democratic Republic, Jason felt himself back in a place where it seemed he had already been long before.

He bought all the available newspapers and settled down at the bar in a café in the centre of town. According to *Neues Deutschland*, the official organ of the old country and still apparently the newspaper with the biggest circulation in the new one, the People's Chamber of Deputies had just elected eight representatives from opposition parties as ministers without portfolio in what Prime Minister Modrow termed a government of national responsibility. As many as twenty political parties and a hundred and fifty interested groups had so far announced their intention of contesting the first free elections in March. Death threats and gallows were being daubed on the houses of Communist Party officials. Over a million East Germans had gone West since 1961, the paper said, fifty thousand of them in the previous month alone. Jason wondered how many of them were Communist Party officials.

He found the private expenditures of the highest-ranking ones listed in the *Sächsisches Tagblatt*. The sums were absurdly monumental, as communism had always been. Two hundred and twenty thousand marks diverted from public funds for Comrade Stoph's greenhouse plants. Three-quarters of a million for Comrade Honecker to purchase a watch that had belonged to Lenin. A hundred million on standby for Comrade Honecker in case an emergency should arise.

Where were the hundred million now that Honecker needed them? Jason groped in his pocket for cigarettes.

'Have one of mine.'

A man sitting beside him at the bar shoved a packet of Camels along the counter.

'Thanks.'

'You're not from here, are you?'

'How did you guess?'

'Everything about you. Different. Spot it at once. Drink?'

'Not just at the moment, thanks.'

It was mid-morning, and the bar was full. An economy with words which Jason registered in the first few sentences the man directed at him turned out to have to do with the effort he was making not to slur his words, even to be able to talk at all. His face was puffy. He was drunk. Probably he didn't know half of what he was saying.

'Drinking all night. Matter of fact. Not been to bed. Packing. I'm off.'

'Oh? Where to?'

'The Soviet Union. Who's your favourite pop group? Mine's Black Sabbath. Nobody sensible to talk to here. People don't understand. Look, let me buy you lunch.'

The man pulled a bundle of money out of his pocket and tossed a couple of bills on the counter. The money, the Camels, the sudden departure to the Soviet Union, a favourite pop group that was a couple of decades out of date – intrigued, Jason accepted the man's invitation and followed him out.

They walked a hundred yards down the street and climbed the stairs to an empty restaurant on the floor above. Jason asked for an omelette. The man asked for beer. He drank his lunch. Jason asked him what he was going to do in Russia.

'Job there.'

'What sort of a job?'

'I work in security.'

'You're a Stasi agent.'

It was a statement rather than a question. Jason waited for a reaction, but the man didn't respond directly to what he had said.

'I can tell that you despise me. All right, let me confess something to you. I *was* a member of the Party. Eh? How about that? An SED member and not ashamed of it. Do you despise me for that?'

'No.'

'There's no reason to, is there? But the witch-hunt is on. Just go out there on a Monday and listen to what they're saying.'

'What are they saying?'

'They're after our blood.'

He lurched to his feet.

'Gotta go . . .'

The man's eyes were red with booze and self-pity and lack of sleep. He couldn't have been more than twenty-eight, thirty at most.

'You despise me, don't you?'

'No, but I wish you'd stop being so sorry for yourself.'

They waited in silence for a moment at the corner of the street. The man swayed and waved his arm in the direction of a steel and concrete building further down the road. There was a high brick wall around it. A crowd of people had gathered at the entrance.

'My file's in there and I can't get at it.'

He saluted with an outstretched arm above his head, his back already turned, already walking away.

Jason waited in the queue until he gathered from the conversation around him that it wasn't a queue; the people were standing there for no particular reason, just out of curiosity. It was understandable. The building surrounded by the high brick wall and with a guard-room at the entrance was the Leipzig headquarters of the Ministry of State Security, the Stasi. Normally people would have given this building a wide berth. They would even have avoided the street in which it stood. But now the Stasi had been driven out.

Jason wondered how they had managed to leave a man in uniform on guard at the entrance to the building. He asked the woman standing beside him, and learned that the man in uniform was a Vopo. In the round Saxon vowels with which she pronounced the word it sounded rather droll. It took him a moment to realise Vopo was short for Volkspolizist, the ordinary police. He found these abbreviations sinister. They were all of the same lineage. Vopo was not particularly droll. Vopo combined with Stasi led back to Gestapo.

He showed the policeman a pass, identifying him as a representative of a defunct West German newspaper, and asked if he could go inside.

'Is it the Citizens' Committee you want?'

Jason nodded. The policeman got on the phone and told the committee there was a West German journalist at the entrance, and could he send him up to talk to Mr Deichmann?

Following the policeman's instructions, Jason walked round to the back of the building, opened the third door he came to and went up a flight of stairs. He heard a door open, and a few moments later a young man with long fair hair came walking along the corridor towards him.

Deichmann, he said, shaking hands, and lightly touched Jason's shoulder to show him the way upstairs. How had he heard about the Citizens' Committee? Deichmann asked. By chance, Jason began, but Deichmann was already saying one could hardly miss the place, it was a landmark, bristling with aerials, you could see them a mile off. He stopped so suddenly that Jason bumped into him.

Pardon, Deichmann said, spreading his hands and speaking very rapidly, as if he were under pressure of time, but what is the Citizens' Committee and why was it formed? Just take a look at the doors.

He waited while Jason inspected one of the doors and confirmed that it was sealed. Deichmann nodded quietly and set off in a hurry, trailing an arm along one side of the corridor and then the other to demonstrate that all the rooms were sealed. He walked in this way, without speaking, the entire length of the building on one floor, went down the stairs at the end of the corridor and came all the way back on the floor below.

Now, said Deichmann, that may seem a long way, but if all the files preserved on microfilm in this building were reproduced as documents on normal paper you would walk five kilometres past them, and that's *after* the Stasi has already destroyed a lot of the material.

It was an impressive demonstration, at risk of turning into a stunt. Probably he had already done it many times, which would explain why he spoke of the five kilometres with what sounded almost like pride, as if the size of the figure mattered more than what it represented.

That was the first objective, Deichmann said as they continued downstairs, to ensure that the files were not tampered with. The Citizens' Committee had been appointed as watchdog, and had occupied the building since December. They made sure that nobody came into the building, and nothing left it, without their permission. The second task was to defuse an explosive situation in which a lot of people would lynch a Stasi man if given half a chance. Don't forget, he said over his shoulder to Jason as they made their way down into the basement, the Stasi was here until only six weeks ago.

It was an eerie reminder, particularly down in the basement of the building. In an alcove stood a bust of Feliks Edmundovich Dzerzhinski, founder of the Soviet secret police. He was framed by shelves of red-bound volumes, with *Aus der Geschichte der Tscheka* printed in gold letters along the spine. Jason smelled stale air as he followed Deichmann along the corridor into a room at the end. Deichmann switched on a light.

'This is where they kept the incinerator. It was still burning the day we arrived. We retrieved what we could . . .'

Plastic sacks stood in a corner, full of scraps of charred paper. Deichmann said they would soon make a start trying to piece the bits of paper together. Jason stooped to decipher a handwritten corner of page.

'Sister-in-law Tuesday next week . . . wants to see the baby . . . sounds like a private letter.'

Deichmann nodded.

'Sometimes they kept the original. The letter never arrived. But usually they made copies. Copies of everything. And parcels. They intercepted parcels from the West. Have a look in here. We call it the delicatessen.'

He opened the door of a room lined with shelves from ceiling to floor. They were crammed with tins, bottles and jars, and all of them contained food. Jason asked Deichmann what they were going to do with all this stuff. Nothing for the time being, Deichmann said. They would do nothing until the elections were over in March.

'In the meantime the Citizens' Committee could do guided tours,' said Jason with a smile. 'It would be a very profitable business, and help to cover your expenses.'

'You're joking.'

'It was just an idea. Who are the people on the Citizens' Committee?'

'All sorts of people. Most of them happen to be Church people.'

'Church people?'

'People from the peace movement organised by the Church during the last ten years. Have you met Friedrich Magirius?'

'No.'

'It would be a good idea for you to talk to him. I could introduce you to him. Is there a number where I can reach you in Leipzig?'

They made their way back upstairs and went outside. It was a relief to get out of the building.

Jason lit a cigarette and wrote a number on his card.

'How many people used to work for the Ministry of State Security?'

'Around eighty thousand. Officially.'

'And unofficially?'

'It's impossible to say. There were informers everywhere. It was everyone's duty in the communist state.'

'As many as a million?'

'Probably fewer.'

'Perhaps more than a million?'

'I can't imagine there were that many.'

'All these people are still here.'

'They're still here.'

Deichmann escorted Jason back to the entrance. Jason gave him his card and watched him pocket it absentmindedly.

'We can't ostracise these people,' Deichmann said.

Jason shook his hand and walked away. Deichmann said something else that he didn't catch. He stopped and turned.

'What did you say?'

'These people are part of ourselves,' said Deichmann. 'Somehow we must learn to integrate them.'

2

On his way to the address Elena had given him, a house in Görlitzerstrasse where Marlene lived, Jason stopped off at the Bebel-Liebknecht House to find out how the discredited Communist Party was faring in the run-up to the election. He asked to talk to the SED campaign manager. The man at reception made a phone call and asked him to take a seat in the lobby.

During the twenty minutes he was kept waiting, nobody left or entered the building. At the Communist Party headquarters in Leipzig, the country's second city, Jason assumed there would ordinarily have been a lot of activity on a weekday afternoon. Now it was like a boarding school where everyone has gone home for the holidays. The rules no longer applied. Yesterday there had still been terrible punishments for offences like running and whistling in the corridors. Now you could run and whistle as much as you liked.

The badness of the art surrounding an ideology is always a warning there will be other things wrong with it. The busts of Liebknecht and Lenin, standing on columns at the entrance and drenched in a weird purple light, formed the centrepiece of a cabinet of horrors. Now that term was over, and the rules no longer applied, Jason could imagine head prefects Lenin and Liebknecht laughingly admitting that the punishments meted out to inmates had only been meant as a practical joke, but on reflection perhaps they were a mistake, after all.

'Mr Gould?'

Jason turned round to find a dapper man in a grey suit, an arm already pointing at his back in readiness to shake his visitor's hand the moment he turned round. The effect was less of a greeting than of a hold-up.

'My name is Kowalski. I'm the PDS campaign manager in Leipzig.'

'PDS?'

'Party of Democratic Socialism, until recently SED. The Party voted to change its name, for tactical reasons.'

'I can imagine.'

Kowalski showed him into a room with the appearance of a sitting-room. It was furnished with a table bearing a smudged tablecloth, a couple of kitchen chairs, and an old sofa whose yellowed foam-rubber upholstery was bursting out of the seams. Jason chose one of the kitchen chairs, with a view of a pantry–kitchen containing a sink and sideboard on the other side of the room. Kowalski sat down opposite him. The window behind him looked out on to a garden where afternoon was already falling.

'So how's it going?'

Kowalski cocked his head.

'I beg your pardon?'

'Your election campaign. I can imagine it must be rather uphill work. What is there in the record of the SED's . . . forty years in office that you think the electorate might want to keep?'

Kowalski took a cigarette out of a pack and held it up between thumb and forefinger, as if showing him an exhibit.

'Three pillars. Social security. Cultural identity of the people of the GDR. And anti-fascism. Those are the pillars we are building on.'

He lit the cigarette.

Jason said, 'But the roof fell in. They aren't pillars. If they were, you'd still be in power.'

Kowalski blew out smoke and said, 'It wasn't all wrong.'

He was silent for a while before he continued.

'People only began resigning their Party membership, I mean in droves, after three things happened. One, they found out how the elections had been rigged last year. Two, they found out how close the connections were between the Party and the Stasi. Three, they found out how much corruption there was in politics altogether.'

The campaign manager fell silent. It was beginning to get dark in the room, but it didn't seem to occur to him to switch on the light. Maybe he hadn't noticed how dark it was.

'Tell me about your election campaign,' suggested Jason.

'Election campaign?'

'What the SED, or rather PDS, is doing to get itself elected.'

'Well . . . of course the Party *could* organise an election rally. Members would come. But it wouldn't be a good idea.'

'No?'

'No. A couple of months ago, back in November, our people were at least given a hearing. Not any more. So then we tried to set up info stalls with leaflets, stickers, that sort of thing. But that didn't work either. Party workers were attacked. From my point of view, as campaign manager of the PDS, we have one distinct handicap. All the other parties share a common goal: our destruction. All the other parties have the same campaigning tactic to promote their own causes: they trample around on us. We get plenty of publicity, unfortunately. Mass rallies, that kind of thing – frankly, I have my doubts. As soon as our candidate opens his mouth and says he's from the PDS the hall will start to empty. Our election campaign can only be a more modest affair, undertaken as quietly as possible . . .'

Jason looked at the sofa with the burst upholstery and said, 'There are limits as to how inaudible an election campaign can be.'

Kowalski nodded.

'I mean, the PDS has got to talk about something,' Jason continued, 'and to be heard talking. What will those things be?'

'One subject on which we've had a lot of criticism from the grass roots, for failing to give it more prominence,' said Kowalski with a stir of enthusiasm, 'is sport. A German Democratic Republic without sport is unimaginable. You asked me what things were worth keeping after forty years. Well, sport is definitely one of them. People's identification with successful athletes is of enormous importance in this country. And as the SED's successor, in some ways still its fiduciary, that's one of the more obvious election assets the PDS can claim . . .'

It was now completely dark in the room, and Kowalski got up to switch on the light.

3

According to his map of Leipzig, Görlitzerstrasse was not far from the centre of town. After a quarter of an hour of driving along the Allee der Sovietischen Freundschaft, Jason realised he must have missed the turning. He turned and followed the road back, stopping every half-mile or so to take a closer look at the street signs. Somewhere on his way back into town, the Boulevard of Soviet Friendship ceased to exist. The road signs had been defaced or taken down. He found one of them on top of an uprooted pole, lying in the grass at the edge of the street.

Once he had left the main roads he found the streets so poorly lit he had to get out of the car in order to read the signs. He imagined this was what cities must have been like at night around the turn of the century. He drove slowly, skirting the pot-holes. Between the muffled streetlamps, shedding no more than a drizzle of light, there were long stretches of total darkness. There were no bars or shops or restaurants; there weren't any cars or people in the streets. By eight o'clock in the evening, whatever life there was in the neighbourhood had already died out.

Görlitzerstrasse was a cul-de-sac. Jason parked the car at the entrance to the street and walked down in search of number 6. Gaps in the line of tall dark houses seemed to show where a house, presumably bombed, had disappeared and not been replaced. He saw that the surfaces of the buildings fronting the street were curiously pockmarked and scarred. It occurred to him that shrapnel or bullets might have marked them this way during street fighting between Soviet and German troops at the end of the Second World War. He realised with astonishment that everything he was looking at here remained just as it had been half a century ago.

Jason couldn't find a name at the entrance to number 6. He walked up to the house, which was set back a little from the road. An old-fashioned vestibule, a sort of open porch with columns, led into the downstairs hallway. Piles of *Neues Deutschland*, tins of paint and building tools were stacked in a corner. A bicycle stood propped against the wall. The floor was littered with dry leaves that rustled and scattered as draughts came scudding in through the open door.

A single bulb burned on the wall, leaving him to infer from the little it illuminated the extent of an unexpected splendour that remained hidden in the dark. Floor, walls, staircase, all seemed to be marble. The caryatids supporting the ceiling on their heads were carved out of solid pillars. Over an archway at the foot of the stairs there was a fanlight whose wafer-thin onyx panels had almost the transparency of glass. A few steps up the staircase, Jason reached a landing surrounded by a balustrade, with the date

1871

inlaid in mosaic on the floor.

He stepped over the date and went on up the stairs into a gradually thickening darkness. He arrived at a door. Jason searched for a bell, and then for a light switch to find the bell. A faint light came through the glass panels on either side of the door. He heard voices murmuring inside.

He rapped against the glass and waited. The drone of voices continued without interruption. Jason rapped the glass again, a little harder, and a voice inside called out, 'Coming! Coming!'

And she was. It was Marlene. He could see the old lady's rocking motions, obscurely, a rising and falling blurred through darkly coloured glass which suddenly lit up as she came plunging towards the door.

4

Jason has made up his mind about Marlene before she turns down the radio, switches on the hall light and opens the door. He has never met her, but already he is sure what she's like. Even if Marlene wished to insist that she was quite different from what Jason thinks she is like, she would not be able to swim free of the net of assumptions, in fact of countless foregone experiences, in which her image is trapped in Jason's mind.

How is this possible?

The net in which Marlene's image is trapped in Jason's mind is that mysterious catch-all intuition, *die Anziehung des Bezüglichen*, the Attraction of Affinities, gravitating to a point of convergence which is both arbitrary and inescapable.

'Coming! Coming!'

Marlene opens the door at the point where all these things – the city, the country, the house gone to decay with the date of the founding of Bismarck's German Reich at the foot of the stairs, the chair in the campaign manager's office, its yellow stuffing bursting out of the seams – are about to converge in the lines on the eighty-year-old lady's face like scars that have been etched by acid. She has no choice. Here is the point of convergence. This is the face with which Marlene must live.

5

'This is Poldi's grandfather. Mining interests in the Ruhrgebiet and Saxony. Poldi's grandfather built the house in 1871. In those days very pro-Reich, bless him, very *Deutschnational*. Oh, and Jewish, as it later turned out.'

Marlene has cleared the dishes. A cigarette in the corner of her mouth, she plunges back and forth between the kitchen and the dining-room table, where Jason sits trapped with a photo album in a yellowish cone of light.

'Görlitzerstrasse in 1914. This is Poldi's Uncle Fritz, with valet, coachman, second gardener, all looking extremely pleased with themselves on the day they left for Flanders. Isn't it crazy? None of them ever came back.'

There are portraits of Leopold from the same year, with full lips and curly hair, wearing a matelot suit, one hand resting on the arm-rest of the chair where his mother sits. Nine years old when Fritz goes off to Flanders, Poldi escapes the carnage, and in 1925 falls scandalously in love instead. He marries 'that dancing creature' secretly in Berlin, remaining there in not unhappy exile until forgiven by the family, and returns with his bride in triumph two years later. Poldi poses smiling in white scarf and topper, a foot on the running board of the open Horch in which Marlene reclines, pouting, an arm flung up behind her head.

'Look at her! *Ach, du lieber Himmel . . .*'

She sways back out of the light and goes plunging into the gloom. Jason watches her progress round the room, hand on arthritic hip, pausing to smooth a corner of the tablecloth, fiddling with bric-à-brac on the dresser, straightening up and peering at something on

top of the tiled stove. Marlene hums a tune while Jason looks down
at her and Poldi in a photo of a group of people in coats and mufflers:
Kurfürstendamm, New Year's Day 1931.

'You were tall.'

'Tall? My dear, I was a *mon*ster.'

Jason laughs.

'That tune you're humming. It's from one of the Comedian
Harmonists' songs.'

'*Richtig!*' Marlene booms.

'What was Berlin like?'

'What do you think it was like?'

'Fun.'

'Everywhere is fun dum-dum-da-dum-dum-dum when you're
twenty-one. Where, where is that stupid brooch I thought I'd put up
here?'

'If Poldi's grandfather was Jewish—'

'Exactly! That was just it. He never *told* anybody. You can imagine
what happened when the race laws came along, and Poldi's father
found out.'

'What happened?'

'He went upstairs and hung himself.'

Marlene swings round, her mouth wide open, making one of her
grimaces. The plug has been pulled out of her face. What is left is an
empty acid bath.

'As *Deutschnational* as his father had been. I mean, he felt it as a
disgrace. Do you understand that? Isn't it crazy?'

Jason turns the page and finds a picture of Görlitzerstrasse 6 with
half the roof demolished. Leopold is standing in the garden with his
hands in his pockets, looking up.

'And Poldi?'

'Escaped to Sweden. Just. I didn't see him for seven years. And
then he went and died. In 1950. He was only forty-five.'

Her face breaks into a grin, as if she is about to cry.

Jason woke up in the middle of the night and couldn't remember
where he was. The smell of old leather reminded him, the hatboxes

and suitcases, half a century old, that were stored under the bed in what had formerly been Poldi's dressing-room.

'He was the same age as I am,' Jason said aloud. He looked at his watch. It was two o'clock. London was an hour behind.

Leaving the door open, he made his way down the long windowless passage by the light in the room behind him. He had made a note of the light switches when he went to bed the previous night, but in the passage he had found none. He turned a corner, and then another, groping in darkness until he came up against the door that led into the hall. He switched on a light and went into the living-room.

The telephone stood on a little trolley beside the sofa. Marlene had bought the trolley specially for it. She was very proud of her telephone. She'd only had it a couple of months, after waiting for ten years. It was the same design as the telephone Jason remembered in his parents' house back in the 1950s. Marlene didn't expect it to work. She was pleased when it did. She told him he would have the best chance of getting through after midnight.

He dialled the number in slow motion, with long pauses between the digits. The line was clear. He listened to the number ringing in London, and then Purdy's sleepy voice

'Were you asleep?'

'Mmm.'

'Sorry. The phones only work at night.'

'Where are you?'

'Leipzig.'

'What's it like?'

'Different. The same. Different.'

'That's clear enough.'

'Listen. There's no time for location-hunting and planning things ahead. No need. You can point a camera at anything and it will have a moving story to tell. Everything is in a delicate stage. No longer frost, not yet quite thaw, suspended somewhere in between. But not for long. Within a couple of months, maybe less, all this will have gone. It won't ever be there again.'

'Let me think for a moment. I'm still in post-production . . . next weekend, and then Monday . . .'

Purdy yawned.

'I could be in Berlin in ten days.'

'Thanks. I'll be in touch.'

The things he had brought for Marlene stood on the living-room table. Tea and coffee from KDW, *Lebkuchen*, a bottle of Gordon's gin. Elena had sent a pair of Moorland fur slippers and a photograph of her mother with the younger children on the estate at Holm. She had been sending parcels to Marlene every year since the end of the war. Jason wondered how many of them had reached her, how many had been diverted by the state security people and gone to stock the delicatessen.

When Marlene had picked up the photo and remembered, her face softened.

'And how is Elena? Is there a picture of her, too?'

Elena had not been with her mother and the younger children on the trek from Silesia in the winter of 1945. She had been at school, cut off by the war, far away in Weimar. Her mother was swept along by the great human river pouring west, refugees in their hundreds of thousands, fleeing from the Soviet army. In the second week of February she reached Dresden, where Marlene found her camping with the children on the station platform and brought them to Leipzig. Thousands of refugees, tens of thousands of civilians, died in the fire bombs that destroyed the city a few days later.

Marlene's house in Görlitzerstrasse was crammed to the roof with refugees. The family stayed there for several weeks before continuing the journey west. The border closed behind them after the Russians had occupied Saxony and Thuringia, and Marlene never saw them again.

She worked as a secretary at a VEB which manufactured agricultural equipment until she was pensioned in 1974. When Marlene reached retirement age she was allowed 'over there'. The regime granted visas to pensioners for visits across the border, in the hope that they would stay there and save the state the cost of their upkeep. Marlene made three trips to visit relatives in Hamburg, which was all she could afford. Elena continued to send her parcels, but they never met.

The story of Marlene's life can be told in a few broad sweeps. Looking for an image that represents her life, Jason finds himself always returning to her face. There are few lines on Marlene's face, but they are etched deep, the grooves along which her destiny has passed.

6

Marlene's house, like the other houses in Görlitzerstrasse, like all the houses everywhere, was rotting from the roof down and turning into a ruin.

The last deed of ownership, which dated from the 1930s, had been in Poldi's name, before the house was taken over by a succession of expropiators: the Nazis, the Red Army, the East German state. None of these occupants cared for the building. They were negligent, even hostile to houses in general, perhaps because houses seemed likely to have their origins in private, privileged, often Jewish money. It was the revolution of envy. Private property was abolished. Abolition became demolition. The owners left, and so did the care-takers. With no one responsible for them, the houses were sentenced to death.

The occupants of the top floor of the house in which Marlene lived had moved out by the end of the 1960s, taking the floorboards with them. Marlene took Jason up to see a simple demonstration. The rain came in through the roof, the damp moved down, the rot moved with it. The floor below had been vacated in the early 1980s. Since then, Marlene had lived alone in the house. Now the damp was in her ceiling, and Marlene, plunging through the rooms, grimaced whenever she looked up and caught sight of the ominous stains.

Who was responsible?

All the Germans, including Marlene, were responsible, because they had started the war that led to all of this. Watching the stains (for which she is unfortunately co-responsible) grow bigger and bigger on the ceiling above her dining-room table thus also becomes an inseparable part of Marlene's fate.

7

The federal film archive in what was then still West Germany was established after the war in Ehrenbreitstein, a fortress overlooking Koblenz at the confluence of the rivers Mosel and Rhine. The site had practical aspects. Reels of inflammable nitrate film could be entrusted to the magazines where formerly gunpowder had been kept dry. The location also had symbolic connotations. Father Rhine was the river of Siegfried and the Nibelungen saga. For a couple of thousand years Germanic tribes had been shedding blood up and down the Rhine where the Romans drew up their *limes* at the outpost of Western civilisation. The bridge at Remagen, not far from Koblenz, was the one over which the American forces had crossed the Rhine in 1945 to liberate Europe from the Nazis and teach the Germans a lesson. The river symbolised a now discredited patriotism. Ehrenbreitstein was thus a good site for the preservation of German history.

Jason was a frequent visitor before the archive moved down the hill to a modern building in the town. He liked the castle. He enjoyed sitting at the cutting-tables in rooms with arrow slits for windows, rudimentarily converted dungeons where the only appreciable source of light was the blue-grey flickering images that rolled off the turntable through the spools and suddenly came to life on the screen.

It was all documentary footage of the Third Reich. There was an eerie cosiness about sitting in the dungeon and feeling safe watching the Nürnberg rallies, the annexation of Austria and the Sudetenland, Chamberlain stepping out of a plane and holding up a piece of paper, arrows in an animated image lunging across a map of Europe; and then a hiatus, followed by the capitulation of Paulus at Stalingrad, the human miles of German prisoners dwindling across the snowbound steppe in a column to the horizon. The impact of that mass of energy, the hubris, the fall, the devastation, the hollowness when the game was up – Jason was spellbound every time by what seemed to be a parable of the futility of human life.

For several days from nine to five he sat there with an American and a Japanese with whom he was researching a TV documentary, watching scenes from the rise and fall of the Third Reich and the judgement at Nürnberg. A reel was on the turntable showing stock footage of the arrival of Hitler's motorcade in Vienna in 1938. The scene was marvellously set. A convoy of large black limousines, shot from a low angle, slid menacingly into view, with Hitler standing in the back of a car, his arm raised, motionless, against a background of seething crowds.

The square in Vienna where the crowds were waiting was then shot from the roof of a building, with the edge of a balcony jutting into the image. For several minutes of one long take, the camera rested on the hundreds of thousands of people cheering and surging tumultuously in the square below, until at last Hitler showed himself briefly on the balcony and disappeared again. As the last yards of the reel snaked through the spools and the loose end began flapping crazily on the turntable, the Japanese man got up from his chair and switched off the machine.

'One is always waiting for Hitler,' he said. 'One is waiting for Hitler to come on stage. It's less interesting when he's off. He kind of makes the show, you know? He's the star.'

'I know what you mean,' said the American.

The three of them of them ambled along the castle battlements to have lunch in the restaurant overlooking the Rhine. It was a bright spring day. From the parapet there was a view for miles.

The American was a TV producer in his mid-sixties. Over lunch he told them how he had been sent to Germany in 1947 as a US army photographer. He was assigned to cover the Nürnberg trials. He said that one of the private pursuits of the trial photographers had been to get right up under the dock where all the defendants were sitting, and have their pictures taken by one of their colleagues.

The photographers had all been souvenir-hunters. Goering, Hess, Frank and von Ribbentrop were favourites. The best souvenirs were the shots of oneself with as many of the top Nazi brass as could be fitted into the background.

'We got to know those guys pretty well. Don't forget, this thing went on for months and months. We hung out with them in recess. We could visit them in prison. So we were really annoyed when we were told that we wouldn't be allowed in to take pictures of the hangings. After all that build-up! We felt we'd been cheated.'

The American took home what he claimed to be a unique souvenir. He had all the defendants' pictures, and all their autographs, on a single piece of paper. He said he was very proud of it.

By the mysterious process of the Attraction of Affinities, Jason met the sons of both Frank and von Ribbentrop within weeks of this conversation.

He was, again, in a castle, and the castle was not far from Nürnberg. Jason had been invited to a wedding. It was a very grand occasion, for which an old German aristocracy Jason had believed to be extinct shuffled out of its corner into the light. On the list at the hotel where the guests were accommodated there were several princes, a sprinkling of dukes, columns of counts and barons. Jason was one of only three commoners present. From the window of his room he watched with interest as quite a few of the aristocrats arrived in antique Volkswagen models, trudging with their battered valises across the hotel car park.

At the banquet that evening they were all transformed. In the expectant atmosphere of the enormous candlelit rooms it was all good breeding and quiet elegance, a palpable stream of self-confidence which had nothing to do with another kind of German assertiveness; and it occurred to Jason as he made his way up the stairs that to be self-conscious in English meant to be awkward, while in German it meant the reverse. The guests gave their names to ushers at the entrance to the ballroom and were directed to the tables where they were seated. Jason wandered round the table until he found the card on which 'Gould' was printed. The card to his left read 'Von Ribbentrop'. For a moment he was taken aback by the juxtaposition of these names. Then his neighbour arrived to claim the seat next to him.

She was a handsome, vivacious woman in her thirties. He found her very attractive. They talked animatedly throughout dinner and then they danced. Her husband was a banker, she said. Jason watched him swirl with her across the ballroom floor. Later they met and chatted for a few minutes. Jason complimented him on his beautiful wife. There was no mention of von Ribbentrop's father.

The son of the Reich's minister in Poland, on the other hand, could talk of nothing else. Frank had just published a book called *The Father*, and Jason interviewed him for a newspaper. The son was the wreckage left behind by the father, and in the book he had written he took his revenge. It was a vision of the father in purgatory. It began with the son imagining the sound of the father's neck snapping as the falling body pulled tight on the noose, and the image of this, his father hanging, was the image that was used to stimulate the son's first experience of masturbation.

The Nazis stole what innocence was left the twentieth century. They tore away the veil that was drawn over the last taboos. No ambiguity remained, no hypocrisy in which to hide. The spectators were horrified and fascinated, and horrified in turn by the nature of their own fascination, and the source from which it sprang.

In the Third Reich, the Nazis re-enacted the myth of Prometheus, the Titan who stole the fire that the gods had hidden from man. His punishment was to be chained to a rock, an eagle gnawing his liver, which renewed itself throughout eternity. The Nazis who stole innocence, and put their torches to the pyres on which the Jews of Europe burned, remained chained to the Germany that had spawned them, and which in punishment found itself gnawed by a swarm of death's-head moths, the flickering celluloid images recording their deeds for all time.

8

B ut there was no joy – why was there no joy?
The wall opened and they streamed out, columns of sputtering little cars that instantly became a symbol, already kitsch, the mascot of the poor relations from the East. Microphones and cameras were waiting to record everything the people from the other side said and did in the moment of their first contact with civilisation. There were tears. There was hysteria. There were emotions. There was the gratifying astonishment of sixteen million new consumers given pocket money to spend and let loose in Western department stores. Western viewers purred over the pictures of the poor relations gawping in front of store windows. What were their impressions? Tropical fruits were given a mention without fail. The availability of bananas became overnight the slogan of a new political awareness. The celebration of freedom was trivialised as a shopping spree. The price tag was the humiliation of the new German arrivals in the face of the enormity of their failure. They were the wedding guests raising their glasses to toast their own funerals.

It was not the situation for joy, and somehow there was not quite the word for it. The *Freude* that still shone in Schiller's poems and Schubert's songs had been ransacked and lost its lustre. *Kraft durch Freude* – Strength through Joy – the NSDAP slogan, exhorted the working masses. One could still hear the word in the lilting cadences of Goebbels. It was one of the words in the German language that had not recovered from its appropriation by the Nazis or its continued abuse by their Cold War successors. *Freude* was stigmatised and had become suspect.

For the people in the East the pressure had gone, but it was a pressure with which they had learned to live. The loss of something familiar, even something unpleasant, preoccupied them more than the gain of something they didn't know, however much *Freude* they were supposed to feel. The rich Germans in the West began to get irritated by the stolidity of the poor relations in the East. Weren't they grateful to be given their freedom, or at last the Deutschmark? Where was their *Freude*?

It was as if the Easterners, accustomed to a lack of things in general, had learned to live at subsistence levels emotionally as well. Perhaps it was safer, because anything other than average might be doctrinally suspect. Stronger feelings could lead to jail. People with stronger feelings risked death to get out of the country. Surrounded by the evidence of paucity and mediocrity that remained inside the country, people's feelings seemed to have succumbed to mediocrity too.

Durch Leiden Freude. Through suffering, joy!

Busts of Beethoven show a scowling man with suffering on his brow. It is Beethoven's image, not only as a composer, but as a German. Joy through Suffering somehow strikes a very German attitude, not because it is restricted to Germans, but because it has been cultivated more memorably by Germans, perhaps, than by others. It is the attitude yearned for by romantics and by adolescents, who are often the same people. It was Joy through Suffering that smuggled Germany into the soul of the sixteen-year-old Jason Gould when, in his first summer with Elena, they went for walks in the forest at Grunewald and read *Die Leiden des jungen Werthers* together.

Goethe's book about the sufferings of young Werther is equally a book about high spirits, about the exuberance of its protagonist. It was conceivably in paroxysms of elation at their own capacity for suffering that young men had followed Werther's example and killed themselves, in a wave of fashionable suicide, when Goethe's bestseller was published in 1774. They were all adherents of the *Durch Leiden Freude* school of thought. It was suffering-through-joy fans who voted slogans like *Sturm und Drang* and *Weltschmerz* into the world vocabulary.

Elsewhere it was the sceptics and debunkers, the unimpressionable men of common sense, who were elevated into national pantheons, but not in Germany. Georg Christoph Lichtenberg or Arno Schmidt, both of them mathematicians who also took the measure of homegrown follies with comparable sarcasm, were not remembered as national figures in quite the same way as Samuel Johnson, Voltaire or Karl Kraus. Lichtenberg looked askance at *Sturm und Drang* and all its works. Schmidt's response to Werther's sufferings was to reach for an ephemeris, establishing that the moon could not have been shining as Goethe claimed on the memorable night when Werther said goodbye to his beloved Lotte. Suffering and joy, and beauty, yes. Suffering and mockery, no.

In 1945 how grisly it must have sounded: *Durch Leiden Freude.* Germans could no longer use the word *Freude* unselfconsciously when it really mattered. They had lost possession of the word. Amputated from the expression of their feelings, they amputated their feelings. *Freude* was trivialised in greetings on Christmas cards. Beethoven's bust came off the mantelpiece and went into the cupboard. The Germans had now disqualified themselves from suffering, too. There was no sympathy. Germans were not allowed to suffer. Too many had suffered on their account.

Joy was the quality whose absence Jason felt most. Joylessness lay at the empty core of a country that might have been defined in terms of what it lacked.

The towns lacked light and colour, advertising, the noise of traffic, places to sit down, places of entertainment or from which to buy newspapers; places at all. The countryside lacked people, everywhere there was a lack of hope. The inhabitants did not by that account seem hopeless, however. The hopelessness of the former German Democratic Republic, the ex-GDR, as it was beginning to be called, was more a topographical feature of the place, something physically appreciable in the landscape, like granite.

By 1989, probably most of the people who wanted to get out had either succeeded in doing so or had been sent to jail. Those who remained had come to terms with the system, some of them more, some of them less. These were the people Jason met and talked to. They worked in schools, in factories, and on farms. For these people, the freedom to come and go as they pleased, regardless of whether or not they would make use of it if they had it, was not the most important thing in life.

Jason asked them all the same question. What is there worth keeping from the forty years this country existed? He was given many different answers, but almost none of them failed to mention social security.

It seemed that for the majority of people social security mattered more than freedom.

Social security as it had existed in the East was something different from what it signified in the West. Not only did it create a society in which no one earned more than twice, at most three times as much as their neighbours did, and in which everyone accordingly lived much closer to the mean, having more or less the same things, and lacking more or less the same things with the same unchanging regularity; it meant not having choices. It meant not being able to and not having to make choices: both the suspension of privilege and the exemption from risk.

It was not just that the social security surrounding them mattered more to people than their freedom. It could only exist in the absence of freedom.

This was the hopelessness that Jason felt like granite in the landscape, a colourlessness and flatness in the cities, where people who had come to terms with the system could live without anxiety, without expectations, without hope or the need for hope. This was the empty core of the country that to him, the outsider looking in, seemed to define itself less by what it had than by what it lacked. It was the destiny of those who had remained.

9

The residential area in Connewitz had been built around the turn of the century. Within a couple of decades an enormous expansion of cities had taken place right across Germany, yet despite the hurry with which they must have been built the houses from the *Gründerzeit* showed a loving attention to detail. Floral designs and stucco mouldings around windows, caryatids supporting entablatures, decorated the façades everywhere. On his way to the house in Connewitz where Rigge lived, Jason frequently stopped and looked around him.

In the cities in the West, isolated houses or rows of houses which had survived the bombs had long since become protected monuments. Here there were miles of them, rotting from the roof down, like Marlene's house; painfully coming apart. In the silent, deserted street under the soft light of the February afternoon they contrived to look elegant in their shabbiness; ageing beauties, specially lit for the occasion by the pale wintry sun, briefly reviving their charms.

He passed through an arch into a courtyard and went into one of the houses. A wooden flight of stairs led up inside it. The wall looked as if it had once been panelled, but the panelling had gone. Someone came up the stairs behind him, carrying a coal scuttle.

Jason crossed a landing and continued up the stairs. There was a cold smell of sweat and cooking in the building, the kind of smell that he remembered from his schooldays. The interior of the house was derelict. Everything that could be removed from the walls and floors had disappeared, probably long ago. He climbed the stairs to the fifth floor, arriving out of breath at the top of the house. There were three doors leading off the passage. Jason looked at the name on the first and moved on to the next.

'I don't think you'll find a name on that door. Can I help you? Who are you looking for?'

It was the person with the scuttle of coal who had been on the stairs behind him. He was a well-built man of around thirty with a clear, rather handsome face.

'I'm looking for Rigge.'

'Ah.'

He came up the stairs and stood facing Jason.

'I'm Rigge. And who are you?'

'Jason Gould. The colonel sent me.'

'The colonel sent you, Mr Gould. And may I ask who the colonel is?'

Jason took an envelope out of his coat pocket and handed it to Rigge. He tore off a corner and opened the envelope with his little finger. As he read the letter Jason noticed a twitch of what seemed to be amusement at the corner of his mouth.

'Come on in. I'm sorry I didn't know sooner. You could have brought this up for me.'

Rigge picked up the coal scuttle with a laugh and opened the door. Jason followed him inside.

'But how does the colonel know where to find me?'

'Didn't Strehlitz send you here himself?'

'No, he did not,' said Rigge with annoyance. 'It was *my* decision to come here. Leipzig was *my* choice.'

'I got the impression from him that he was co-ordinating all of this.'

'Naturally. That's the impression he always wants to give.'

Rigge carried the scuttle over to the stove in the corner of the large room and stoked it with the coal he had just brought upstairs.

'When did you last actually meet the colonel, Mr Gould?'

'We spoke on the phone a few days ago. But I've not seen him for many years.'

'Coffee?'

'Thanks.'

Rigge went into another room. All it contained was a sink, a draining-board, a gas cooker and a coffee machine. It was the kitchen. The rest of the apartment seemed to be equally bare.

'How long have you been here?' Jason asked Rigge.

'Just over a month, since the beginning of the year. Not much to show for it, is there? But I don't know how long I'll be here. Leipzig is a more convenient base for me than Berlin. And incomparably cheaper. This place costs eighty marks a month. That's East marks, of course. You have to carry the coal up five floors, but even so . . .'

Rigge went to the window and looked out.

'Strehlitz is an old man. And the trouble with the old men is that they can't let go. I'm indebted to the colonel. His influence was great. But this is not a time for old men. The colonel's time is past.'

He handed Jason a mug of coffee and they went back into the next room.

'In his letter he says I can trust you, although you are not one of us. Why do you want to talk to me?'

'I know about the movement's past,' said Jason. 'I would like to find out how you see its future.'

'Just as a matter of interest, as it were?'

'As it were.'

'Why should I want to talk to you?'

'Because through me you can reach a wider audience. I make television documentaries. I write articles and books. It *is* as a matter of interest, in fact, of personal as much as professional interest, which has to do with the fact that I've been living in Germany for most of my life.'

Rigge looked at him mockingly.

'Don't you risk being compromised?'

'No, I don't think so. But perhaps you do.'

Rigge smiled.

'I suppose you could say they feed off one another,' said Jason. 'The exhibitionist and the voyeur, and to some extent both are compromised. Both are protagonists for the mass audience that is watching, which is also compromised by its involvement in both sides of the relationship. It's the relationship of this age. Do you think we have much choice?'

Rigge lit a cigarette.

'And why me?'

'Von Strehlitz has been running his private academy since 1950, and considers you to be one of the most promising alumni of that academy in forty years. Not exactly as Führer material, I gather, but as an organiser. And then, as always, there is the background making it a personal, rather than merely an ideological issue, and it is the personal background that interests me.'

'The fact that my parents were refugees?'

'Their home is now in Poland. Surely a relevant detail in any right-wing nationalist's biography.'

He shook his head.

'It's not my parents.'

'Who, then?'

Rigge got up.

'We can talk, but preferably not in here. I could do with some fresh air. Shall we take a walk?'

Rigge had lived in the former GDR until he was fifteen. He still retained some of the conspiratorial habits he had learned from his parents, he told Jason when they came down to the street, which had come in useful later in life. On whatever side of the border, he was careful where he talked. Whether it was the Stasi in the East, which was of course still here, even if it had receded further into the background, or the *Verfassungsschutz*, the watchdog of the constitution in the West, there were always listening ears.

His family had escaped in 1974 and joined his grandfather in Würzburg, where they lived for a year before moving to West Berlin. Rigge's grandfather had just gone into retirement at the time. Perhaps that was the reason why he began to speak more openly about things he had kept to himself for as long as he remained active in public service. Rigge spoke very affectionately of this grandfather, the long conversations with him, the 'special books' he kept on a shelf in his bedroom, their attendance together at the evenings hosted by the *Landsmannschaften* – Silesian expatriate circles in which Rigge's mother and father apparently took no active part. His parents were hard-working people, politically oblivious in their single-minded pursuit of money. Probably they had little time for their son. Jason could envisage the scenes Rigge was describing because he already knew them from the families of the previous generation. These were the people who had never talked, whose children had grown up in an incriminating silence.

But the grandfather talked, and to Rigge it sounded good, the enthusiasm of the old man vividly recalling what in retrospect, at least, had been the best years of his life, 'when we were still somebody', and not the defeated nation that people seemed to be apologising for the whole time. It was all shored up by the revisionist histories of Diwald and others, which he took off the bedroom shelf and gave the boy to read. Jason appreciated that the grandfather must have given him a sense of identity and a feeling of home at an age when the boy had effectively had neither. When Rigge moved to Berlin, it was his grandfather who gave him the introduction to his next mentor, Botho von Strehlitz, a former staff officer in Hitler's entourage.

'How did you come to meet him?' asked Rigge.

'Through my father. My father knew him.'

'And handed you on to him.'

'But not in the direction I think you're suggesting. I was never one of the colonel's young men, not in any respect.'

'Still . . .'

They reached a pub on the corner of the street. Rigge opened the door and Jason followed him inside.

'One takes it for granted here, or at least I do, but it's interesting to note a sort of continuity on the enemy side, as it were, as well. Look at some of our loyal friends in Canada, for example, or the United States. In the GDR the transition was more fluid than in the federal republic, because ideologies provide much better camouflage. You just put a different label in the blank, Zionist instead of Jewish, for example, and come out in support of the Arab countries. Dozens of the Marxist ideologues who ran the media here had their training in the Third Reich, you know. They could service the propaganda machine here just as well by making the appropriate substitution. What'll you have to drink?'

'A beer.'

Jason sat down and looked round. It was an empty, sepulchral room, mournful with neglect. This country was full of empty spaces, blanks in people's minds, which Rigge wanted to fill.

He came back with the drinks and put them on the table.

'So what are you going to write on your labels?' Jason asked.

'The word *Volksgemeinschaft*, in big letters. That's the headline. We want a people's community again, no more of this individualist, democratic rubbish where it's every man for himself.'

Rigge took a sip from his glass.

'Two. Political action to support this. Quit the European Community. Put the national interest first. Three . . .'

He held up his hand and counted the points off on his fingers. Watching him, Jason was reminded of Kowalski making his points at the SED headquarters, and he wondered why enumerating one's points when speaking was such a widespread German habit.

'. . . solidarity with many of the principles of national socialism during the Third Reich, notably the legitimacy of the state as deriving from the Führer's authority alone.'

'Hitler derived everything from himself. He was *there*. Who have you got? Michael Kühnen?'

'Wait until this country has collapsed. Wait until Mitteldeutschland has become a part of Germany again. History shows that the situation always brings forward the man for it.'

'I'll wait.'

'And then, of course, the repatriation of all foreigners. We believe in the purity of race, and that nationality must be defined by race.'

'Back to the laws of 1913?'

'They still apply.'

'Anachronistically. The most backward nationality laws in Europe,' said Jason with irritation.

The remark slipped out, and he saw it was a mistake. Rigge's face had immediately hardened.

218   **DESTINY**

'Not for us. We shall enforce them, and a lot more thoroughly.'

'Who is this "we" and "us"?'

'Oh, the names change, the groups come and go, but it's always the same people, and they keep on coming,' said Rigge airily, turning a beer mat between his fingers. Jason could feel him slipping away. The sense of collusion that had been there until now, and which was indispensable to get Rigge to talk, had suddenly evaporated.

'Do you have a name now?'

'Not yet. When I have enough people here, I shall found another party. Then the party will be given a name.'

'How are you going to mobilise people?'

'By bringing them together for a common purpose, which needn't be overtly political at first, getting them interested and winning their confidence. It's easier for me because I grew up here. What d'you suppose all the kids are doing now that the youth organisations here are closing their doors? They're used to having their free time arranged. They're used to group activities. There'll be more and more discontent as the old system crumbles and there's nothing to replace it. Wherever there's discontent you can easily mobilise people by making their problem your own. And then you turn it round.'

'What does that mean?'

'Then you make your solution theirs.'

Rigge looked at his watch.

'I'm sorry, but I've got to go. Would you be interested in taking a look at one of the projects we're starting up?'

'I would.'

The two men got up and left the pub. It was a damp, foggy evening. The dim white light from the streetlamp hung like a shred of cloth in the dark. For the past twenty minutes they had sat in the pub alone. Outside there was nobody in sight either.

'This is a ghost town,' said Jason.

'The ghosts of the past. They're coming back. Which direction are you headed?'

'I'm not sure. That way, I think. That's where I left the car.'

'Come round tomorrow at around nine o'clock. We'll drive down to Chemnitz. See you then.'

'See you then.'

He watched Rigge cross the road and turn the corner. It was only after he had gone that Jason was able to fill in the blank in his memory and remembered that Chemnitz was the former name of Karl-Marx-Stadt.

10

The head of Karl Marx on a terrace overlooking the centre of Karl-Marx-Stadt was up for sale. It was a gigantic bronze, the size of a semi-detached house. On the stone plaque in front of which the head rose massively out of the pavement, with a rather comical effect, as if the rest of Karl Marx was still trapped underground and struggling to get out, it said in a dozen languages: 'Working men of all countries, unite!'

Working men walked past in the morning sunshine, however, and paid no attention to Marx's plight. They were more interested in what the two young men might be offering for free at the table they had set up just down the road. Rigge and Kronenberger were in fact collecting signatures for a referendum to give Karl-Marx-Stadt back its original name, Chemnitz.

Within weeks of the country's collapse, towns and the streets and squares in them, political parties and organisations, even people, were peeling off their old names and sticking on new ones. Soon the debate would begin about the name of the country itself.

'We want to blot him out,' Kronenberger told Jason. 'We want to erase Marx, and the memory of him, and of all his works.'

Kronenberger had never met Strehlitz. Jason wondered if the colonel would have regarded him as 'Führer material'. He talked emphatically, even passionately, about the need that had suddenly arisen to change the name of the town. Kronenberger was a good speaker who had been given his rhetorical training by the communists, and as a former secretary of the German socialist youth organisation FDJ, he had until recently used his skills on their behalf.

The gigantic bronze head of Karl Marx, staring out over the modern town that had been built on the ruins of the old one and which still bore his name, would not have deigned to turn even half an inch to take note of Kronenberger and his referendum. Struggling to get out of the pavement, but sinking inevitably, Marx would have gone down calling Kronenberger a traitor.

11

Would Marx have been right? Was Kronenberger a turncoat, or *Wendehals* – turn-throat – in the new word that needed to be coined at the time in order to cope with the hundreds of thousands of Kronenbergers, as if this were a new situation rather than essentially the old one that had already been there back in 1945?

'*Ich bin Deutscher,*' he told Jason when they took a break from collecting signatures and had lunch in a café. This statement was quite different from Jason telling Kronenberger, 'I'm British,' or the person at the next table saying 'I'm French.' It implied the further words (often expressly added, as in this case) 'and I'm proud of it.' It was doubtful that Kronenberger meant he was actually proud of his nationality. It meant that he was what he was, and didn't want to have to keep on apologising for it. It meant that Kronenberger wanted to be normal.

There were quite a few Germans who still regarded Willy Brandt as a traitor. For others, Karl Herbert Frahm was a hero, a patriot precisely because he had gone into exile (and taken a new name), fighting Nazi Germany in order to defend the fatherland. Inside the country, there were many who would not accept this distinction, but outside Germany Brandt was entirely above suspicion. Only he could afford to run an election campaign under the slogan: 'Germans, We Can Be Proud of Our Country,' as he had done in 1972. Brandt had to keep on reminding his countrymen of the need, for their own self-assurance as a people, to accept the notion of fatherland. Probably he reiterated this point because he believed that a nation that was ashamed of its national identity and disowned it was as unstable as one that kept trumpeting it, and that if the political centre failed to claim the national issue for itself, it would become the property of national extremists, a nettle no one else would touch.

But Brandt's reminders of the fatherland embarrassed his countrymen. Talk of the fatherland was taboo. Germans on either side of the border went about their business and pretended to be somebody else. In the socialist republic they were officially not Germans but 'socialist human beings', members of an international class brotherhood. In the federal republic, often abbreviated as such or referred to by its initials, camouflaging Germany, they became 'members of an economic community', proud, perhaps too proud, of being Europeans. People called Germans, living in a country called Germany, did their best to disappear.

Rigge was quite right when he said to Jason, 'You just put a different name in the blank.' Finding one's orientation in Germany is like using a map on which the names of the towns and roads are not the same as the names one reads on the signposts. At moments in German history, most recently in 1989, it *is* this situation.

Germany's dilemma is the amoeba's dilemma. It doesn't know what shape it is, because its contours keep on changing. Sprawling across the middle of Europe, as much East as West, Germany remains amorphous, a provisional state of affairs by definition. Uncertainty about the shape and size of the country to which they belong is the conundrum of the Germans. Marx denouncing Kronenberger as a traitor (or, for that matter, conservative nationalists denouncing Willy Brandt) raises the question: traitor to what? Is the German identity defined in terms of territorial integrity? Integrity of culture? Integrity as a *Volk* or nation? The uncertainty leads the Germans to question, to overestimate and then underestimate the sense of their own identity. Germany is always still somewhere on its way, a country that has never arrived at its national destination.

12

Gas lamps were burning in back streets on the outskirts of the town in the middle of the afternoon. Jason drove round the pot-holes, looking at houses in an even worse state of decay than those in Leipzig. From windows everywhere hung banners in black, red and gold, invocations of hope and prosperity dressed in the colours of the West German flag. Many of the trucks passing in the street had the flag draped over their fronts.

Country roads were cobbled and lined with trees, the state-owned land on either side empty for miles. Stopping at a layby to look at a map, Jason got out of the car to stretch his legs. Wandering across a plot of wasteland, he found himself in a graveyard. No church or other building was in sight. The graves were not memorials but registers, marked only with a name and a date. In a corner of the graveyard there was a compost heap strewn with rubbish. Jason had never been in such a loveless burial ground. It was difficult to imagine the living coming here to look after their dead.

He walked on down the track into a copse and glimpsed a big house through the trees. Groups of people were coming towards him across a grassy slope. In each group there was an adult accompanied by three or four children. There was something different about the children. Jason had sensed it from a long way off before he could see it. It was how they walked. Their movements weren't fully co-ordinated. When they reached the edge of the wood they were quite close to him. They seemed to be children from a home who were being taken for a walk by their teachers. He heard the adults speaking to the children in slow, clear voices. Jason watched them come abreast of him and walk on down out of sight. Seeing the handicapped children, and the isolated house where they lived, Jason remembered similar places in the country where he had spent his own childhood, and he was sharply aware of his own wholeness then, his freedom now.

In the hollow of the copse he followed a curve of the track, and suddenly his path was cut off, shorn off with the grass and the copse. It came to an abrupt end on the edge of a cliff. Beyond stretched a devastated landscape. It was how Jason imagined the surface of the moon. Strip-mining had razored away the earth a hundred feet deep, leaving a greyish-brown plain scarred with geometrical canyons. Nothing grew on this plain as far as the eye could see.

Arriving back at Leipzig, Jason had to postpone the journey to Berlin. Deichmann, the man who had shown him round the Stasi headquarters, had left a message with Marlene, asking him to come to the new Town Hall at six o'clock that evening for a meeting with the Church leader and chairman of the Round Table, Magirius.

Deichmann met him at the porter's lodge and led him through vaulted passages across a huge, neo-Gothic hall. It was the sort of town hall that an affluent, assertive bourgeoisie had erected as a monument to itself almost everywhere at the end of the nineteenth century; bombastic, magnificently built, the marble genuine but the style a fake, a revival of that romantic medievalism to which Germany in particular had been so susceptible. Deserted at night and shadily lit, it was a spooky place.

The Round Table had already been in session for an hour when they reached the conference chamber. Jason looked admiringly up at a ceiling with beautiful inlaid floral designs and rosettes in gold, imagining a camera tracking down over the panelled walls to the parquet floors and the marble fireplaces at either end. The Round Table in fact turned out to be lots of tables arranged in a square at which some twenty or thirty men and women were sitting. Chairs were set up in rows at one end of the room for people like Deichmann to sit in as observers. Some of the observers wore Vopo uniforms.

Jason was not interested in the discussion that was underway. He was much more intrigued by the mixture of people participating.

The debate was about whether or not the members of an advisory committee seconding the Round Table until the communal elections in May should be paid a salary out of public funds. From the fussy, bureaucratic protocol that characterised the discussion one would never have guessed that a revolution had taken place only a couple of months before. The mayor and the municipal government had been sacked, and the people sitting in this room now ran the city.

Between the representatives of the old parties that had been corrupted by their collusion with the discredited regime and the countless new parties that had sprung up out of the political rubble that was left, now confronting one another across this table, there was an atmosphere of animosity and mistrust. Youthful, long-haired representatives of the new left, sitting in on behalf of parties with names like Democracy Now and New Forum, would be the beneficiaries of any resolution that shored up the reform movement, which the old guard, putting as good a democratic face on the proceedings as possible, stubbornly continued to sabotage.

The dean of East Leipzig was one of perhaps not more than half a dozen people whose neutrality was trusted and who had the authority to chair such a meeting. Magirius was an energetic, middle-aged man with a lock of black hair he was continually brushing out of his face, as if the job of removing obstacles that threatened to obstruct the discussion had so completely taken possession of him as to become a personal mannerism. As chairman he was forced to intervene frequently, reconciling, soothing and chivvying along, sometimes with a lash of heavy sarcasm. In the end, when all else failed, he spectacularly lost his patience. The size of the salaries in question stood in no proportion to the size of this discussion, he said emphatically, or to the size of the municipal purse out of which they were to be funded. Considering the dramatic situation of the people on whose behalf they were supposed to be taking action here, this kind of temporising and petty-mindedness was a relapse into the old ways that he understood all of them had agreed must change. The chairman was in favour of the motion. Was there a majority in favour? Votes against? A few hands went up. Then the motion is carried, the chairman said, and suggested they now took a break.

Deichmann introduced Jason to the dean in the corridor outside the chamber, where coffee was served. Jason was impressed by Magirius and would have liked to talk to him at greater length, but they were continually interrupted by people with questions about the Round Table agenda. They arranged to meet instead at the dean's office in a couple of days, and Deichmann invited Jason back to his house for supper.

13

Ilona Deichmann moved slowly and quietly and had a warmth of manner which radiated across the room in waves. It was an enormous attic room, a family bazaar, littered with toys and battered furniture and the leftovers of the day, still lying where they had been dropped by the three small children who were now asleep in the next room. She took Jason in to see them after supper, sprawling in cots arranged one on top of another. Ilona covered them up again with the blankets and closed the door.

'People may tell you it was the ideal state for working mothers,' she said to Jason, 'but it's not true. Not for me. Didi, aren't you going to offer us anything to drink?'

Deichmann got up and went to a cupboard.

'We never did things their way. Oh, you could. You could do things your own way, if you made a little bit of an effort. How long have we been married, Didi?'

'Nine years,' her husband answered, head inside the cupboard, his voice muffled.

'Have you got children, Mr Gould?'

'No,' said Jason. 'I like children, but I've never had children of my own.'

'Well, in this country, you probably would. Then you'd be given somewhere to live, you see. Of course, that's not a reason for having children. But if you're going to have them, the sooner the better, because then you can apply to the state for family accommodation. That's how most people here think. You have a right to it. But I was already twenty-five when Charlotte was born.'

Deichmann put an array of bottles on the table and explained what was inside them. His wife sat on the sofa, watching her husband with what Jason thought was an expression of amusement, just the hint of a smile at the corners of her lips.

'Why have you brought them all over here? Do we need to see all of those bottles? Mr Gould is going to get the impression we're alcoholics, and will write something critical about the drinking problems they have in socialist states.'

'Do they?'

'Oh, terrible.'

Ilona laughed.

'The drinking is the least of the problems, but it's the one you see on the surface. Well, anyway. What was I saying, Didi?'

'You wanted to tell Mr Gould about the nursery where you worked.'

'Oh, yes. When Charlotte was born I had a year off and continued to receive my salary. After the birth the mother would normally go back to work and leave the child in a state care centre, but that's not what I did. Not after all I'd seen – I used to work in one of those places.'

She took a sip from the glass and put it on the table.

'The place where I worked we looked after babies in the one-to-three age group. They were left there by the working mothers on Monday morning and picked up again on Friday afternoon. They were weekly boarding babies. Imagine! Normally we had one member of staff for ten babies, but at night there were only two of us on duty in charge of sixty children. Well, you can imagine what it was like. Sixty cots in one room, each with its little mound. Some of the older children woke up in the night and cried and cried. It was heartbreaking. When Charlotte was one and it was time for me to go back to work, and I imagined her lying in one of those sixty cots, I thought no, not for us. You can't do that to a child, can you?'

'No,' agreed Jason.

'Didi earned quite a decent salary, and we had some savings, so we could make a go of it. And that was the first thing that sort of edged us out of the mainstream, because all mothers, nearly all mothers, went back to work when their year was up. The state did everything to encourage them to do so. I suppose I would have as well, if I hadn't known. Anyway, I didn't, thank God. It was the same thing again when the children reached kindergarten age. State kindergartens were free, of course, but we didn't want to send ours off to one of those places. People say they had no alternative, but they did. There were kindergartens run privately by the Church, and you had to pay, but you could make ends meet by doing without something else.'

'So that's how you got involved with the Church, and the politics that went with the Church?' asked Jason.

Ilona nodded.

'There was all that business about re-armament, and the Church was organising prayers for peace, and the next thing we knew we had become dissidents, undesirable elements in our socialist society. But all Didi and I had wanted was more of a say in the education of our children. You see how easily one thing leads on to the other. The next is that Didi will be out of a job. I expect lots of people soon will be. But with us it'll be voluntary. We're going to do things our way. Didi's going back to school to study theology. Having come this far . . . Didi's going to become a pastor, aren't you, Didi?'

She took her husband's hand and clasped it in her lap, the smile that always hovered at the corners of her mouth beginning to spread its wings, as if it had alighted and now settled permanently on her face.

14

Half an hour before the five o'clock service began, the Nikolaikirche was packed. The people waiting in the church were expectant but quiet. The times of conspiracy and persecution they associated with this building were now over, and the atmosphere within its walls seemed to be a reflection of their triumph. It was a beautiful church, flooded with light. The columns along the centre aisle soared, like a sharp intake of breath, floating the roof, detached among airy shadows above.

Friedrich Magirius walked quickly to the lectern in the centre aisle and at once began to talk. His subject was the fate of Erich Honecker. No doubt everyone here had heard that the former dictator and his wife had just been offered asylum by the Church, Magirius said, and he was aware that the present mood in the country would make the Church very unpopular. He could understand people's feelings. But the Church was there to help everyone in need, 'Everyone,' he repeated with emphasis.

Standing at the lectern in a dark suit, the dean of East Leipzig gave the impression less of pastor of this church than of a layman invited to address the congregation. There were no flourishes. His appearance was unobtrusive and matter-of-fact. He spoke in a monotone, as if delivering a bulletin, but sometimes the compact voice could dramatically shift its register, unfolding an unexpected resonance and power.

'Two destitute people have been given a roof over their heads. Despite the injustice of the regime for which they were responsible, despite the hypocrisy of the Socialist Party they represented. When I hear people demand that Honecker and his wife should be handed over to the authorities, I wonder if it's a scapegoat they're demanding in order to clear themselves. Sometimes that is my impression.'

There was a pause for the interpreter for the deaf, who was standing in the aisle in front of Magirius, to catch up with what he was saying.

'The hymn we shall now be singing should be on the sheet you will find in front of you. It's not such a problem getting copies printed as it used to be in the past.'

A murmur of amusement rippled through the congregation, and everyone stood to sing the hymn. Magirius then read the lesson. His text was the passage from I Corinthians 13. Charity had never been a more topical subject, he said, than it was on this Monday afternoon, a clear reference to the mass demonstration that would be taking place that evening in the square outside the church, as it had been every week for many months past. There was no mistaking that in recent weeks the mood of the crowd had become shrilly inquisitorial and increasingly nationalistic.

When the service was over Jason went to the dean's office behind the church. Three eager women, generating the friendly, somewhat fussy atmosphere that seems to surround clergymen everywhere, sat at their desks in an overheated room. A plump lady with a stooping gait, one hand sliding her necklace back and forth, got up and went discreetly ahead, her head bowed, like an usher. Jason was shown upstairs and asked to take a seat in the passage.

Magirius appeared ten minutes later, apologising and breathless. Standing there in his crumpled dark suit, he seemed a much slighter figure than he had at the service. He was nervous and awkward, with none of the authority Jason had seen him demonstrate as chairman of the proceedings in the Town Hall or as pastor in the church. It was like meeting an actor in his dressing-room after watching his performance on stage. He was almost not recognisable as the same person.

'Isn't it a little warm in here? Would you mind if I opened the window?'

Magirius sat down on the bench under the window and crossed

his legs, leaning slightly forward, his shoulders hunched, his eyes shifting restlessly. It was a defensive, even wary attitude, and Jason wondered why.

They chatted for a while about the dean's various responsibilities in Leipzig and Jason mentioned the difference he had noted between the Church in West and East Germany. Here the Church struck him as a more vigorous institution, he said, presumably because it had more urgent needs. He told Magirius that in a few days he would be meeting a man in Berlin with whom he was making a documentary about the changes that were taking place in the country. In its role as unofficial opposition under the Socialist Party's dictatorship, the Church had played an important part during the past ten years in helping to bring those changes about. Nobody knew that better than the pastor of the Nikolaikirche, who had helped to set rolling a ball which had gained nationwide momentum the previous autumn and had finally led to the overthrow of the state. Had the Church become a political forum by accident or design?

'The gospel isn't in a vacuum,' replied Magirius without a moment's hesitation, as if reading his text off a teleprompter. 'It's addressed to real people in real life, of which politics is a part. Our job is to show the relevance of the one to the other. Religion is not something that exists in its own right. That is the foundation, as it were, of the building we hoped we should see rise after everything that has come to a head in these past few months. How did it all begin? It began with the escalation of the armaments race in the early eighties, which took place against people's wishes. I arrived in Leipzig at that time to take up my new position. Before that I had been working in an effort to bring about reconciliation between Germany and the outside world, because of the wrongs we had done in the war. I was pleased to find a lot of people already active here in the same endeavour, and it was these people with whom I joined together in an undertaking called Prayers for Peace. The only place people could give voice to their concern was in the church. Whenever they ventured out on to the square to hold a vigil with candles, the police intervened, and they fled back into the church. It became our task to give these people protection.'

'And that began here in the Nikolaikirche.'

'That began here. But not only here. It's thanks to Wonneberger, from the Lukaskirche, that people spoke out against the state for failing to honour the Helsinki Charter of Human Rights, which the GDR had ratified on paper but continued to ignore in practice. Wonneberger was moving outside the bounds of accepted opposition from the Church, and although, of course, that's wholly to his credit . . .'

Magirius shifted in his chair, and Jason sensed that they had touched on a sensitive spot.

He listened inside himself to the echoes of that phrase 'the bounds of accepted opposition', which in a German context could never be disentangled from the question of the bounds of expected obedience. Jason had heard rumours around town that the dean had given less support to the opposition in the past than might reasonably have been expected. There was some resentment that he had afterwards reaped what was seen as the glory which rightfully belonged to his more outspoken colleague from the Lukaskirche. Jason had the impression that here, too, Magirius wanted to make amends, and that making amends one way or another had been the entire business of this German pastor's life.

Jason felt sympathy. Here was a man who was a native of Dresden, and almost certainly had his own losses to mourn in that city. The circumstances of his birth had cast him in the role of apologist for crimes committed by others in the name of his country. Jason wondered about the ambiguities of such a position, in which the high moral tone must surely be under cross-examination by contrary instincts of self-preservation, as was only natural, and how in time this kind of self-denial must become almost intolerable. Or was there satisfaction, perhaps even an outlet for inadmissible vanity, in the psychology of atonement? The pastors, after all, were now the true celebrities of this country, which went some of the way towards explaining why people like Deichmann were eager to give up their jobs and hurrying to take holy orders. There was even a recognisable physical mould in which they were cast, with the long hair and gaunt wildness of a John the Baptist after his sojourn in the desert,

as one might imagine him in a Dürer etching. Had something akin
to *Durch Leiden Freude* resurfaced in the disposition of Germany at
the close of its disastrous century, some kind of wellbeing in the
humiliation of atonement, some kind of masochism?

'That, at any rate, was Wonneberger's achievement at the time,'
Magirius continued, 'while we at the Nikolaikirche took a different
view. We were against the idea of turning the Church into a platform
for political discussions. For whatever we did, we were answerable to
the authorities. To them we spoke as citizens of the state, not as
people of the Church, when we told them what we regarded as the
ills in this society. Church leaders in Berlin took up these issues
with the authorities time and again, to no avail.'

'Yet they continued to respect the sanctuary of the Church . . .'

'The state didn't dare intrude inside the church.'

'Why did the opposition emerge from Leipzig in particular?'

'The opposition that gathered in the churches of Leipzig was
itself formed by the problems of this city, which were even worse
than elsewhere, but protest movements had independently got
underway in other places as well, of course. The decay of cities and
the pollution of the environment, these problems were particularly
acute in Leipzig. Things began to get tense with the extradition of a
group of people from Berlin early in 1988, and from the spring of
that year until the mass exodus in the summer of 1989 the prayers
for peace were at the centre of the protest movement. It gave people
hope, and courage. With the exodus of thousands of refugees that
summer, the atmosphere was transformed overnight. For the first
time people had the courage to take their convictions out of the
churches and on to the streets. All of this happened so late with us
because those who might have had the force and energy to change
things had already left the country.'

Magirius sat hunched over the table and looked at Jason. There
was a pained, haunted look in his eyes.

'It's bad when houses are left to become ruins, but houses can be
repaired. It's bad when the environment is polluted, but industry
can be changed. But when people have been misdirected for forty
years, and have learned to shut themselves off only so that they can

somehow muddle through, damage has been done which it will be
very difficult to repair.'

A sudden surge of voices reached them through the window,
reminding him of the demonstration now taking place in the square.
What the voices were chanting was unmistakable, even at a distance.
It was the chant with which it had all begun.

'*Wir sind das Volk! Wir sind das Volk!*'

'What the people claiming to be the people want is unification of
the two German states,' said Jason, with a nod in the direction of
the window, thinking: *Volk*, idealised and transcendent, symbolising
a unity beyond any political reality. Where had he read that? He
turned back to Magirius and asked: 'Do you see an alternative?'

'With the sudden opening of the borders something was done to
us all at once that should have been done gently and gradually,'
Magirius answered. 'I don't wish to be misunderstood – it is now too
late and the opportunity for the alternative has gone, and I regret
that it has – but this is the most irresponsible action one could have
taken. People here are wholly unprepared to cope with the mirage of
the golden West. All they can see is their share of the riches. They see
unification just round the corner, tomorrow or the day after. The
expectations are so enormous that any suggestion of rolling up one's
shirt-sleeves and having a go at something new—'

Magirius broke off.

Jason said: 'I admired the way you chaired the meeting in the
Town Hall. It was refreshing to see the representatives of the new left
sitting at the same table as the chief of police and giving him a piece
of their mind. But you had to shove the motion through.
Democracy, fine, but only if it doesn't cost anything. The old guard
wasn't giving an inch.'

Magirius shook his head.

'I have to say I'm discouraged. We shall go the way of least
resistance, and that will be reunification. Even if Brandt speaks of the
two German states growing together, some of us here feel strongly
that they should still be growing together as something *really* new,
something that was never there before. Our history is already so
burdened that any fusion of the two states as one must inevitably

cause misgivings about what direction a united Germany will take. I thought we were laying the foundations for a new building, a sovereign, democratic and independent Germany within the borders of our former republic, but during the last six months I have watched what we were building being overwhelmed and swept away, a makeshift hut carried off like a straw, as if a dam had burst.'

The rhythm of the crowd's roar was changing. Moments later the pounding syllables of its new chant came thundering over from Karl Marx Square. *Deutschland, Deutschland!* By the time Jason reached the square he had difficulty making his way through the crowd of fifty thousand people now gathered there. He was quickly sucked into it, unable to move forward or back as the people around him, swaying in mass delirium, took up the refrain, '*Deutschland einig Vaterland*', and the colours unfurling, black, red and gold, seemed to echo the chant in the pennants snatched at angrily by the wind that swept across the square.

15

From Dresden Jason drove north through the Niederlausitz into Brandenburg, trying to imagine how it had changed since Elena had lived here, and then turned east. He followed the border up until he arrived at Holm, shortly after noon. A few miles to the east of the village lay land that had belonged to the estate. It had been a part of Germany until the end of the war. Now it was in Poland.

The two large country houses in a park surrounded by a brick wall were visible from the end of the village street. Looking north, he could see the roof turrets and the church spire just as they were indicated on Elena's sketch. At the south end of the village she had marked a farm, and the name Kruse. The farmhouse was still there, set back from the road. It was in Kruse's driveway, if Kruse's it still was, that Jason had just parked his car.

He stood thinking for a few moments, then walked back to the car and took out a map. He went down the track into a courtyard enclosed by farm buildings. He turned and looked round.

A man was sitting on a bench outside the farmhouse, smoking a cigarette. Jason wished him good day and said he was lost, and asked for directions to Berlin.

'Oh! That's a way.'

They spread his map out on the bench, and the man pointed and explained. A woman came out of the house with a cup of coffee for the man, who was presumably her husband. Finding Jason squatting beside him, poring over the map, she asked him if it was his car out in the driveway, and would he care for a cup of coffee while he was here?

'A black Audi, very smart,' she said to the man, and then the man wanted to go round and have a look at the Audi, too. They were amazed to hear that already a car like this could be rented in Leipzig.

The couple was called Kruse. Jason had noticed the white enamel plate on the door by the bench while the man was giving him directions. He looked about thirty-eight or forty, so the young man whom Elena remembered farming the land when she lived at Holm as a girl must have been this man's father. They sat talking in the sun. Jason asked him about the farm. At first Kruse's answers came reluctantly, in a trickle, and then the words began to pour out of him in a torrent.

Kruse said that his family had been on the land since the end of the eighteenth century. After the war, under state agricultural planning, his father had been driven to the brink of ruin. There was no specialisation, and farm management became totally uneconomic. Farmers were required to deliver quotas of almost everything, not only grain and livestock, but vegetables, wool, tobacco and spices.

By the time Kruse was growing up, in the 1960s, the policy had been reversed to the opposite extreme. Specialisation became the order of the day. His father looked after livestock that did not belong to him on land that had been turned over to the co-operative and was no longer effectively his either. Many farmers had fled to the West and taken jobs in the cities. Kruse stayed on. He went to university, studied agricultural engineering and became the senior administrator of the Holm co-operative in the same year his father died.

'Each of us did his own job without knowing what the others were doing. We were cogs in a machine. But because there was no co-ordination, the cogs were just turning in space, and not driving a machine at all. The scale on which things were done here was simply too large. You never got a picture of the whole. I had a relatively well-paid job, but I couldn't stand it, the inefficiency and the waste, and I asked for a transfer. I became a swineherd instead. With my training as an agricultural engineer! People become careless when they don't have a personal responsibility for what they're doing. I'd see things get broken on the farm and it made me angry, because in my heart I still thought, had always thought, of the farm as mine.'

'Didn't it make you angry that you couldn't come and go as a free person?'

Kruse shook his head.

'Growing up here, one accepted things as one found them. With the farm it was different, because Dad was there, always reminding me that it was really his, and that one day it would be mine. But as for the rest . . . I didn't have the feeling I wasn't a free man.'

'And now?'

'Now I get up in the morning and stand at the window looking down into the yard, and it's a different feeling, a feeling I can't describe,' said Kruse.

When Jason looked up in the silence that followed he was surprised to see tears running down Kruse's face.

It wasn't until the end of their conversation that Jason asked about the two houses at the far end of the village in the park that had once belonged to Elena's family. The family had lived there even longer than the Kruses had been on their farm. Kruse said he was heading up there himself, to the co-operative, and would give him a lift on the tractor if he wanted to see the place.

On Elena's sketch of Holm an avenue of linden trees extended from the gate to the first of the two large country houses set back in the park, but all the trees had gone. Kruse brought up the subject of the linden avenue himself. He was familiar with it from photographs. According to his father, the lindens had been felled, along with all the other old trees in the park, in the cold winter of 1947, when the villagers had nothing else to burn.

Perhaps it was the lack of trees, in winter the lack of any other vegetation, that made the house appear so stark, as if the treeless avenue leading up to it had ditched it there in the emptiness, almost out of spite.

The banked stairway that Jason remembered from old photographs his father had taken on his visit to Holm in 1934 had disappeared. It must have been dismantled. It had once led up from either side to the entrance of the house, which was now used by the co-operative as an office. All the windows on the upper floor were

shuttered. Jason followed Kruse up some concrete steps into a dark
hall with muddy floorboards. Notices hung on the wall above a row
of rubber boots. A length of washing line hung from a hook in the
wall behind the door, the noose at its end presumably used to slip
over the handle and hold the door open in summer. Everything here
was makeshift, and the makeshift had endured.

Kruse went clattering into a room at the end of the hall; an enormous room, perhaps formerly a ballroom. Stripped of furnishings
and curtains, the empty room echoed their footsteps as they came in.
Another provisional encampment, a desk with a couple of chairs,
stood against the wall just inside the entrance. An iron stove on
thin legs, looking like a stag-beetle, squatted in front of the fireplace,
a pipe sticking out at one end leading up the chimney. That was all.
They glanced round the room and went out again.

Kruse disappeared in search of the person he had come to talk to
at the co-operative, and Jason wandered over to the house on the
other side of the park. Kruse said it had been converted into an old
people's home.

He remembered Elena telling him that the two identical houses
had been built in the late sixteenth or early seventeenth century for
twin brothers. Their similarity was echoed in the noticeboards just
inside the entrance. For some reason it was less dark here, and a strip
of lighter colour, running round the noticeboard like a frame, was
clearly visible, marking the spot on the wall where a larger picture
must originally have hung. The corresponding room at the end of
the hall had been turned into a refectory. Two women were already
laying the tables for supper, although it was still early in the afternoon. The evening meal was served at seven, he had read on the
noticeboard, and inmates were requested to be punctual. Everything
smacked of the brisk regimen one would expect in a hospital.

Upstairs there was a smell of beeswax in the passage, and a glint
of recent polish on the floorboards showing on either side of the
carpet, made of jute or some coarse material, which ran down the
middle. He walked down the corridor in the direction of a faint
sound of music. The new doors let into the wall at intervals along
the passage indicated the conversions that had taken place here.

Many smaller rooms had been made out of a few larger ones. He passed a door which stood half open, giving him a glimpse into the room where the music was coming from. Reaching the end of the passage, he turned and made his way back, pausing at the half-open door to look inside the tiny room.

An old lady sat with her back to him on the side of a bed. She was picking up framed photographs that stood on a table beside the bed, and dusting them with a handkerchief. One by one she held them close to her face, as if to see them better, and replaced them carefully, arranging them in a semi-circle on the table. He watched her in silence for a few moments, with a pang of sadness that mushroomed and spread inside him as he continued down the passage and went back outside. On the opposite side of the house he came across the other old people on the glass-panelled terrace, facing west. Wrapped up in coats and blankets, they sat stiff and motionless in the disused conservatory like winter plants, drowsing in the afternoon sun that poured over the lawn and rolled back the melting frost, leaving a powdery white margin, like a tide-mark, untouched in the shadow along the house.

1990
September to
October

1

Elena stood on the terrace outside her house and felt the heat rising off the stones. It was a hot autumn afternoon. Not a leaf stirred in the vineyards around the house. From the Montreux end of the lake she looked towards Geneva in the haze. There must have been something of a breeze blowing below. White sails dotted the lake, but not perceptibly moving, reminding her rather of starched napkins standing on a table.

She moved along the terrace from window to window, closing the shutters. She moved back, stooping to water the plants along the house wall, and looked out under the brim of her hat at the Mont Blanc Massif, blocking out the sky on the far side of the lake. Upwards of two thousand metres, yesterday's rain had fallen overnight as snow, dusting the summit and the surrounding peaks with a sprinkle of white that sparkled in the afternoon sun.

Elena went back into the house to finish packing her suitcase. She was reluctant to leave the house: she liked its beautiful surroundings, and the beautiful objects inside it. She liked its smallness. The house fitted her. She had Sophie to thank for it.

When she was so ill after Jens died she came and stayed with Sophie for several months. They drove along the lake, and Sophie noticed the little house for sale among the vines. She rang the agent and arranged to view the property. It was a winter afternoon. Elena stood in the little room upstairs overlooking the terrace and saw the lake and the mountains beyond. A muted shaft of sunlight slanted into the room. Inside her exhaustion Elena felt something stir.

She bought the house. Buying it proved to be the turning point. At the time it wasn't certain if she had recovered or was going to die.

For months she just seemed to linger, unsure whether she wanted to make the effort. After selling the big old house in Grunewald and buying an apartment nearer the centre of Berlin, Elena still had enough money left over to buy the house. She didn't tell Jason. She wanted it to be entirely her house. It is the house where I shall retire, she said to herself. The previous year, when she turned sixty, she had moved permanently from Berlin to the village overlooking Lake Geneva.

'You'll get lonely there,' Jason objected.

'No I won't. There's Sophie just down the road. And for quite a lot of the time you'll be coming to stay.'

The house was built into the side of the hill. A terrace of white stones jutted out into the vineyard. House and terrace formed the single open space on a hillside covered with vines. Looking down on it, as she reached the top of the village street and turned on to the main road, Elena was reminded of the house in Grunewald in the clearing in the forest.

She arrived at the outskirts of Geneva in half an hour. There was a lot of traffic in the city centre, and it took as long again to reach the clinic tucked away in the old town. No one was in the waiting-room. She heard the cars pass in the street below, the sound of doors opening and closing and people walking down the corridor. Elena liked coming to the clinic. It was a safe enclosure where she felt relaxed. People here looked after her.

At last she was able to place herself in someone's care, and the burden she had carried all her life seemed to be taken from her shoulders.

2

In the place called Gethsemane stood her mother's bed, but her mother could not sleep, for her soul was sometimes exceedingly sorrowful, even unto death. The pastor came to Holm and read the lesson in the chapel. Once a fortnight, the family and the staff assembled there for the service. Elena's ancestors lived on in the inscriptions on the chapel walls. Her mother had told her that. Those were her words. Although they were dead, her ancestors lived on. They lived on as part of the ritual that was celebrated once a fortnight in the chapel at Holm, thanks to Him, whose love was so great that he laid down his life for mankind, including Elena's ancestors. He had redeemed them, so that they might partake of everlasting life.

The chapel, like everything at Holm, lived on in Elena's memory with a richness of detail unsurpassed by recollections later in her life. It was a cool, dark enclosure, compounded of odours that could still prick her nostrils, causing her to differentiate between the leather and dust of the prayerbook and the dankness of the green mould growing at the bottom of the chapel wall. These impressions characterised the place called Gethsemane, a cool dark greenness whose dank smell gave warning of something lurking, the betrayal of Jesus after he had gone to the garden to pray with his disciples. Gethsemane was the place of sorrow, and so was her mother's bedroom.

During the times Sophie was overcome by *Schwermut*, Elena was brought to her mother's bedroom and listened to her lament. When they were overcome by *Schwermut* and became exceedingly sorrowful, her mother sought refuge in her bedroom, Christ in the place called Gethsemane. They both suffered from the same sickness of the soul.

Elena froze, immobile, struggling to stay awake. She must stay awake at all costs. This was why Sophie fetched her into her bedroom, to share her sorrow and listen to her lament.

In the chapel the pastor read the lesson that became engraved on Elena's heart. She felt compassion for Christ in the cool dark greenness of the place called Gethsemane where he went to pray with his disciples. He asked them to watch and pray with him, but the flesh was weak and they fell asleep. Christ came upon one of the sleeping disciples and asked: 'Sleepest thou? Couldest not thou watch one hour?' Elena felt shame and sorrow for the weakness of the disciples' love. She saw herself sitting upright at the end of her mother's bed, locking her fingers and gripping her knees tight in order to stay awake. Had she been in Gethsemane, Elena would not have fallen asleep. She would have gripped her knees until the knuckes went white. She would have comforted Him.

In the mythology Elena created for her life, the place called Gethsemane became a permanent installation. It took shape around that bed where her mother spoke to her of her troubles at night, and Elena sat rigid, gripping her knees in order to stay awake.

She envisaged herself as a clearing in the forest. Surrounded by darkness, she was the space full of light through which the forest breathed.

In Elena's mythology of love ran a strong current of discipline, of duty and self-sacrifice. In her dramatisation of love she cast herself as the heroine who sacrificed herself for her love of others.

The mythology of love as self-sacrifice imposed an obligation not only on Elena but on those to whom she entrusted herself. There was a strong framework of idealisation within which she loved, and expected to be loved in return. For Elena, love became inseparable from compassion. Love acquired and retained for her a specific meaning.

The meaning of love was to stay awake in order to give comfort to the person whose soul was sorrowful even unto death.

3

The past lived in Elena, but Elena did not live in the past.
When she met Jason at Grunewald station, it was not Jason who travelled back into the past to discover the resemblance to her mother but her mother who came forward to be incarnated in Jason in the present. From the moment her mother was able to live on in Jason, Elena felt less need to remind herself of her mother in order to keep her memory alive.

Because the past lived in Elena and not Elena in the past, it changed as her life changed. At different moments in her life she saw the past in different perspectives. She reappraised it. She saw a different past.

A figure in the background, one that had always been obscured by her mother in the foreground, came forward into the light after Jens' death. This was not her grandmother, who remained the shadow in Elena's memory that she must have been when Elena was a child at Holm, but the person who had been Holm's bright and tranquil spirit, Aunt Etta.

Etta stood for the sense of permanence that surrounded Holm. She embodied constancy, with a serene trust consolidated under conditions of life which had not greatly changed on the estate during the centuries before Elena was born. Behind the turbulence that began to rumble as the estate moved forward into the twentieth century, the greater turbulence of war, famine, inflation, social unrest, the smaller turbulence of Sophie's divorce and unhappiness after returning to Holm from Berlin, Etta had guaranteed continuity in the family's life at Holm. Yet not until later in her own life did Elena recognise how important Aunt Etta must have been for the clear sense of identity that Elena possessed even as a child.

When Jens died, she felt his absence in death more strongly than she had felt his presence in life. It was only with the distance of years, when at last Etta's figure emerged from the background, approaching her with hurried, belated steps across the enormous sunlit lawn of her childhood, that Elena understood what had drawn her to Jens.

Jens was Etta's messenger. He brought back to Elena Etta's reassurance of continuity. Around her he recreated the level landscape that had surrounded Holm. But the levelness accompanying Jens remained by its nature unobtrusive, associated with a quality of flatness that spread out and had already gained too much ground in their married life before Elena became aware of it.

As a young woman, she felt herself to be living in a landscape of dramatic contrasts. She had a rising and falling rhythm, rising steeply to meet challenges, falling off sharply from disappointments. In the dramatisation of Elena's life, she contrived to remain a heroine even when her theme was self-effacement and she made sacrifices that went unrecognised.

When the texture of her life seemed to her to have become too thin and flat, she could turn reproachfully on Jens in her disappointment, in much the way her mother had turned on Etta, whose equanimity sometimes bordered on indifference, and ask sorrowfully, 'Sleepest thou? Couldest not thou watch one hour?'

Sometimes Elena was left with no option but to make herself the object of her own compassion. Surrounded by flatness, she had to devise pretexts for her rising and falling rhythm which were sometimes so artificial that they made her seem like a woman it was impossible to please. Afterwards she would respond to the provocation she had initiated; she showed remorse, did penance, was as good as gold.

If Elena saw herself as the clearing full of light through which the surrounding forest breathed, this image was nourished in her by Etta, not by her mother, on whose behalf the image took shape. Sophie's original image, the first, ineradicable image of her mother, was one of darkness in the forest and the wind passing through the branches making a sound of *Vergänglichkeit*, sorrowful even unto death.

Both images, of the forest labouring in darkness and the clearing full of light through which it breathed, were inherited by Elena from the two persons to whom she was closest, her mother and Aunt Etta. Both images were carried on by their successors. Instinctively she recognised the old patterns from her childhood when they reappeared, and she was able to sustain them throughout her adult life. She had chosen them. The same level landscape of tranquillity she associated with Etta surrounded Jens. The same rising and falling rhythm of her mother's sway of feelings, a butterfly opening and closing its wings, hovered over Jason the moment she first saw him, and settled on him for life.

In this convergence of patterns, perhaps attributable to an obscure force of Attraction of Affinities, there was a clear sense of order in Elena's life. She recognised the limitations of her own, of the human scope. She did not expect variety. Her deepest ties would always be formed around resemblances to the ties that had been there first. The thread running through the pattern (which Elena recognised as the thread of her destiny) could only be so clear because of the clarity that was in Elena herself. Inside herself she felt a space in the forest that was full of light and a sense of purpose to her life that she could only have described as the will to happiness.

4

When the war ended, Elena was confronted with the documentary evidence of the German crime almost casually, in a newsreel, which was shown before the main feature starring Ginger Rogers and Fred Astaire – a stupendous, unbelievable shot of bulldozers shoving a pile of skeletons into a pit.

Elena didn't stay for the main feature. She felt unable to watch. She left the cinema. She was sixteen, and it was a death sentence. She felt sure the immense pile of corpses with which she had been confronted would block out whatever trivial happiness might have been awaiting her on the other side for as long as she lived – for the remainder of her entire life.

She felt herself called upon to hold a vigil on behalf of the holocaust dead. Beside her mother's death in an air raid at the end of the war, the deaths of countless relatives and friends and the disappearance of Holm behind the Iron Curtain, she mourned the millions murdered in the concentration camps as if they had been her own dead. It was as if the nights spent watching on her mother's bed had been in preparation for this infinitely greater task.

She lived in Berlin-Grunewald, not far from the station where the Jewish population of the city had been transported to be murdered in the camps, and she could feel them wandering around in the forest, the restless souls of the dead, returning to the place from which they had set out. She thought daily of them. She thought good thoughts for them in a place that was full of light. She consoled and appeased them, reprimanding herself if she even briefly forgot them. 'Couldest thou not watch one hour?' Elena heard the pastor's voice in the chapel at Holm, and she burned with shame. She kept up her vigil for ten years.

When she lapsed she would burn with shame, a sharp, physical pain as if she had been stung all over her body. But she did not feel guilty. She felt compassion in the face of the holocaust dead, and shame when she discovered they sometimes slipped out of her consciousness. But guilt never found its way into Elena's mind.

There was a lot of talk of the German guilt, and Elena did not know what to do with it. What did that mean, German guilt? Both the national pride before the war and the national guilt after it were alien categories to her. They did not fit into her understanding of things, and she had no use for them. She did not know any women who had use for them. Men had made them up. It was men who got excited about them.

Elena followed the legal hair-splitting that accompanied the question of war guilt, and found the intellectual constructions of law artificial and distasteful, deplorable, in the face of a tragedy whose victims she mourned as if they had been her own dead. In the course of all the abstract analysis and argument that screened off the subject, the victims were already beginning to disappear, after only a few years.

For Elena what mattered was sorrow. There was that feeling first and foremost, and for a long time after that came nothing else.

Perhaps it was by an Attraction of Affinities that Elena found herself drawn into the café in Vienna where she met the woman who had the same name as her mother. Sophie was ten years older than Elena, at thirty a woman while Elena at twenty was still a girl. She was Jewish, with one sister, one co-survivor of the extended family that had lived in Vienna before the war. All of these qualities – the Jew, the survivor, the friend who was at the same time a mother figure – converged in the person of Sophie to make possible Elena's eventual release from the bondage in which she was held by the holocaust.

Elena fell in love with Sophie, in many strands of love it would have been impossible to untwist from the baffling skein of admiration and envy, humility, a yearning for approval, a yearning for redemption, both the sensual fascination and the feelings of repulsion aroused in her by a woman she felt in so many ways to be alien.

Sophie was a bohemian. She couldn't cook or sew; sloppy at home, she became extraordinarily stylish the minute she stepped out of the door. She ate in restaurants, spent her evenings in bars and clubs, where she always found men (in those days, they were all Americans) to pick up the tab. She surrounded herself with an aura of luxurious femininity that fascinated Elena, who kept nothing more alluring than soap on the bathroom shelf, and who at twenty still wore her hair in plaits.

For several months she stayed in Sophie's apartment and kept house for her. She wanted to serve, and Sophie, with a mixture of amusement, affection and shrewdness, readily allowed her to do so.

When Elena was a little girl she had heard someone say that true beauty was always coupled with lack of vanity. With every glance in the mirror, a woman forfeited something of her beauty. From that day on, Elena made a point of not looking in mirrors. She took care not to look in mirrors in the same way she took care not to fall asleep when it was her responsibility to watch on her mother's bed in Gethsemane. Not looking in mirrors became a fulfilment of duty. Having a goal, and the ambition to reach it, and the will to do so – this was Elena's character. Of course, it was partly because it happened to have been shaped that way by her Prussian upbringing, but it wasn't just that.

The war had interrupted her education, and it was not resumed after the war ended. Intellectual stimulus and challenge were things she had to learn to provide for herself. Setting herself tasks was an activity that allowed her to compete against herself. She busied herself; she issued challenges to herself. The conversations she held with herself, the competitions she held against herself, were a measure of her imaginativeness and self-sufficiency. Elena's way of not looking in mirrors also shared something of the superstitious but playful way she still took care not to step on cracks in the pavement, even when she was twenty.

Sophie taught Elena to look in mirrors. She gave her expensive perfumes and showed her other ways of doing her hair. Elena looked in the mirror to please Sophie, but she kept her fingers crossed when she was doing so, telling herself that it didn't count.

One might imagine Sophie and Elena as figures in a fairytale. Sophie's role is that of the wicked stepmother. Jealous of Elena's purity and beauty, she attempts to corrupt her. Sophie gave Elena the cup to drink from and waited for the fateful drop that would be her doom to fall between cup and lip, but it never did. Elena was incorruptible. She was like a charmed figure in a fairytale, guarded by a talisman which warded off all harm.

What was the secret of Elena's innocence? What was her magic talisman? Sophie tried to find out. Sometimes she asked Elena to come into her bed, so that she could breathe in her scent and surround herself with it when she fell asleep. The young woman in the bed beside her felt so light, she herself by contrast so heavy and dark. Sophie put her arms round Elena and drew her to her breast. She felt herself dark and heavy, a forest encircling a fragrant clearing that was full of light.

Sophie's exhalations, all the darkness and sorrow that came streaming out of her, passed through Elena and seemed to be purged. Sophie saw it through her tears, through all the horrors she had behind her, baffled that such a thing was possible.

She saw a brightness at the core, despite the horrors a will to happiness which Elena mysteriously preserved inside herself.

5

Sophie married a rich American who had made a fortune with patents in the textile industry, and moved with him to Geneva. They lived in a palatial villa on the lake with a house in the grounds for the cook and the butler. Her husband also bought Sophie an apartment in town for the times when she preferred to be alone. Occasionally she stayed there overnight, and always when Bill was away on business. Bill had bought the apartment in her name – it was one of the conditions she had his lawyers set down in black and white in the marriage contract.

Bill was a friendly man from a small-town background in Missouri. Elena liked him, and he liked Elena. She had an open invitation to come and stay. For Elena the house was wonderland. It had an elevator, a cocktail bar with a bowling alley, a movie theatre where Bill watched pornographic films with Sophie, and a bathroom made entirely of glass. Bill liked to bowl and to watch movies, especially westerns, but these things bored Sophie.

When Elena came to visit she played bowls and watched westerns with Bill, otherwise he usually did so on his own. Sometimes be brought clients home and played bowls with them, but Sophie never joined in. When Bill came home from the office she never got up to fix him a drink. Mostly she wasn't even there. Sophie never did anything for Bill, except sit and watch pornographic films with him, at least in the first few years of their marriage.

It amused her to see Bill and Elena playing bowls together. At dinner one night, in the Alhambra patio, she suggested they had an affair. She came out with it just like that, in front of the butler and Bill's business partners and their wives. Elena felt ashamed for him, but Bill laughed it off.

Why did Bill put up with it? Why had he married Sophie in the first place?

'I'm the zany in Bill's menagerie,' Sophie once said casually to Elena. 'He's a collector of exotic items. Hadn't you noticed?'

Elena was attracted to Sophie because she was so different from herself. She stood outside, looking into Sophie's life with Bill, surrounded by what seemed to Elena to be fabulous wealth, each of them isolated within the contractual arrangement they called marriage, each of them the acquisition in the other's menagerie (Bill always in the row behind Sophie in the house movie theatre where they watched pornographic films, because Bill needed that to be able to make love to his wife), and Elena, looking in, felt like a voyeur, repelled and excited at the same time.

Sometimes she became Sophie's accomplice. They stayed overnight at the apartment in town, to have a girls' night, Sophie told Bill, although she was in fact meeting a lover. When Sophie had lovers in the apartment, Elena lay in her room and read. Afterwards, when she met Bill, Elena always felt uncomfortable about having deceived him, but Sophie didn't care.

Elena invited her to Berlin, but Sophie said she would never set foot in Germany again. She met Jens and Jason only once, at the chalet Bill owned near Martigny. Sophie and Bill were always very generous to Elena. They told her to take the chalet whenever she liked, and Elena came down one summer with Jason and Jens for a vacation in the mountains. Bill drove over with Sophie for lunch. It wasn't a success. Elena tried to bring together two sides of her life, and they didn't match.

But it was because Sophie was so different from her that Elena found herself drawn to her. When Elena saw how different Sophie's life was, how different things could be, she questioned her own. She saw that there were alternatives to the quiet existence she led in Grunewald, surrounded by the forest. When she was staying with Sophie in Geneva she was able to stand outside her own life and look at it as if it were a stranger's. She saw the chronic shortage of money in that other person's life, the meagreness of its pleasures, the lack of excitement. Was she really such a domestic person, *häuslich*, as

Sophie called her, or had she made a virtue of necessity and become so?

When she sat talking to Bill about business, markets and finance, subjects that Elena intuitively grasped and for which she felt she had a talent, she realised how much she had been prepared to do without for the sake of what she had. The whole structure she had built for herself around what she thought of as her destiny suddenly seemed questionable. Had she perhaps clung to it because she was afraid of risking something else?

Mightn't she just as well have had other priorities in life, run a business and made money, or married someone like Bill and used his money (to so much better effect than Sophie, who let it run through her fingers)? Shouldn't the sense of arrival she had ruled to be irrevocable from the moment she met Jason have been brought up for review like everything else? Was her loyalty to these former goals perhaps rigidity, the strength of character she had always assumed to be her greatest asset in fact a liability?

As the years passed and the likelihood of Elena pursuing any of these alternatives dwindled, she stopped asking herself these questions. It is as it is, she said to herself.

After ten years of marriage Bill divorced Sophie. The private detective he had hired to follow her showed him explicit photographs documenting his wife's affair with another man, or rather, with half a dozen other men. Sophie's mercenary view of her marriage was nothing new to Elena, but still she was upset by her friend's coldness when it came to her separation from Bill.

She was now able to appreciate Sophie's calculating foresight, how smart of her it was to have ownership of the penthouse Bill had bought for her written into their marriage contract. Ten years on, the penthouse was worth two million dollars. Sophie moved out of the lakeside villa and into the town apartment without the slightest ruffle to her life, as if her marriage with Bill had been in preparation for this day.

Bill married again a couple of years later and moved back to the States. He still came to Geneva once or twice a year on business, and always invited Sophie out to lunch.

With good humour and affection the two women watched each other gradually ageing. They were such opposite types that there was never any rivalry. The friendship thrived on its own improbability. Sophie stopped trying to persuade Elena to jump overboard and do something crazy with her life. Elena no longer waited for the catastrophe that had always seemed to be hovering just round the next corner to happen to Sophie. They could let one another just be.

Elena's view of her friend had gone through many metamorphoses during the thirty years they had known each other. At first she had seen in Sophie the martyr, the survivor of the holocaust who could do no wrong, whom no amount of riches could compensate for what she had suffered and forgone. Elena fell in love with the beauty of Sophie's suffering. She felt her compassion was called for, and it allowed her to come into her own.

This idealised version of Sophie was broken by the callousness with which she had behaved in her marriage. Elena saw her as a cold bitch with the morals of an alley cat. For a time she saw both Bill and herself as victims who had been exploited by Sophie.

Later on again, when Sophie told her of the fetishism at the core of her marriage, of the precise sexual arrangements Bill had required of his wife, which, for a while, she had been able and willing to satisfy, Elena began to appreciate the other side of the case. She was astonished, in retrospect, to find how discreet Sophie had been at the time about what was going on in her marriage. Thinking about why she was astonished, she realised it must be on account of the implicit condescension with which she had come to regard Sophie.

It took Elena a long time to disentangle herself from the notion that you got your deserts according to how you had lived. The catastrophe she always felt to be imminent in Sophie's life was really a projection of what Elena regarded as Sophie's just deserts for living as recklessly as she did. In another sense, Sophie had exactly the life she deserved. There were no contradictions between what she wanted and what she got. It was easy for Sophie to detach herself from her boyfriends because she was never attached. Men always paid for her because it was clear she expected them to. Sophie would not be thrown by any experience because no experience ever went more than skin-deep.

Elena peered into her, trying to make out the depths. But there were no depths. Her life chattered on, a fast, shallow stream. Elena's life, by contrast, flowed on like a broad and deep river.

As they grew older, each of them became more of what they were already. Elena broadened and deepened, and wondered about the purpose of her life. Sophie grew hectic and brittle, and didn't wonder about anything at all.

6

Her name was called out over the intercom and Elena went in to see her specialist, Dr Korol. They were old friends. They were the same age, and called each other by their first names. Aleksandr Korol was Russian. He had fled from Moldavia in the 1960s. Now the Soviet Union was breaking up, Aleksandr would be able to return to Moldavia for the first time in a quarter of a century. Elena would be able to return to the family estates in Holm after an even longer absence. They at once began talking animatedly about these things, as if this was the purpose of Elena's visit.

'I don't know if I shall go back,' said Aleksandr. 'On the contrary, the flow seems to be the other way. Relatives of mine who were on holiday in Berlin this summer decided to stay. Just like that. They have left everything behind them and are asking the Germans for political asylum. Imagine. Russian Jews coming to Berlin and asking for asylum. Thousands of them. There couldn't be a clearer sign of how the times are changing. But as for me . . .'

He stood looking out of the window. 'Perhaps I am afraid of what I shall find if I go back to Russia. And you, Elena?'

'I've been back over my grandmother's estate so much in my mind. I can still see it all so clearly.'

She smiled.

'It's as if I never left.'

'But you have a house there, property the family can claim back.'

'The estate falls under the Soviet land reform carried out between 1945 and 1949, so it's not covered by the law dealing with the restitution of confiscated properties. And besides,' Elena shrugged, 'I have a house.'

'And you are happy in it?'

'Yes.' She smiled. 'Does it show?'

Aleksandr came over from the window and sat down at his desk. He picked up a file and opened it.

'Yes, it does. There has been no deterioration. No metastases have developed. The condition is stable, I am very happy to report – against all my expectations six months ago, to be frank with you – that the cancer has gone away. Why, how, I have no idea. The body . . . you know, an old word for the body was bone-house. Perhaps because you are happy in your house.'

Aleksandr accompanied Elena back to the entrance and strolled with her down the drive to where she had left her car.

'You will be staying in town?'

'For a few days. With an old friend. And then back to Berlin for a couple of weeks.'

'But not to Holm.'

'Not to Holm.'

'It may be a wise decision.'

Elena got into the car and wound down the window. 'What do you think? Should I come back and see you in the spring?'

'I'm always happy to see you, Elena.' Aleksandr laughed. 'But no, it's not necessary. Come when you feel like it. Just come for a chat. Any time in the next twelve months.'

Elena took off the sunglasses she had just put on and remained silent for a minute. 'You mean there could be a recurrence?'

'There could be.'

'Are you hiding anything from me?'

The doctor smiled and shook his head. 'No, I am hiding nothing from you.'

'Goodbye, Aleksandr. And thank you.'

Elena drove down the hill through the old town and pulled in at the side of the avenue bordering the lake. She heard the cars roar past behind her, smelled the fumes of gas and watched a startled flock of pigeons snatch flight over the lake as she walked down the promenade. She leaned over the balustrade at the water's edge, stopping time for a moment, absorbing all the sensations of being alive, collecting herself, before she stepped into the phone booth and called the number in England that Jason had left her. Listening to the phone ringing, she imagined the hotel somewhere on the south coast, the seafront that Jason had described to her, his daily walk to the nursing home, where Magnus was dying. She wondered—

Her train of thought was interrupted by the receptionist answering the phone. She asked to speak to Jason Gould, but the receptionist said he was no longer there. Mr Gould had checked out of the hotel and returned to London only that morning.

7

The cab stopped at a set of traffic lights, and Jason looked out of the window at the familiar streets of Berlin with a warm sense of wellbeing. His gaze drifted across a vacant plot of land to a poster dimly illuminated on a wall. A single word was printed on it, set off in white letters against a diffuse background.

Deutschland.

Jason came across the poster again the next day. He began to notice it in various places, in slightly different forms, throughout the city. He passed it in a couple of shop windows. He saw it from a train, blown up on hoardings around a building site. *Deutschland*, unadorned, a word printed on a diffuse background.

Someone must have started a campaign.

The poster had a curiously unsettling effect. What did it signify? Who was behind the campaign? What was this country in a word, naked, or was it neutral, without a democratic republic or a federal republic attached to the name, Germany pure, not East or West or anything? What would it taste like – *Deutschland* served straight? Was it something old or something new? An encouragement or a threat? What parts would be joined together that October, to form what whole? Was it a union? A reunion, and if so of what? Where was the Germany one could wish back?

Germany before the fall, that was what one wanted back.

There was no way around the word on the posters which were cropping up all over the city, for Berlin was still, or would be once again, the capital of this rediscovered country for which one was going to have to find a name. In some versions of the poster there was a question-mark appended to the word.

Deutschland?

One had to look and see. A time came for the bandages to be removed. The patient who had been patched up and put together again looked in the mirror for the first time.

8

Deutschland before the fall, that was what one wanted back, but there could be no return to that place, one had to go on through the fire to the place on the other side. The aftermath was still smouldering, and would go on smouldering for a long time. The trail of powder laid by Michael Kohlhaas on the border between Saxony and Brandenburg led through a department store in Frankfurt back to Brandenburg, where only recently it had ignited again.

The week that Jason returned to Berlin from the south coast of England, where he attended his father's funeral, housing that had been designated for refugees in the Cottbus area was set on fire. The hostel was still empty, but there were others that were full, and would soon be burning, and soon you could read *Deutschland* on the poster by the light of the flames that were springing up around the country. This was the way the international press read *Deutschland*, perhaps the only way it was able to read it. Germany, smouldering, always made the news.

Purdy, his cameraman for many years, arrived with him from London, and together they journeyed through the rump of the communist state during the last weeks of its existence. They were looking for Rigge, the neo-Nazi Jason had met through an introduction supplied by Strehlitz at the beginning of the year, who, within a month of the Berlin Wall coming down, had gone East to establish a political base, but in Leipzig, not in East Berlin.

There was no trace of Rigge at the house in Connewitz where Jason had met him in February. The apartment he had occupied was empty. No one knew where he had gone. Jason found the pub where Rigge had taken him for a drink, and he began asking around.

Eventually he met someone there who told him where he could find someone else. This person told Jason that Rigge had moved to Chemnitz, formerly Karl-Marx-Stadt, and gave him an address where Rigge had been living.

They found a large, decaying house on the outskirts of the town. The girl who lived on the second floor was out to work during the day, the neighbours said, and told Jason to come back in the evening. He waited with Purdy in a café across the road for a couple of hours. He saw the girl coming, guessed it might be her, and intercepted her on her way into the house. She said she had no idea what he was talking about. She didn't know who Rigge was. Jason followed her up the stairs. He said he had an urgent message for Rigge from a grandfather who lived in Würzburg, and could she pass it on. She said he could pass it on himself, and shut the door in his face.

Jason pressed the buzzer. After a while the girl opened the door and asked him to come in. They stood in the corridor inside the apartment. The girl leaned against the wall, her arms folded, waiting for Jason to speak. The corridor they were standing in, and the rooms leading off it, as far as he could see, were empty. It was an apartment that had nothing in it. When it became clear that the corridor was as far as her invitation extended, Jason began explaining who he was and why he wanted to see Rigge. The girl interrupted him. Rigge was no longer living there, she said. He had moved to Dresden a few months ago. She didn't have an address.

They drove on to Dresden the same night. Jason took the wrong exit and they got lost on the outskirts of the city. At three o'clock in the morning it was a dark wasteland of a town. The streets often had no signs, and where they did, there wasn't enough light to read them by. Purdy had to get out of the car to inspect them by torchlight. At some point they crossed the Elbe, and Jason followed the river back into the centre of town. He recognised Semper's reconstructed opera house. This was the landmark he'd been given to help him find the hotel when he called up en route to make reservations.

Jason had a contact in town, a local correspondent for the Berlin newspaper *TAZ*. The man's name was Schulze. Jason called him in the morning and asked him if he had any information about Rigge. Schulze said he didn't want to talk over the phone. He asked Jason to come to an address not far from the Zwinger, the palace where the rulers of Saxony had formerly lived.

A dozen buses with West German number plates stood parked in front of the palace. It was a magnificent building. They looked round it on a warm autumn day before going to meet Schulze. Crowds of tourists were feeding the ducks from the bridge over the moat at the entrance to the palace. They were all from West Germany. The Zwinger and Semper's opera house were what the tourists wanted to see, both of them buildings that had been bombed and beautifully restored. The restorations, not the ruins, were what the German tourists came to Dresden for.

The bombed church beside the Zwinger wasn't even a ruin. It was a pile of rubble, fenced off on a strip of wasteland. For a mile or two around the city centre, the restored palace must have been about the only building now standing as it had stood before the fire-bombing of Dresden on a February night in 1945. The elderly West German tourists came to see this one restored building, got back into their buses and drove away. Jason watched Purdy climb over the fence on to the church bomb-site and begin to film the modern city centre across a foreground of rubble.

In the East, the impression of a place patched up and somehow running on under provisional management until business was back to usual struck Jason much more strongly than it ever had in the West. In Dresden, in 1990, he felt closer to 1945 than he had felt when he arrived in Berlin in 1961, the year the wall was built. This feeling of proximity to the war was like the ruined church, a pile of rubble that had been shoved aside but still remained in view. Beside the ruins stood a baroque palace so seamlessly restored to the past that it betrayed nothing of the destruction that had intervened.

Journalists, particularly journalists from abroad, came here as scavengers. There was a tendency to look at the city for the evidence of war ruins, and to define the present by what had risen in the ruins' place. The present became, tendentiously, a replacement for the past, something patched up until normal business could be resumed. The present was the small, always provisional annexe of the gigantic building which was the past.

Jason was aware that although the preoccupation with war ruins was a true and legitimate interest, it also perpetuated a cliché in which the image of Germany remained frozen, leaving one little scope to modify that image with reference to what there had been before and afterwards. This was Purdy's frozen interest in the ruins. They cut off his view of all that had preceded them in Dresden's history.

Jason left Purdy filming the ruins and walked to the address Schulze had given him. The house was surrounded by scaffolding. Inside, a corridor led all the way around. There were lots of doors leading off it but no indication of what was behind them. Jason tried some of the handles. They were locked. He went upstairs. He found a girl sitting on the landing, who said the editorial office of *City Magazine* was one floor up. Jason remembered that Schulze was on the staff of this magazine – he just worked as a stringer for the newspaper in Berlin.

At this moment a man appeared at the top of the stairs and said in a theatrically quiet voice that he was the person Jason was looking for. Schulze was short and had a round face, with close-cropped hair and rimless spectacles, through which he looked at Jason, unblinking. The resemblance to the Bert Brecht icon was remarkable, and it had obviously been cultivated by Schulze. Brecht's close-cropped hair and rimless glasses were once popular in the West, too, but that had been twenty years ago, it occurred to Jason, and, suppressing a smile (he was fond of Brecht and already found himself becoming fond of Schulze), he went upstairs to meet him.

9

Jason followed Schulze into a smoke-filled office where three men sat working in silence, but Schulze only went in to fetch a tobacco pouch from his desk and came straight out again. 'We can talk better in here,' he said, and showed Jason into a room down the passage containing nothing but two chairs and a table with a lamp and a phone that seemed to have found their way there by chance.

Nowhere in this other Germany did he receive a sense of things belonging. Jason found himself in an atmosphere that was always fugitive and provisional, as if taking place on the spur of the moment, unintentionally, or even against the will of the people who inhabited these rooms. There was a lack of co-ordination between people and their surroundings. Perhaps for this reason his perception of them seemed fragmentary. Jason took a good look at Schulze (with whom he felt sympathy on account of his resemblance to Brecht) as he sat at the borrowed desk, and decided that this was what was missing – the background in which people belonged and which put them in a perspective he could recognise. He wondered if the destitution he saw around him in the exteriors was something that continued all the way through to the core, to a destitution inside people that was all the worse for being invisible.

'. . . Michael Kühnen was here,' Schulze was saying.

'Oh? What was he doing?'

Schulze produced a quizzical smile. 'Kühnen and your historian David Irving, for the second time in twelve months. Always a welcome guest in right-wing circles. Surely you can't have missed—'

'I've been out of the country for some time. Not *my* historian, by the way. Tell me about it.'

'Well, Kühnen held a neo-Nazi rally, only that's not what it was called. The title he gave it was German Unity and Social Justice, or something like that, in order to get round the ban that would otherwise have been imposed by the local government. Kühnen's ploy and the city council's weakness, or complicity, or however you choose to describe their favourable reaction, have generally been interpreted as a sign that Dresden is a hospitable place for people with right-wing ideas.'

'Is it?'

Schulze shrugged. 'Let's just say it's a hospitable place. Live and let live. It's a city with a tradition of sensuous pleasures. People are willing to find a compromise so that their ability to enjoy life won't be impaired.'

'Pulling down the blinds when the Nazis march past?'

'People don't need blinds for that. They can look and still not see. I covered the march for the magazine. There were one or two voices of protest along the route. The rest was silence. As you know, Dresden had a reputation for . . . let's call it backwardness, even during the GDR days.'

'Because it's tucked down in the valley? People's TV sets were unable to receive the West German stations that everyone else was watching?'

'Exactly. Anyway, for various reasons the Nazis felt comfortable here, and they stayed. Rigge arrived with the first wave that came this summer.'

'Did he come on his own?'

'No. He came with a man from Chemnitz by the name of Kronenberger.'

Schulze rolled up the cigarette he had been turning in his fingers and licked the paper.

'They were allies at first. Both were affiliated to a party called Deutsche Kraft, which was founded in Augsburg earlier this year. They came here to start up a Dresden branch. The new party was a breakaway from the FAP and saw itself as a successor to all kinds of other right-wing groups, from the FAP and NPD to the Republicans and followers of Kühnen. Kühnen wants to act as a catalyst, spawning so many new groups that it's impossible to keep track of them, or him, for that matter. He doesn't seem to care about the names. But if you stay in one place and keep watching, you'll see the same old horses and riders coming past again and again. We're watching them go by on a carousel, the old performers in new disguises.'

'Rigge too?'

'Sure. Formerly a member of the FAP, and before that of the Order of Germanic Youth, or whatever that thing was called which was founded by Strehlitz.'

'It was called the Bismarck Youth.'

'Whatever. It's always the same old stable with the same old stink coming out of it. Every country has its sewer, and this is the German sewer. Open commitment to the national socialist ideology, to the state whose authority is invested in the *Führerprinzip*, and so on and so forth. The incorrigible Nazis, new or old, who have this sort of thing on their agenda, don't count for more than two or three per cent.'

'Ten or fifteen.'

'That's the sympathy belt. I mean the untouchables, the hard core. And for me that's the point. Even revival movements require an element that is new and different if they are going to generate real energy. The kind of energy you need can't be generated by the past.'

'No?'

'Not by something in the past alone. The need for the movement has to be generated out of the present, and the needs of the present are different from the needs of the past. Nowadays we no longer have a background of authority which a *Führerprinzip* has to slot into, for example. That kind of attitude to authority just isn't there. The context has changed. That's why I can't see this resurgence of neo-Nazi activity as the writing on the wall. All I can see are graffiti.'

'And Kronenberger?'

'Kronenberger's something else again.'

'In what way?'

'I'm coming to that in a minute. Excuse me . . .'

The phone was ringing. Schulze picked it up and answered it. He said he was busy at the moment and would call back.

'I'm trying to get hold of Rigge, but nobody seems to know where he is,' Jason said when Schulze was off the phone.

'No. Rigge is a mystery. He simply disappeared.'

'Having come to Dresden with Kronenberger this summer to start up a local branch of Deutsche Kraft.'

'Right.'

'Are there any conjectures as to why Rigge disappeared? Might he have gone underground, for example?'

'He was more likely withdrawn.'

'Withdrawn?'

'There are people who believe Rigge wasn't a Nazi but an agent working for the *Verfassungsschutz*.'

Jason was astounded.

'Who knows?' said Schulze. 'An agent might be planted on the scene for various reasons. Officially, to keep tabs on what's happening. Unofficially, as an *agent provocateur*, helping to bring about a situation evidently serious enough to warrant counter-measures that would not otherwise be justifiable. Did you ever meet Rigge?'

'Yes.'

'And Kühnen?'

'Regarding Kühnen,' said Jason, 'there was something I wanted to ask you. The last time I saw him out he was looking haggard. He had obviously lost a lot of weight. The rumours are—'

'AIDS. It's not a rumour any more. It's definite.'

'So it's true. Führer dies of AIDS. Not a good headline for the supporters of the movement.'

'But it all belongs together. Think of Röhm and the SA. Comradeship, the cult of the physique, homosexuality, the cult of leather, gangsterism. Cynical friends of mine in France point out how dull Germany would be without these things. What would Germany's fascination be without them? It has to preserve them to preserve its image. The SS man in black uniform – a parade uniform he would have seldom worn, incidentally – has become an ineradicable part of the icon. Imagine Marilyn Monroe telling her producers she had decided to turn herself into a brunette.'

'What can you tell me about Kronenberger?'

'He and Rigge came here at the same time to start up a Dresden branch of Deutsche Kraft. They fell out. Kronenberger left, and within a very short space of time he had set up his own outfit in Cottbus.'

'Outfit?'

'You can't describe it as a political party. It's more like a gang. A kids' gang. Some of them are in their twenties but most are still in their teens. Kronenberger has mobilised four or five hundred members within a couple of months of arriving in Brandenburg. It's the same old Nazi ideology on top, but it's driven by a modern energy. It's the *Herrenrasse* ideology grafted on to the mood of underground fanzines. It's all about cult and fashion, with Kronenberger as the icon, not a political leader but a rock star.'

'What's the new angle on this?' asked Jason.

'The attraction of the Nazi paraphernalia is its power to shock. The "Sieg Heil" and the salute are sexy because they're taboo. For these junk kids the Nazi stuff is very far away, maybe not something with a real historical existence, more something that's part of the national mythology with a terrific aura of taboo. It's in-your-face to the rest of the world. The national mythology bit is important, because when everything else breaks down – your family, your chances of a job, the communist state and all it taught you to believe in – not much seems to be left other than the myth of a shared folk origin with which to shore up your identity.'

It was interesting to hear what Schulze had to say. He talked about these things differently from the way a Western journalist would. There were no pieties. There was no treading warily around subjects still booby-trapped with taboos.

'Look at the fantastic publicity they're starting to get. They meet to compare their press cuttings.'

Jason smiled.

'I'm serious. This is how you advance in your disillusioned, no-future peer group. This is where the prestige is. Wait until reality TV gets in on the act. These kids aren't reading *Mein Kampf*. They've never heard of it. They read *Tempo* and *Bravo* and stuff like that. There's a gigantic conspiracy going on here, between no-future kids who want attention, a public that craves to be entertained and people like you and me with a story to sell.'

'I spoke to Rigge earlier this year,' said Jason, 'and a lot of what he said didn't sound historical at all. No yielding of former German territories in the East, and that's a big slice out of Poland, Czechoslovakia and the Soviet Union. Repatriation of all foreigners. Modification of history's judgement of the role of Germany in the twentieth century. None of these issues were on the agenda twenty years ago. All of them are at least on the fringe of, perhaps closer to, the mainstream debates in Germany today. Have you seen those "*Deutschland*" posters that have started showing up everywhere?'

Schulze shook his head. He had rolled himself another cigarette and was brushing bits of tobacco off his knee. 'Isn't all this a part of the adjustment process set in motion by the end of the Cold War? I think so. Should we demonise readjustment? Are all the decisions taken in 1945 irrevocable? Obviously not. Take the fate of the Baltic states, for a start. How might their secession from the Soviet Union affect East Prussia, for example, now geo-politically isolated from the rest of Russia? What happens to all those buffer zones between Eastern and Western Europe that have now lost that function? I don't see these issues as having been invented by or as belonging to the right wing alone, do you? The old order has vanished, and anything becomes possible. Politely but firmly, we have to resist the stereotype that has been imposed on us as part of the demonisation of *Deutschland*.'

Schulze got up. 'I have to see someone briefly. Would you mind waiting here for about ten minutes?'

'I might as well get along, too. I was thinking I should go to Brandenburg to take a look at the situation there myself. I was wondering if you could suggest how to get in touch with Kronenberger.'

Jason followed Schulze out into the corridor and together they made their way downstairs.

'He's a bit unpredictable. Changes his mind at the last minute and doesn't show up. I must have a think about the best way to approach him.'

'I read in the paper that some of the people picked up in connection with the recent attacks on refugee hostels in Brandenburg were card-carrying members of Deutsche Kraft.'

'Oh, sure. Most of them are skinheads – I mean, a really violent bunch. Look, is there somewhere I can reach you?'

Jason gave Schulze the number of his hotel and thanked him for his help. He left the building and returned to the ruined church to find Purdy, but there was no sign of him. A wind suddenly got up, chasing the low ceiling of cloud across the sky, and on his way back to the hotel it began to rain.

10

It was raining on the evening Jason pulled up outside the house in
Dresden Neustadt. Schulze had given him the address. It was a
rambling, derelict house, dating from the turn of the century. Most
of the slots for cards showing the lodgers' names on the board at the
entrance were empty. There was no card for Petra, who lived on the
top floor. Petra was Rigge's girl in Dresden. Jason called her for help
in finding Kronenberger, and she said she was planning to go to
Cottbus for a Deutsche Kraft meeting that weekend. If he gave her
a lift she could take him there.

Purdy's camera was already running when they made their way
upstairs and Jason knocked, and Petra opened the door in her
underwear. Jason had asked her in advance about the camera and
Petra had said she didn't care. Jason had the impression she enjoyed
playing to the camera; overplaying, in fact, because the whole thing
was a performance, beginning with the way she stood casually in the
doorway in her bra and told them to come in.

'It's not my apartment,' she said, as Purdy followed her through
the living-room into the bedroom. The reason she disowned the
apartment became evident when they saw the decor and the souvenirs that decorated the bedroom, the photo of Hitler standing
with folded arms on the wall over the bed, the Nazi memorabilia on
the shelves, the book entitled *Deutsche Heimatlieder* in Gothic script
on the bedside table. 'Whose apartment is it, then?' Jason asked her,
and Petra laughed and shrugged. She was sitting on the bed, painting her toenails. How about the decor, Jason asked again, did she like
it? Would she keep it if the place was hers? Petra thought she might,
describing the decor as *ganz niedlich*, rather cute. She got off the bed

and moved to the mirror to do her make-up. Purdy knelt on the floor beside her, his camera looking up at her in profile. Jason stood behind her, talking to the face in the mirror. It was the face of a nineteen-year-old, barely lived in. Her hair stood up on her scalp in red and greenish tufts.

'You're a hairdresser, aren't you?'

'Yeah.'

'Do your own hair?'

'Do I what?'

'Do you do your own hair?'

'Daniela does. The girls do each other's hair.'

'Does Daniela advise or just do what you tell her to do?'

'Just as it comes. We just have fun.'

Jason grinned. 'Hard to tell which bits have been done and which haven't.'

Petra laughed. 'Is this going to be shown on TV?'

She was buttoning up a military-style tunic and Jason asked her if she knew who Hitler was. She said of course she knew, and Jason asked her if she didn't mind sleeping under the picture of a mass-murderer, even if the apartment wasn't hers. Petra thought Hitler wasn't as bad a guy as history made him out to be. Purdy was backing down the stairs, filming her as she descended, but he stumbled and had to ask her to come down again. So as they were coming out of the apartment, Jason repeated his question about sleeping under the picture of a mass-murderer, and Petra repeated her answer, but Purdy wasn't satisfied with the shot, so they had to do it a third time. When they were down the stairs Jason said in English to Purdy that the girl was already giving them enough of a performance without getting her to do takes again, as if the whole damn thing was scripted or something, because they were doing a documentary, not a feature film.

In the car he asked the girl fake disbelief, jokily, how all that old horror-movie Nazi stuff could turn her on, and Petra said they needed someone like Hitler again to clean up the country, to rid it of all the trash, the niggers and gypsies and foreign trash that loafed around and were paid for doing nothing. 'How does all that shit get into your head?' Jason asked, but not aggressively, more as if he were kidding her. Petra was squirming around in the front seat, trying to fix a strap crosswise over her tunic from shoulder to waist. Under the tunic she was wearing a blouse with a black tie, and she had stuffed her black trousers into the top of her boots, so that it looked as if she were wearing riding britches. Petra said her grandad had been there and told her it was the best time of his life; there were parades, there was work for everyone and young people were taken care of; people had ideals to live for, not just for themselves, and there hadn't been all the drugs and crime and stuff there was today. Jason got the feeling there was an odd mix in Petra's answer, half *kitsch* and half naïve yearning, because it was something like a lost innocence that Petra missed, and which she was longing for. He asked her if she was a member of Deutsche Kraft. She said no, but it made no difference that she wasn't. She'd been to the Kühnen demo and marched in the front row with Rigge; they'd all given the Nazi salute, so for sure the police had her on their files as a militant extremist, but what the hell. Jason wondered aloud if she'd had fun and Petra said it was a group thing, so yes, in a way it was fun, but her parents didn't like her getting mixed up with Nazis and they gave her hell when she showed up at home. Out of the blue she said: 'We'll get the eastern territories back,' and when Jason asked her whether she thought Poland was going just to hand them over or what, she was silent. Jason asked her if she'd be prepared to go to war to get the eastern territories back. 'We'll negotiate for them,' said Petra.

They had been driving off the main roads for the last half-hour. The empty, ink-black countryside, interrupted at intervals by a dimly lit village street, rushed past with hardly a sign of life. They were nearing the outskirts of Cottbus when Petra asked Jason to pull up at a restaurant by the road so that she could ask for directions to the pub where the Deutsche Kraft meeting was being held. She said she'd never been there before and she didn't know the area too well.

The restaurant was brand new, made entirely of glass. The sign 'Miami Beach', between two neon palm trees, flashed on and off from the roof. It was a Saturday night and the place was full, as if the entire population of the desolate country through which they'd been driving had been packed into Miami Beach. Jason got out of the car to stretch his legs.

From outside, looking into the brightly lit interior, Purdy tracked Petra's walk through the restaurant to the counter, where she talked to one of the waiters. It was only now that Jason realised what she was wearing. She had dressed herself up to look like a Nazi stormtrooper. She had improvised the costume, and, however ludicrous it was, the effect of the sight of someone in Petra's get-up on the people inside the restaurant when she walked in out of the night was electrifying. They turned and stared at this apparition from the 1930s. The whole place froze for the few moments she was in there talking to the waiter; watched in disbelief as she marched back out. 'What's the big deal?' she asked Jason as they got into the car and drove off. She sniggered. 'Everyone looked like they'd seen a ghost. Hey, papa, have you got a cigarette?'

They overshot the turning they were looking for and arrived in Cottbus, got lost in the miles of identical apartment blocks arranged barrack-like around the city centre, and had difficulty finding their way back out of town. They found the turning at the second attempt. It was easy to miss, not even a country road, just a dirt track through the fields. It led through the woods and emerged in a clearing where it came to an end outside an inn. A lamp with a yellowish beam hung over the entrance.

It had stopped raining. Wisps of steam rose off the tarmac in the aftermath of the rain. Jason told Purdy it might be better to keep himself and his camera out of sight for the time being. He made his way with Petra across the courtyard between the parked cars, and as he walked through the orchard beneath the dripping trees towards the outbuilding where they had been told to go, anticipating a picture of a soldier with strong jaw and high cheekbones which would be hanging there with a familiar caption underneath, Jason thought of the room where Strehlitz used to hold his assemblies of the Bismarck Youth thirty years ago, and he realised that this place in the forest was where it had reconstituted itself, the hydra with many names.

Through the trees he glimpsed coloured lights under the eaves of a building resembling a barn. Two garden gnomes, cap in hand, turned smiling faces upwards to welcome Jason at the entrance. Involuntarily he was reminded of the woodcutter's children in the fairytale, arriving at the gingerbread house. Nothing could have represented better those *kitsch* traditions enshrining German cosiness. Nothing could have seemed to him more sinister at that moment. 'The god whose hand let iron grow, he had no love of slaves.' Jason stood outside for a moment, looking through the windows.

He opened the door and stepped into an interior that might have been part of a low-budget film set, so effectively, with just a few improvising touches, had an atmosphere been created extraordinarily evocative of the Third Reich.

11

What is this barn in the middle of the forest? And what is Jason Gould doing there?

The barn with the smiling garden gnomes at the entrance is part of an iconic German landscape. The red, white and black garlands hanging from the rafters; the hundred or so young men with military haircuts and black leather jackets – souvenirs such as a swastika or an iron cross on a ribbon hanging here and there around someone's neck – sitting on benches at rough wooden tables drinking beer; and in particular Kronenberger's softly spoken question, 'Are you a Jew?', as he looks up at Jason while inspecting his identification papers: all these are quotations from a landscape embedded in the diffuse background on the *Deutschland* poster.

All these elements have been there before. The Nazis play-acting in the barn in the forest quote role models from the Third Reich. Copies of copies, layer upon layer around the originals (which were themselves quotations from the past), they accumulate tradition; just as Schulze does, whose rimless glasses quote Brecht, or Caspar David Friedrich, quoting figures in *Teutsche Tracht* surrounded by oaks and runic stones, creating tropes in an idealised landscape, or Kleist quoting Luther and Kohlhaas. They all subscribe to a German iconography, not just incorporating but reinventing the national past.

Identity as an involuntary process of accumulation, layer upon layer: one of these layers is the Third Reich. How can the always inexplicable ever be forgivable, the always unforgivable ever be explained? What a blot on the clean and tidy German copybook! One wishes it could go away. One wishes one could bring back the dead, and the civilisation that was murdered with them. It has to be included, however. Otherwise the iconography becomes a fake.

But what does Jason Gould think he is doing here?

And what answer will he give to Kronenberger's question?

12

Jason reaches the barn in the forest in a very roundabout way, via Berlin, where he arrived the year the wall was built, and which he watched being taken down thirty years later. He is in the barn because he has no alternative to being a figure in the German landscape. He has become part of it along with everyone else, inextricably embedded in the diffuse background on the *Deutschland* poster. In fact he has become so caught up in it that there are times when he shares the German sense of resignation at being unable ever to escape it.

Layer upon layer, he has involuntarily accumulated the traditions, layer by layer, the German identity, including the chapter of horrors in the national biography. It is not personally his biography, but what does that mean? He has of necessity become identified with it, from the moment he acquiesced in that process of *Anziehung des Bezüglichen*, an Attraction of Affinities that brought him together with Elena at Grunewald station and kept him forever after.

Jason says yes to Kronenberger's question without having time to think about it. For a moment his life has hung by a thread.

Not that he is in any physical danger at this moment. He is taking his part in the play alongside Kronenberger, whose muscular henchmen, waiting in sinister poses in the background, are also part of the play. Jason is not a Jew, despite an aura of Jewishness that lingers around the name Gould. He could be Jewish, for all he knows, but this is not why Jason says yes to Kronenberger's question.

In the moment when everything converges on a single issue and his life hangs morally by a thread, there is no room left to manoeuvre, either/or, either a Jew or not a Jew, in the Nazi play that is being acted out by Deutsche Kraft in Kronenberger's barn, it is Jason's destiny to say yes, an act of identification that has become inescapable.

And what does Kronenberger do?

He folds Jason's identification papers neatly along the crease and hands them back to him.

'What can I do for you, Mr Gould?' he asks politely, giving no sign of remembering that they have met before.

Jason explains the situation. He is making a documentary on the resurgence of neo-Nazi groups. He would like to have an interview. A cameraman is waiting outside in the car. Kronenberger nods and takes out his diary.

'Tomorrow at one o'clock? Are you familiar with the Novotel on the next exit from the autobahn?'

'Well, actually I was hoping—'

'My fee is four hundred marks an hour, no cheques or credit cards.'

'I beg your pardon?'

It takes Jason a moment to rally.

'Is that the going rate? Is that what *Spiegel* and *Stern* magazine pay you?'

Kronenberger shrugs. 'Well? Would one o'clock suit you?'

Jason looks at Kronenberger with his pencil poised over his diary and an expectant look on his face, and suddenly he sees through the masquerade. He sees a bit-part actor on the make, dressed up for a play in a ramshackle barn, demanding entrance fees from a greedy audience for as long as the going is good and they are fool enough to pay his price. Jason sees himself as Kronenberger's accomplice, making a living out of Kronenberger's show, writing reviews on behalf of Deutsche Kraft. And he sees the public behind the lights, voyeurs in the shadows, craning their necks when the old stripper who's had herself lifted takes off her bra and pulls down her knickers. Jason shakes his head and turns away. He begins to take in the extent of a gigantic con trick. But Kronenberger is a busy man, and has no time for Jason now. Striding to the stage, where he climbs the stairs and takes the microphone, he has already forgotten Jason, does not even hear the door close behind him as Jason leaves the barn and disappears into the night.

13

The older generation was dying – that summer von Strehlitz and Holger's father, deprived of the satisfaction of witnessing the official reunification of the two countries in October, and a few weeks later Magnus Gould, who didn't care either way. Jason was there for his father's end in a nursing home in England. It came slowly. Jason had been anticipating it long before. Magnus must have, too. He died with dignity, a little frostily, turning away from life with something like an expression of cold distaste for what he saw when he took his last look back. Strehlitz, the old Nazi, died without forewarning. The colonel gave everyone the slip, ducking suddenly out of his life before he could be held accountable for it.

Jason, who went to visit him in the spring before he died, was once again baffled by the arbitrariness of fate. The least deserving seemed to be the best rewarded, nowhere more so than in the grace with which they were allowed to die. The old Nazis lived on and on throughout a serene twilight of old age, financially well provided for and in almost obdurately good health. It seemed they would never die. They lived on and on, and so did their works, enshrined in miles of propaganda and documentary footage that was still able to emanate an extraordinary malevolent power. The Third Reich had created myths and set up icons, used the technology and established the style for packaging and merchandising the twentieth century.

Mythologies remained exempt from the ravages of time. At eighty, Botho's power to fascinate the young was apparently still undiminished. Walking up the stairs to the house in the leafy street off the Kurfürstendamm, Jason stepped back into a world with which he had first become acquainted thirty years earlier, when he was sixteen.

Botho's manservant, Tiedke, still stood in the hallway, chasing away the shadows with his gong, and Jason's youthful successors, members of the colonel's private corps, came downstairs for meals or filed into the assembly room to be edified by the colonel's harangues on *Deutschtum*. In 1961, von Strehlitz had been listened to by his audience as a protagonist in the events of quite recent history, but for his acolytes thirty years on, he had become not merely a mentor but a living legend. Here was someone who had actually taken part in quashing the *putsch* against Hitler in July 1944, which in the perspective of right-wing Germans in 1990 was an event already passing out of history into myth. Von Strehlitz himself had joined the icons.

In the thirty years between his first and last visit, Jason had seen and documented the backstage view of the icon many times, the smoke-filled public houses and provincial halls where the old troopers held their one-night stands, their impudence, their glibness, their false conviviality, their false history, their falsification of everything, their heartlessness and sentimentality, their indefatigable *Geltungsdrang* – the craving for attention from anyone, anywhere, at whatever cost. Court appearances sustained political opportunists like Strehlitz, bold-faced in their (usually correct) assumption that the German law establishment would implicitly be on the side the nationalists claimed to represent. The cases left an unpleasant smear in the legal annals, a long trail of paper that was just so much garbage – lies, slanders, endlessly reiterated self-propaganda, earning the defendants fines, suspended prison sentences, at most six months or a year inside; and always, of course, prominent headlines.

Jason wondered they were not worn down by the absurdity and the shabbiness, the hopelessness, the loss of human dignity, that accompanied such a life. But it was almost immaterial what the heirs of Hitler did or didn't do. They lived by proxy, parasites on the still powerful emanation of evil that exuded from the testament of the Third Reich. They lived at the expense of the modern media, still hypnotised by the masterclasses of Goebbels and the monster his propagandists had invented, which placed the Nazi spectre under a magnifying glass and then responded to the enlargement with magnified alarm. The Third Reich icon, the mass parades, the mass confidence, the mass death, the mass everything, had emancipated itself and become self-perpetuating, one of the endlessly self-multiplying images that were the key signatures of the twentieth-century nightmare.

Jason was as inextricably caught up in this spiral as anyone else, but being aware of it he became prone to the illusion that he was also in control of it. Strehlitz was categorically not a person one could number among one's friends, and after his early days as a guest in his house Jason had kept that resolution. At intervals of two or three years, however, in response either to his father's inquiries or at the colonel's request, Jason had returned to the house to see him. Such errands provided pretexts, at least, for his visits. But the kind of curiosity that lingers around a taboo lingered here, too, making it easy for Jason to comply. A ghoulish interest still hovered in the room with the crossed sabres hanging over the mantelpiece and the picture of the square-jawed soldier, created in the image of the God whose hand let iron grow because he had no love of slaves. This room, and the symbols it contained, had helped to furnish Jason's biography. They could not be taken back out of it without leaving a gap.

A more problematic ambivalence lay in Jason's feelings about Strehlitz himself. What was one to do if one happened to have taken something of a liking to such a man?

The reaction of Magnus had been to keep in a bottom drawer the letters that Botho continued to write him throughout the 1930s, and which ceased only with the outbreak of war. Jason found the letters in his father's papers after his death. They had moved with him, from England across a lot of Africa and back home again, from one place to another, for half a century. Jason had already learned from Botho that he had been in love with his father. Magnus had apparently not answered the later letters, but he did not discourage Botho from writing them, either, punctilious as a schoolboy in the Christmas cards he dutifully dispatched to Berlin with a round-up of the year's news. Magnus never told his son of the letters. It was extraordinary for Jason to imagine Magnus reading them. It was extraordinary for the son to have to come to terms with the father's sexuality, the fact that he had desired and been desired by men as well as women. The references in Botho's letters to assurances that Magnus must have confided to him in writing after their meeting at Holm in 1934 were unambiguous.

The letters from Botho lay together with the letters from Sophie Romberg in the same bundle. While her letters were simple, a little pale, wistful at most, the letters from Botho were glowing. Something in Magnus had been willing to receive them, and had wanted to keep them. He had not been just a passive recipient. Dangling the annual Christmas card in front of Botho's nose, he had artfully encouraged him to keep up the flow. Why were they in the same pile as the letters from Sophie? Jason imagined Magnus reading them side by side, assembling a montage in his mind. The persons and the feelings overlapped. There was no clear division. Jason found himself having to revise the cast-iron pedigree of the branching tree he had considered his destiny. The father's sentimental journey back to Germany after the war in the guise of the son had been inspired not only by an abortive love for a dead woman but also by a romantic attraction to a homosexual who was a Nazi.

In the weave of history there are infinitely many such personal attractions, an attraction and convergence of affinities it is impossible to distinguish and segregate from the overall pattern.

Had Magnus ever condemned? Had he ever passed judgement? Not a single word. It was not for him to speak. For Botho was wrapped up in his father's own secret. Magnus couldn't come out into the open about the one without disclosing the other.

Botho had made an accomplice of Magnus's son, too. Jason hung around on the fringe of the smell that came out of the room in Botho's house where the corpse was hidden, because he found the smell of corruption irresistible. He made a living out of it. He became a licensed purveyor of it. By the time he could own up to this admission he was already compromised, but had there been any alternative to finding out by experience that values were inherently ambivalent, and that what seemed to be clear was actually diffuse, and had to be disentangled by force? It had taken Jason all this time to understand that the only way out for him was to quit altogether.

14

When Jason emerged from the barn in the middle of the forest, that was already what he was doing. He was leaving Deutsche Kraft behind him forever. He was mentally washing his hands of the matter. The metaphor brought to mind an image of his friend Holger, doing literally just that at the police station to which he was taken on the day Katje was shot on the street in Berlin and died bloodily in his arms.

Holger had quit sixteen years before. He came out of the castle that was the law, because he had to learn to be vulnerable.

Holger found a new mythology on which to rebuild his life; or rather, he interpreted an old one in a new way. When Siegfried bathed in the dragon's blood that made him invulnerable, a leaf fell between his shoulder blades, leaving him mortal after all. This was the spot where he was stabbed as he stooped to drink at a fountain in the Odenwald (or, in Holger's version, as Siegfried stooped to wash his hands of the whole insufferable Nibelungen affair).

For Holger, this was the hero of German myth (revised edition); a mortal, a naked man in the forest with a leaf sticking to his back, looking not merely vulnerable but rather absurd, as men are bound to do when they emerge from a bath in dragon's blood with a leaf sticking to their backs; a man who accepts his mortal status, and who does indeed die; not a hero any more, just a human being.

15

It was six years since they had last met, before Holger moved down south to the country. He came out of the farmhouse on a damp afternoon and peered through the fog up the garden path along which Jason was cautiously advancing, holding aside the branches the rain had bowed down into the path. Seeing Holger standing at the door in slippers and a lumpish handknitted pullover, Jason was so amused by his old friend's ridiculous appearance that he couldn't help smiling. Holger, for his part, saw a plump middle-aged man, fussing about getting his trousers wet. Jason was so different from the taut, highly strung boy he remembered from their first meeting in Berlin (whom Holger could suddenly envisage in front of him), and at the same time so reminiscent of him, that he seemed to be less Jason than a caricature of him. Seeing this caricature, Holger burst out laughing, exactly as Jason recalled him laughing at the sight of the old man who tried to walk through the glass door of the café on the Kurfürstendamm the day they first met. Both of them were caricatures of the young men they had been on that occasion.

'*Nicht sein kann, was nicht sein darf . . .*'

It was Jason who quoted Morgenstern to Holger this time, a magic formula, closing the circle.

Holger embraced him and led him inside. Jason registered the embrace as something new. Beyond shaking hands, Holger had avoided touching people in the past.

'Can you stay overnight?'

Jason shook his head.

'I was driving along the autobahn to Berlin when I saw the sign, and I just, you know, I mean quite spontaneously . . . I have to get back tonight.'

'But you'll stay for dinner.'

'I'll stay for dinner. Where are the children? And Ingrid . . .?'

'They're out shopping, but should be back in an hour. In the meantime . . . you know, I always wanted to show you the view we have from upstairs. It's the best thing we have to offer guests, and like you they all seem to come on a foggy day.'

Holger showed Jason up to the library he had built in the roof of the house, and the view there would have been from it but for the fog, and in a sense this View But For the Fog remained the commanding presence in the room for the next hour, just as it did in Holger's life.

Jason scrutinised his friend for telltale signs – slurred speech, a slight limp – betraying that he had once been involved in a near-fatal accident and was fortunate to be alive at all. Katje's death, followed by Holger's conviction for aiding and abetting a terrorist, had meant the end not only of his career. It had undermined his entire existence. But for that accident, he would now look back upon his life as having been . . . a disaster. Was that a paradox? Not in the least! Holger knew that this was what interested Jason (friends who looked up old acquaintances did so with the curiosity not just of friends but of voyeurs), and he came straight to the point.

'It looks like a retreat. It looks like the end of the world, and perhaps even further than that when you see it in this fog. Well, of course it is. But . . .'

He turned away from the window, tapped Jason on the chest and said in a confidential tone of voice: 'I no longer have a false bottom in my suitcase. I no longer live by double standards. I have nothing to conceal any more. So hasn't it been worth it?'

Jason was touched by the question. Holger wanted his reassurance, and he gave it.

The children were quick and forthcoming like their father. Jason could feel a brightness in the house, an agreeable disorder, the merging of people, a sense of home. Only Ingrid, the casualty in Jason's life, remained distant. Had she ever forgiven him his abrupt departure from the Istanbul hotel, subsequently from her life, with the feeble excuse that whatever had been between them was just a mistake?

'How nice to see you, Jason,' she said, and her kiss just brushed his lips. He wished it could have been possible to tell Ingrid that it was exactly in this, the directness with which she came up to him and kissed him on the lips, and the lightness in how she did so, an intrusion already turning into withdrawal before he was aware of it, that Jason knew why he had been in love with her, and could still taste that love, even when it was no longer there.

'How is Elena?'

Jason was left alone with Ingrid while Holger was in the kitchen preparing supper.

'Elena has made a remarkable recovery, it seems . . .'

'Seems?'

'Nothing is certain for more than six months at a time. But she lives on the bright side. She has a will to happiness that is independent of the physical state of her health. Perhaps independent of anything.'

'Of you, too?'

'That is her nature.'

'And you? Are you independent of her? The two of you independent of each other and still living together in a little house in Switzerland?'

There was a mocking tone in her voice. A smile came and went on her lips, quizzing him. Jason smiled back.

'No. I am not as independent of Elena as she is of me. Elena is a free person. She is free in a way that I have never been, because it is not in my nature. I am defined by my constraints. Elena is defined by her freedom. That is the difference. Wherever I am, I am there by necessity. Elena is there by choice.'

'Is she?' Ingrid frowned. 'Perhaps she tells herself she is there by choice.'

She stood at the door looking out into the garden. 'I tell myself I am here by choice, that we live in the country, that Holger stays at home and looks after the children while I work at the local hospital, and our whole life takes place by choice. But I know that we are defined by our constraints, as you put it, and that all we can do is to make the best out of a situation we did not originally choose.'

'But that's the difference, Ingrid. Elena is there by choice because she is able to believe she is. She believes she is a free person.'

Ingrid turned from the window and Jason saw that she had been about to say something to him but had changed her mind, for at that moment Holger came into the room to announce that supper was ready.

Jason crossed the old frontier between West and East Germany in the early hours of the morning. It was a route he had driven dozens of times, always with an unpleasant feeling in the pit of his stomach when he saw the searchlights at the border, the border guards in their grey uniforms and fur caps, the cars waiting in silent columns, engines switched off, gradually freezing, a thin layer of snow on the ground. In his memory this border crossing always took place in winter.

Now it was a mild autumn night. A strong warm wind was blowing. The cars on the autobahn slowed down as they were routed through the old waiting area where only recently they had been forced to a standstill and subjected to sullen scrutiny, but no one stopped at the deserted border post now. The rows of arc lamps remained unlit. A door on one of the outbuildings swung to and fro in the wind. The cars sped away across the dark Thuringian countryside en route for Leipzig and Berlin.

This was where the demarcation line had been drawn after the war, the Americans to the west in Bavaria, the Russians in Thuringia to the east. A giant furrow was ploughed at random through the fields and woods, dividing towns and villages; a fence was erected for a thousand miles, the earth sown with mines. Where there used to be nothing a border came. People attempting to cross the border were shot. Thousands of soldiers were needed to guard the border. It was a thousand-mile scar that remained terrifyingly numb, physically so, appreciably so, a coldness that nothing could warm, for half a century.

The border was a trip-wire in the consciousness of the people who lived on either side of it. It triggered off an awareness of fundamental differences. Here and there, freedom and captivity, life and death. The border was a permanent state of emergency to which people became accustomed. It grew into something ordinary. The numbness became entrenched in their consciousness. The extraordinariness became a banality.

Now there was no border, but the cars still had to slow down, as if filing past a memorial, paying their respects to the border that had been. In a year or two the road would be straightened, and the cars would no longer have to slow down. The border would disappear. But what of the border as trip-wire in people's consciousness?

Growing up after the war, Holger had turned himself into a sort of mental customs inspector, always on the lookout for suitcases with false bottoms, because people with double standards, past and present, led double lives. The habit became ingrained, and one day he realised he had imperceptibly acquired double standards himself. The suitcase with the false bottom was his own head. But the running commentary that used to go on in Holger's head, the sceptical *hinterfragen*, the habit of asking what might be behind the appearances of his fellow Germans prospering in the years of the 'Economic Miracle' – where had she been? What had he done? – gradually exhausted itself and fell silent.

Holger exhausted himself and fell silent, going into early retirement in the country. His father, whose Nazi past had shamed him, died; Magnus died, von Strehlitz, one by one the individuals died and suddenly a generation had disappeared, and the age that had lived through what they had said and done, and in the end through what they remembered, disappeared with them.

The former GDR exhausted itself and fell apart. It remained as a habit of thought, although it was no longer there. The cars slowed down at the zigzag in the road marking the border checkpoint, behaving as if the border was still there, although it no longer was, and the day the road had been straightened out the people in the cars would keep their foot on the accelerator, not hesitating for a second, not even thinking about it, because on the road ahead nothing was there.

16

Jason was still shedding the journey, not just the leisurely drive down to Switzerland from Berlin, but the weeks before on the road with Purdy, images of the changing political landscape, the lives of his friends, his father's death. When he and Elena joined up in Berlin three months had passed since they had last been together. On both sides there was a sense of being not quite aligned. They quarrelled. Elena was inordinately hurt by Jason's forgetfulness over a number of things she had asked him to do in England, and Jason responded to her reproaches brusquely, hurting her even more. These were the rituals of collision and withdrawal, of hurt, remorse and forgiveness, as if after every longer period of separation the terms of their coming together had to be negotiated again.

On their way south they stayed overnight with Marlene in Leipzig. The old lady was so moved when she opened the door and saw them standing there that she wept tears of joy. She had good news for them, she said with a wink and a grimace, leading them upstairs to see the changes that had taken place. In the summer, a young couple had moved into the house where Marlene had been living alone for the past few years, and had begun to renovate the top floor. A proper overhaul of the roof would have to wait until the next spring, but at least they had succeeded in stopping the leaks, put in a new ceiling and restored the floorboards which the last tenants had taken with them twenty years earlier. The bank had agreed to make her a loan with the property as collateral, for Marlene's title to the deeds was clear and within weeks she expected to have the house restored to her by the courts.

Compared with the stricken woman Jason remembered plunging

arthritically up and down the kitchen when he visited her at the beginning of the year, Marlene now moved around the house with remarkable speed and agility. All these encouraging developments, and the hopes they opened up for the future, had made the old lady look years younger. Only her old way of grimacing was unchanged, unable to smooth out, adapting to the otherwise relaxed expression that had settled on her face. Standing in the garden, she looked up at the house and exclaimed happily, 'Can you believe it? You've pulled through, old thing. After sixty years! Hurrah!' – still grimacing, as if saying something she found distasteful.

The following day they stopped at Speyer to look round the cathedral and to have lunch. Afterwards they fell asleep on the bank of the river in the afternoon sun. Jason could smell the coolness of the river in the lengthening shadows when at last he woke up, and he guessed that it must already be getting on for evening. Elena had disappeared. Soundlessly the river flowed. He could feel the evening cool. He watched a group of people strolling in the poplar avenue on the far side of the river pass slowly out of sight. Twenty minutes passed, and Elena still hadn't returned. There was not a breath of wind. Nothing in the landscape stirred.

Jason began to feel uneasy. He looked across the Rhine into the shorn fields, rising gradually towards the distant hills. The harvest had been brought in. Then Elena stepped back into the landscape, restoring vanished familiarity, mending the interrupted peace. Are you all right, he asked. She said she had to walk miles to find a toilet – absurd! Jason again asked her if she was all right, and smiled when she told him why she'd been away so long. But waking into the sudden emptiness on the riverbank that afternoon had been like a premonition of Elena's death.

They followed the Rhine upstream and decided to spend the night in a village not far from the Swiss border. The room in their hotel had a balcony looking out on to the river. Jason stood out there smoking, talking through the open door to Elena inside the room. What's that popping? she asked. Fireworks, he said. Fireworks? Jason reminded her that it was Unity Day. The two German states were now officially united as one, and celebrations were taking place all over the country. Elena came out to watch the fireworks exploding over the Rhine. Look, she said, pointing. *Schön!* The rockets released sprays of sputtering coloured stars that drifted soundlessly through the night and were snuffed out in the river.

Elena settled in at once, but for Jason, still coasting on the momentum that had brought him there, it always took him a few days in the house before he felt he had arrived. Life going on outside still interested him more. There was a fine view of the lake from his study upstairs, and Jason, supposedly working at his desk there, spent most of the time looking out of the window at the mountains and the lake, absorbing the different landscape around him. They were sailing the last of the autumn regattas on Lake Geneva the week that he and Elena arrived. He watched the brightly coloured sails of the yachts swarm out of the harbour and unfurl in stately procession, sliding out of the shadows of the mountains into the sunlight, taking off suddenly across a sheet of bright water.

In the middle of October they closed down the lake. The boats were brought to the marina and hauled up out of the water. Jason and Elena drove down through the vineyards and went for walks along the shore. Enclosed in mist, the lake was perfectly still.

On the terrace of the house in the vineyards it was still mild enough to sit outside in the middle of the day. The morning mist rolled back, revealing the lake and the mountains soaring up on the far side. Sophie, Dr Korol and an old schoolfriend of Jason's who now worked in Geneva came for lunch. Elena sat with her hands in her lap, her eyes closed, the sun warming her back. She listened contentedly to her guests' talk, keeping her eyes shut for no other reason than that to do anything at all would be to risk disturbing a perfect balance. She could feel a slight breeze getting up, and heard the vines rustling under the terrace wall. Dr Korol was pointing, naming the villages on the opposite shore for the benefit of Jason's friend.

'Look!' said Jason, and, involuntarily opening her eyes, Elena saw the surface of the lake below ruffled by a sudden breeze as a single yacht with billowing white sails flew swiftly out from the shore.